Another of Cheryl Bo
marriage-of-convenie

An innocent visit to the Duke of Aldridge's to request a donation for her war widows puts Lady Elizabeth Upton in the midst of a most shocking scandal. . .

The Duke of Aldridge offers for his best friend's sister, Lady Elizabeth Upton, after a mix-up sends her to his bedchamber—just as he's emerging from his bath. She most certainly does not want to force the duke's hand, but how can she bear the shame her scandalous behavior has cast upon her dear brother, the Marquess of Haverstock?

Once she agrees to marry her childhood heartthrob, Elizabeth realizes she wants nothing more than to win her husband's love. But capturing his heart is no easy task when former loves threaten to destroy the fragile bonds of their marriage.

Some of the praise for Cheryl Bolen's writing:

"One of the best authors in the Regency romance field today." – *Huntress Reviews*

"Bolen's writing has a certain elegance that lends itself to the era and creates the perfect atmosphere for her enchanting romances." – *RT Book Reviews*

Lady By Chance (House of Haverstock, Book 1)
Cheryl Bolen has done it again with another sparkling Regency romance. . .Highly recommended – *Happily Ever After*

The Bride Wore Blue (Brides of Bath, Book 1)
Cheryl Bolen returns to the Regency England she knows so well. . .If you love a steamy Regency with a fast pace, be sure to pick up *The Bride Wore Blue*. – *Happily Ever After*

With His Ring (Brides of Bath, Book 2)
"Cheryl Bolen does it again! There is laughter, and the interaction of the characters pulls you right into the book. I look forward to the next in this series." – *RT Book Reviews*

The Bride's Secret (Brides of Bath, Book 3)
(originally titled *A Fallen Woman)*
"*W*hat we all want from a love story...Don't miss it!"
– *In Print*

To Take This Lord (Brides of Bath, Book 4)
(originally titled *An Improper Proposal)*
"Bolen does a wonderful job building simmering sexual tension between her opinionated, outspoken heroine and deliciously tortured, conflicted hero." – *Booklist of the American Library Association*

My Lord Wicked
Winner, International Digital Award for Best Historical Novel of 2011.

With His Lady's Assistance (Regent Mysteries, Book 1)
"A delightful Regency romance with a clever and personable heroine matched with a humble, but intelligent hero. The mystery is nicely done, the romance is enchanting and the secondary characters are enjoyable." – *RT Book Reviews*

Finalist for International Digital Award for Best Historical Novel of 2011.

A Duke Deceived
"A Duke Deceived is a gem. If you're a Georgette Heyer fan, if you enjoy the Regency period, if you like a genuinely sensuous love story, pick up this first novel by Cheryl Bolen." – *Happily Ever After*

One Golden Ring
"*One Golden Ring*...has got to be the most PERFECT Regency Romance I've read this year." – *Huntress Reviews*

Holt Medallion winner for Best Historical, 2006

The Counterfeit Countess
Daphne du Maurier award finalist for Best Historical Mystery

"This story is full of romance and suspense. . . No one can resist a novel written by Cheryl Bolen. Her writing talents charm all readers. Highly recommended reading! 5 stars!"
– *Huntress Reviews*

"Bolen pens a sparkling tale, and readers will adore her feisty heroine, the arrogant, honorable Warwick and a wonderful cast of supporting characters." – *RT Book Reviews*

Also by Cheryl Bolen

Regency Romance

A Lady by Chance (House of Haverstock, Book 1)

The Brides of Bath Series:

The Bride Wore Blue
With His Ring
The Bride's Secret
To Take This Lord
Love in the Library
A Christmas in Bath

The Regent Mysteries Series:

With His Lady's Assistance (Book 1)
A Most Discreet Inquiry (Book 2)
The Theft Before Christmas (Book 3)

The Earl's Bargain
My Lord Wicked
His Lordship's Vow
A Duke Deceived
One Golden Ring
Counterfeit Countess

Novellas:

Lady Sophia's Rescue
Christmas Brides (3 Regency Novellas)

Romantic Suspense

Texas Heroines in Peril Series:

Protecting Britannia
Capitol Offense
A Cry in the Night
Murder at Veranda House

Falling for Frederick

American Historical Romance
A Summer to Remember (3 American Historical Romances)

World War II Romance
It Had to be You

Inspirational Regency Romance
Marriage of Inconvenience

Duchess by Mistake

(House of Haverstock, Book 2)

Cheryl Bolen

Duchess by Mistake is a work of fiction. Names, characters, places, and incidents are the products of the author's imagination or are used fictitiously. Any resemblance to actual events, locales, or persons, living or dead, is entirely coincidental.

DEDICATION

For my sister Suzi, a life-long lover of books, for all the help she's given me over the years

Prologue

Charles Upton, the Marquess of Haverstock, gazed across the breakfast table at Anna. Finally, the colour had returned to her cheeks after months of grieving for the babe they'd lost before it ever drew breath. Even though they had been married for nearly two years, he could never grow tired of gazing upon Anna's beauty.

He'd been told she was the image of her mother, a spectacularly beautiful French noblewoman who'd captured men's hearts as easily as snapping twigs beneath her feet. How fortunate Haverstock was that he'd married his youthful Anna before she'd had the opportunity to ensnare men with a single glance. And how profoundly grateful he was that he was the first and only man to whom she'd ever given her love.

One of the footmen silently appeared at his side and handed him a single letter. The handwriting looked vaguely familiar. By Jove, it looked very much like that of Aldridge! How could this be? The letter appeared to have been brought by a page and bore no marks of having come through the post. Had he returned from Italy, where he'd been for nearly five years?

Brows lowered, Haverstock flipped it over. And he saw the seal had been stamped with a sword, the Duke of Aldridge's symbol. Haverstock smiled and tore open the letter which bore the duke's crest.

My Dear Haverstock,
I'm posting this from Dover and I expect it will reach London before I do. I look forward to seeing this noted beauty you've wed, and I confess to having the devil of a time picturing sensible Lydia uniting herself with Morgie. These eyes of mine yearn to behold my dearest friend after so long an absence.
Aldridge

"You won't believe who's back in town," Haverstock said to his wife.

"Allow me to try." She put down her newspaper and eyed him with shimmering brown eyes. "A friend of yours?"

He nodded.

"One whom I have never met?"

"Correct again."

"Can it be the Duke of Aldridge has returned from Italy?"

"You know me too well, my love." He took her hand and brushed a kiss on the back of it.

"I wonder if he brings the Contessa with him?"

"I seem to recall hearing that she's gone back to her husband."

Anna's long lashes lowered. "Your ducal friend is very naughty indeed."

"But I daresay you'll warm to him. Women always do. He's very charming--even if he is a profligate." His and Anna's marriage was built on impermeable bedrock. He never need fear she would look at another man.

Not even Aldridge, whom women found

irresistible.

"I certainly hope he doesn't try to corrupt my upstanding husband."

"We're very different. Especially now." Haverstock wanted but two things now: to be a family man and to do whatever he could to defeat the French.

The footman returned to the chamber at the same time as Haverstock's last maiden sister took her place at their table. "Another letter for you, my lord."

He and Anna greeted Cynthia, who had lately taken to using her given name of Elizabeth in honor of the recently deceased aunt for whom she'd been named. He cast a glance at the letter the footman placed in his hand and easily recognized Morgie's neat script. Until recently Morgie would have just stepped next door when he needed to communicate with Haverstock, but since Lydia's lying in, Morgie rather hovered at her side like a damned lap dog. Haverstock could have searched the three kingdoms and never have found a finer husband for his favorite sister than Morgie was to Lydia.

Tearing open the letter, he read.

It' all over town. Aldridge is back!!

A mischievous look on his face, he met his wife's gaze. "You'd already heard about Aldridge, hadn't you?"

She giggled as she nodded.

"Knew what?" Elizabeth inquired, her teapot frozen in mid-pour.

He looked at his sister. "The Duke of Aldridge has finally returned to England."

Chapter 1

How in the deuce had so many learned he was back in England, Philip Ponsby, the 5th Duke of Aldridge, wondered as he began to scan the pile of fresh correspondence upon his desk. He had told but one person, and he knew without a doubt Haverstock wasn't one to gossip. *The servants!* He'd sent ahead to have them ready the house. The chain of servants' communication was far superior to that of their masters, though their methods eluded him.

Thankfully, Aldridge House did not smell musty even though he had been away for five years. That was one of the dubious advantages of being the eldest of eight. His siblings often used the London house, trotting up to go to the theatre or to meet eligible suitors at Almack's. It was the latter--and its endless procession of eligible misses wishing to unite themselves with the Duke of Aldridge--that had sent him packing for his long sojourn on the Continent.

Yet he had to admit it felt devilishly good to be back in the country of his birth. Until he'd seen the white cliffs at Dover and the spire of Westminster Abbey, he had not realized how thoroughly he had missed England, dreary skies and all.

Once that vile Napoleon had stuck his own

usurping family on the throne of Naples, Aldridge had realized how grave was the threat to his own country from the Corsican monster. If Napoleon could plunder his conquering way across Europe, what was to stop him from overrunning the British Isles?

Aldridge, for one. There was nothing he wouldn't do to keep that from happening. Before the week was out, he would present himself at the Foreign Office and offer his services to the Crown.

In the stack of letters, an utterly feminine script caught his eye. He'd been away from England for so long now he could not remember any lady's handwriting. Curious, he opened the missive. It was just one page. One sentence, actually. From Belle. Annabelle Evans. Five years ago, she'd been the most beautiful courtesan in all of London. The last he'd heard, she was under the protection of the Duke of Benson.

Aldridge,

I shall call on you this afternoon on a matter of importance.

His glance flicked to the case clock upon his chimneypiece. Two o'clock. He really wasn't up to seeing anyone after the long, uncomfortable journey, but he could not refuse to see Belle. She had long ago done him a good turn. No doubt, she wished now to be repaid. Had she lost her fine good looks? Was she destitute? Would she ask him for money? He shrugged. He was a very wealthy man. If the woman was in need, it would give him pleasure to assist her.

He rang for a servant, and when a youthful footman who was long of leg and broad of shoulders appeared, the duke requested a bath to be prepared in his bedchamber. Damn but he was tired. And he felt as if he were coated in dust and dirt from Dover road.

While water was being heated and carried to his tub, he would scan the remainder of the letters. After finishing with them--and delaying composing any responses--he trudged up the broad marble staircase to his private chambers, pleased to find his bath ready. With assistance from Lawford, he stripped off his clothing, then eased himself into the warm bath in front of the fireplace.

"By the way, Lawford, instruct Barrow that if a lady calls, he should bring her here."

"Very well, my lord." Having been with Aldridge since he'd left Oxford, Lawford was used to ladies of the demimonde showing up in his master's private chambers.

Lady Elizabeth Upton would say it was surely Divine intervention which had sent her to the modest lodgings on Miser Street early that day. But in reality it was the kindness of her brother James. An officer in the Peninsula and the brother closest to her in age and affection, James had written her a letter to ask that she see to the wellbeing of the young widow and child of a slain soldier who'd served under his command.

James had written, "*It was my understanding that the marriage between Harry Hudson—one of the best soldiers in His Majesty's Army—and his wife was exceedingly strong. He always stressed that if anything should happen to him, he wished for me to see that she and their little girl were looked after. Obviously, I cannot do that from Spain, but I know I can count on my favorite sister to undertake this commission in my stead.*

Obviously, if there is great need, I shall want to do whatever I can for the widow."

There was nothing Elizabeth wouldn't do for her brother. Armed with the widow's address, Elizabeth availed herself of her eldest brother's coach to call upon Mrs. Hudson. When the crested Haverstock coach turned onto Miser Street near Covent Garden, Elizabeth's gaze was riveted to a most forlorn looking woman. She judged the woman to be near her own age of one and twenty. One hand clasped that of her little girl, whom Elizabeth judged to be three; the other clasped a bulging case, much like Elizabeth's valise, but much shabbier.

Without even hunting for Number 12, Elizabeth felt certain she had found James' widow. She indicated for the coachman to stop and opened her coach window. "Mrs. Hudson?" she inquired.

The woman halted and turned to eye Elizabeth, a brow raised in query. "Yes?"

"Would you permit me to carry you to your destination? It seems my brother, Captain James Upton, served with your husband and had a very high opinion of him."

Tears sprang to the fair woman's green eyes. "My Harry was a very fine man." As she swiped away a tear, Elizabeth noticed the young widow still wore a simple gold wedding band. She noticed, too, the woman's clean muslin dress was patched. Elizabeth's heart went out to the stricken woman. "Harry wrote to me of how much he admired Captain Upton." The woman was possessed of a genteel voice.

By then the coachman had gotten off the box and opened the carriage door. Which was a good thing for Mrs. Hudson because rain was beginning to fall. "Please come sit with me," Elizabeth said.

The woman and her daughter climbed in and sat opposite her. Elizabeth could tell from the little girl's curious gaze that this must be the first time she had ever been inside a carriage. "I am Lady Elizabeth. What is your name?" Elizabeth asked the angelic looking child with copper tresses.

"Louisa."

Elizabeth eyed the mother. "Your daughter is lovely."

Mrs. Hudson's eyes still misted. "She takes after my husband."

How sad that this woman had lost the husband she obviously adored. Elizabeth's gaze went to the woman's bag. "Are you going somewhere?"

Mrs. Hudson burst into tears. "We've just been evicted from our lodgings. . ." Mrs. Hudson tried to calm herself enough to offer assurances to her worried daughter. "It's all right, pet. Mum's all right."

It occurred to Elizabeth that she must have been evicted for failure to pay rents. Which meant that she likely had no place to go. "Where will you live?"

The woman shook her head. "I don't know what we'll do." A fresh wave of tears overtook her.

Elizabeth reached across the coach and patted her. It seemed like a miracle that she came to Miser Street at the exact time Mrs. Hudson was forced from it. "Please don't worry. That's why I've come today. Captain Upton wants to ensure that you and Louisa are looked after." Elizabeth had not the slightest notion what kind of sum would be needed to pay the woman's rent, but she thought the pin money in her reticule should go some distance. "How much money should you need in order to return to your lodgings?"

"I am behind eighteen guineas—and that's not counting this month."

"Allow me to go speak with your . . . proprietor." Elizabeth disembarked from the coach and scurried across the puddled pavement to Number 12.

Though Mrs. Hudson and her little girl were spotless, that was not the case with the foul-smelling rooming house where they resided. On the first floor, a rain-splattered Elizabeth made the acquaintance of Mrs. Preble, a seemingly well-fed, middle-aged woman who wore a widow's cap. Elizabeth explained the plight of the unfortunate Mrs. Hudson.

"It's coin in me pocket that puts food on the table, not a soft heart." There was a hardness in the woman's face.

"If you allow Mrs. Hudson to finish out the month, I shall pay you twenty pounds, which includes what she owes—and happens to be every penny I can lay my hands on." By next week Elizabeth hoped to procure lodgings in a decent neighborhood for Mrs. Hudson. The area around Covent Garden was no place for a genteel woman and child.

Mrs. Preble's eyes brightened. "Till the end of the month it will be then." Her gaze darted to the reticule Elizabeth was opening. She dumped the entire contents on the nearby desk top. Coins of every denomination and varying shades of metal made a small mountain. It looked like much more money than Elizabeth knew it was.

"It should be twenty pounds," Elizabeth said.

As the coach rattled across the busy city, a sense of exhilaration courses through her. Helping Mrs. Hudson and her dear child had given Elizabeth more joy than anything ever had. Assisting at Anna's sewing school had made her feel useful, but not like today.

For some time now she had grown tired of the Great Husband Hunt. She must resign herself to spinsterhood. She would, after all, end up being the maiden aunt like her namesake, Aunt Elizabeth. Only once had Elizabeth ever fancied herself in love, and he had not returned her ardor enough to offer for her hand.

No, make that twice, she thought. As a very young girl she had pined away over her brother's friend who just this day had returned to England after a five-year absence. From the age of twelve until the year of her presentation, she had dreamed of capturing the handsome duke's heart. Given that there was an eleven-year age gap between her and Aldridge, him having been interested in his friend's twelve-year-old sister was as impossible as a dry Scottish spring. *Perhaps if he had been in England the year I was presented. . .*

It would do her no good to dwell on what was done and could not be undone. She no longer believed a husband and family of her own were necessary to her happiness. Her joy would come from helping war widows like Mrs. Hudson.

Throughout the snarling carriage ride, she began to form a plan. She would go through all of James's letters to identify those who were killed, and with Haverstock's help she would go to the War Office and seek the direction of each of those widows.

But first she to find a way to procure a large house in a respectable neighborhood. Her home for war widows and their children could brighten these family's lives, just as Anna's sewing school had done so much to better the lives of women and children in the East End.

"I have come to the conclusion I shall never wed." Elizabeth regarded her beautiful sister-in-law as the two sat in Lady Haverstock's scarlet study penning letters later that afternoon.

Anna looked up from her gilt escritoire. "You can't mean that. You're but one and twenty years of age. There's much time for you to find someone you love as much as I love Charles."

It stung rather that Anna had not assured her of Captain Smythe's love. It seemed Elizabeth had been the last to discover the dashing officer had no intentions of plighting his life to hers--after stealing her heart before he returned to the Peninsula. "The only man I ever fancied myself in love with did not return my affection, and I've not met another since who would tempt me to give up the life I've grown happy with."

"That man wasn't worthy of you. Pray, pet, if you just be patient you'll find a great love."

"I think not. In recent weeks I have chosen to emulate Charlotte and do good works."

"There's one significant difference between you and Charlotte. She has a husband to whom she is happily married."

Elizabeth shrugged. "I don't need a husband in order to have a full, rewarding life in the service to the less fortunate."

"I cannot say that I haven't noticed how much time you've been spending at our sewing school."

Elizabeth shrugged. "Someone had to step in with those poor, unfortunate souls when Lydia was breeding." It pained Elizabeth to speak to Anna of her sister's recent confinement for she knew how devastated Anna was over the loss of her own babe.

"You've done much good," Anna said.

"I mean to do more. Has it not struck you that there are a great many officers' widows who have become destitute? Many of them have lost not only their beloved husbands but also their homes."

Anna nodded sadly. "How can you alleviate such a grave problem? You're but one person. One very young person--with no fortune."

It was true that Elizabeth had no fortune. Dear Anna was dipping into her own fortune to provide dowries for each of Charles's sisters. "I have given this much thought. I may not have fortune, but by virtue of my birth, I have access to many noblemen with deep pockets, and I mean to play upon that strength."

"What have you in mind?"

"This very afternoon I have located a large house in a respectable neighborhood. It can easily accommodate ten families--provided the children share chambers with their mothers."

"And how do you propose to pay for it?"

"It belongs to the Duke of Aldridge, and I mean to ask for its use. After all, because he's Charles's oldest friend and because I've known him all my life, I believe I can persuade him to help. Despite his debauchery, he *is* noted for his generosity.

And it helps that he's one of the richest men in the kingdom."

Anna's dark brows lowered. "I'm sure he's not really debauched. If that were the case, I don't think Charles would be as fond of him as he is."

"Perhaps I've used too strong a word. The privileged man does behave in a scandalous fashion."

Anna nodded. "I do look forward to meeting him." She dipped her pen in the ink pot. "Tell me, is this house of his in Mayfair?"

"Oh, no. Nothing that fashionable. It's in Bloomsbury. The homes on Trent Square have belonged to the Dukes of Aldridge for generations. I learned that the last occupant of Number 7 Trent Square has recently died, and it has become vacant."

"How fortuitous, then, that the duke's returned to London."

Indeed it was. Elizabeth need not tell Anna she planned to call on the duke. Anna would object. Resigned to being a spinster, Elizabeth had no wish to continue acting like a miss on the Marriage Mart. She was a woman now, and she was embarking on this new chapter of her life. Alone. Elizabeth would take sole responsibility for this scheme, and she refused to solicit Anna's money for this endeavor.

Anna looked at the clock upon the chimneypiece, then stood. "I told Lydia I'd come see the babe this afternoon. Will you come with me?"

Despite that Anna had lost weight in her grief over her own babe, Elizabeth thought she'd never seen a more beautiful woman than her brother's dark-haired wife. Huge brown eyes thickly fringed with extraordinary lashes were set in a flawless oval face. Every bit as striking as her huge eyes was the sheer whiteness of her perfect teeth.

Poor Anna was already attached to Morgie and Lydia's infant son. It was such a pity she had no babe of her own. She would be as wonderful a mother as Lydia was proving to be. "I saw little Simon only yesterday. There are other matters that demand my attention."

Sometime after donning a dress which matched the periwinkle colour of her eyes and topping it with a matching pelisse suitable for calling at Aldridge House, Elizabeth found herself knocking upon the door of that fine house on Berkeley Square. She wondered how many times Charles had passed through this door during his two and thirty years. Since she had only come out three years previously, she had never had the opportunity to pay a call upon the duke, owing to his long absence from England.

The white-haired butler who answered her knock looked as if he'd been in the employ of the Aldridges for at least two generations. He quickly offered her a tight smile and spoke before she had the chance to offer her card. "Please come in. His grace awaits. If you will just follow me up the stairs."

She supposed with this being the duke's first day back, he was entertaining callers in the drawing room. She had not considered that she would not have him all to herself. It would be difficult to make her bold proposal to him in a room full of people. Her brother had once said the duke did not like to have his charities acknowledged, preferring anonymity.

Her gaze lifted to the massive chandelier that glistened above, then she began to follow the stooped-over butler as he mounted the stairs, his movements slowed by age. All the way up the impressive, iron banistered staircase portraits of long-dead Aldridges stood almost one on top of the other and seemed to be staring at her.

To her surprise, when they reached the first floor he did not stop but continued mounting stairs to the next level. Though her experience with ducal residences was limited, she was unaccustomed to finding a drawing room so far removed from the home's entrance. In most of the houses with which she was familiar, the third level was reserved for bedchambers.

They reached the third level. It was slightly less formal than the second level, actually looking remarkably like the third--bedchamber--level at Haverstock House. The butler turned to the right and shuffled along another corridor until he reached the first paneled and gilded door. It was closed. He teetered to a stop and turned to face her with a somber countenance. "You will find his grace in here." Then he began to retrace his steps.

She drew in a breath, reached for the door handle, and opened it.

She heard a splashing sound before the door was fully open. How peculiar. When she had clear view of the room, she gasped. There in its center, framed by the fireplace behind him, the Duke of Aldridge was emerging from his bath. His long, glistening, gloriously formed body was completely naked.

In her entire life Lady Elizabeth Upton had never seen a naked man in the flesh. Though her first instinct should have been to run screaming from the chamber, she was frozen to the spot, unable to remove her gaze from . . . the manly part. And so much more. From his wide shoulders along his burnished skin and muscled limbs, the dark-haired duke exuded a masculinity like nothing she had ever seen.

A flood of memories of her former adoration of this man many years ago walloped her. She felt the heat climbing into her cheeks and knew she should flee from the profligate duke. Yet, like a compulsion to watch a grim sight not suitable for female sensibilities, she was incapable of turning away.

"You're not Belle!" he said, snatching his toweling and covering the lower portion of his statue-worthy body. His voice held a note of incredulity.

No doubt, Belle was a lady of the demimonde. What a wicked man he was! To think, his first day back in the kingdom he chose to spend with a woman of *that* sort.

At the sound of his voice, she realized how shameless she must appear. And how very improper it was for her to be there. She came to her senses, let out a full-fledged scream, turned on her heel, and fled down the stairs.

And came face to face with her brother.

"Haverstock!" she cried.

His brows lowered with concern. "What's the matter, Lizzie?"

She tossed her head back in the direction of the duke's private chamber. "That man! He's thoroughly debauched." Then she scurried down the stairs. Never again would she come to this . . . this temple of profligacy.

***

Aldridge was having the devil of a time trying to remember where he had seen that chit before. No doubt, she was a lady of Quality. He'd likely scared the poor thing senseless. There had obviously been a serious misunderstanding.

As soon as he called for Lawford, Haverstock came striding into Aldridge's bedchamber. When he saw that Aldridge was without clothing, his facial expressions thundered. "What in the hell were you doing with my sister?"

Oh, damn! That's why she looked familiar! The duke grimaced. "It's not what you think."

Haverstock's gaze raked over him from the top of his wet head down the full length of his nakedness. "Oh, isn't it? My god, Aldridge, she's an innocent! How could you?"

By then Aldridge's valet had come striding in with fresh clothing for his master, and Aldridge began to dress. "It seems I owe your sister an apology. Cynthia, is it not?"

"You know very well it was Cynthia! Only she now uses her given name of Elizabeth."

"I assure you I have no dishonorable designs on your sister."

Haverstock regarded him thoughtfully for a long, silent moment. "Then are you saying your intentions toward Elizabeth are honorable?"

"But of course. What do you take me for?"

"It appears I shall now take you for my brother-in-law."

Just as his sister had done a moment earlier, Haverstock spun around and fled from the chamber.

Aldridge wanted to call after him, wanted to reason with him, but what could he say?

A rush of thoughts flooded his brain. It was

his own damn fault this debacle had occurred. He was the one who'd told Lawford to instruct poor old, hard-of-hearing Barrow to admit a lady into his bedchamber. It had never occurred to him an innocent young lady--and not the worldly, corrupted Belle Evans--would show up at Aldridge House his first afternoon back in London.

Philip Ponsby, the 5th Duke of Aldridge, had been born to extreme privilege, and accordingly, was accustomed to the gratification of all his wishes whether they be the acquisition of a new thoroughbred or a Rembrandt. Even infirmities that had struck other young men of his acquaintance had never visited him. He had also been favored with tolerable good looks and the ability to attract lovely lasses who had no knowledge of his exalted rank. But this afternoon as he stood only half dressed in his bedchamber, he was numbed by an overwhelming sense of bereavement.

For he knew he would enter into a marriage neither he nor the shocked young lady desired. It was not only the honorable thing to do, it was also what he had to do to restore his friendship with the only fellow whose friendship had ever mattered to him.

He must own that in the hinterland of his brain, he'd realized that upon returning to England he would have to settle down and see to securing the succession. Two and thirty years was more than enough time to sow his wild oats.

At this point in his life he was resigned to marriage. But he had never thought that the selection of the future Duchess of Aldridge would be snatched from his own hands. For the first time in his two and thirty years, he felt powerless.

Chapter 2

Elizabeth Upton had never been so humiliated. Every member of her family--save for her brother in the Peninsula and her married sister in Cornwall--had learned of her indiscretion. Because she had exercised the unsound judgment of visiting a bachelor without benefit of a chaperon and, therefore, been exposed to . . . an *exposed* man, it was thought that she had been compromised.

All of her claims of innocence had fallen on deaf ears.

Upon her return to Haverstock House, she had positively refused to speak to Haverstock about the matter. Really, it was too, too embarrassing. She had not been able to purge from her memory the vision of that . . . that *appendage* between the Duke of Aldridge's slender waist and his muscled thighs. The very memory of it sent heat to her cheeks and a breathlessness to her lungs.

Even statues of well-formed Greeks she'd seen in the British Library managed to conceal the . . . the shape of that particular endowment. And though she was no expert, she thought perhaps the Duke of Aldridge in every way was more. . . well, *more* everything than the average well-formed Greek.

After she'd sent away a raging Haverstock, his

gentle wife had come to Elizabeth. Anna at least listened to Elizabeth's defense but assured her that Haverstock would accept nothing less from the duke than marriage. "It's not right that he not marry you after you've . . . well, after you've seen things no maiden should see."

Once Elizabeth had sent Anna away, Lydia then came and told her she must marry the duke. In her two decades, Elizabeth had never dared not to obey her wise and much-respected eldest sister. But today she sent Lydia away with vehement refusals to do as her sister bid.

Next, her sister Kate had come to assure her of her stupendous good fortune in securing a--forced though it was--proposal from a duke! Really, Kate insisted, Elizabeth was the most fortunate lady in the kingdom. Being Elizabeth's least favorite sister as well as the sister whose mercenary opinions generated the greatest animosity, Kate, too, was sent away.

That night Elizabeth refused to leave her bedchamber. She even sent away untouched trays of food that kindly Anna had sent up.

Aldridge never would have believed his first night back in London would find him standing behind closed doors in Haverstock's library, begging the hand of his youngest sister. Or was she the second youngest? Deuced if he knew. She'd been but a babe in arms the first time Aldridge had come home from Eton with Haverstock, who was then Lord Charles Upton. There must be a dozen years separating Aldridge's age from hers.

She had still been in the schoolroom when he left England five years earlier. In the ensuing years she had come out, and despite that she was in possession of a pretty face and figure had failed to attract a husband.

To his great misfortune.

Nevertheless, in the past half a dozen hours he had resigned himself to this marriage. Ever pragmatic, he had enumerated the advantages to this alliance. First, it would unite his family to that of his greatest friend. Secondly, the Haverstocks were an old family of lineage nearly as noble as his own. Third, this Elizabeth-Who-Used-to-be-Cynthia was prettier than most of the young ladies of his acquaintance. And, fourth, if she was in possession of even half the intelligence of her plain elder sister, Lydia, he would count himself fortunate to be wed to so sensible a woman.

Haverstock sat behind a sweeping desk, glaring. His anger obviously prevented him from extending the courtesy of asking Aldridge to sit. Consequently, Aldridge stood there feeling much as he had as a twelve-year-old standing before the headmaster.

"You must know one of the reasons I've returned to England is to seek a wife, and it would give me inordinate pleasure if you'd do me the honor of allowing Lady Elizabeth to become my duchess."

Still staring at him, Haverstock rose, then a smile slowly lifted as he stuck out his hand. "Welcome home, brother."

The two shook hands.

"Won't you have a seat?"

Aldridge dropped into a nearby chair.

"Damn, but it's good to have you back," Haverstock said.

"It's good to be back. I'm looking forward to meeting your marchioness. Word of her extraordinary beauty reached me in Italy."

"I hope one day your marriage to Elizabeth will bring you the happiness Anna's brought me." Haverstock grew solemn. "Despite her extraordinary beauty, I wasn't in love with Anna when we wed, but I soon fell under her captivating spell."

It was a pity Aldridge would never be as besotted over Elizabeth as he'd been told Haverstock was over his wife. "I pray that you're right."

Haverstock's countenance brightened. "Did you know Morgie and Lydia have a son?"

"I did not. As fond as I am of Morgie, I never credited him with having such good sense as he demonstrated by marrying Lydia."

His comment launched Haverstock into a chuckle. "They are uncommonly good for each other--and devoted to one another."

Aldridge shook his head. "I cannot picture Morgie as a father."

"Nor can he. I don't think he quite knows what to make of the little fellow, but in his own way, Morgie's very proud to have a son."

Now Aldridge grew solemn. "What about you? Is your Incomparable breeding yet?" As soon as the words were out of his mouth, Aldridge regretted bringing up a possibly painful subject.

Haverstock's face shadowed. "We're just in the second year of our marriage. Anna's young. There will be time."

Aldridge had obviously touched on a sensitive topic. Beastly of him.

At the thought of the three life-long friends

having sons, something deep inside of Aldridge unfurled. Neither his horse winning the stakes nor his winning bid for the *da Vinci* had made him feel as exhilarated as he felt at this moment contemplating a son of his own. "It's delightful to think of our offspring growing up as close to one another as we have been all these years." Now why had he gone and babbled such?

"I hope that means you'll not be leaving the country anytime in the next twenty years."

A smile on his face, Aldridge shrugged. "That depends. I mean to offer myself at the Foreign Office."

"By Jove, that's the second-best news I've heard in a long while. We can put your analytical mind to good use on cryptology."

"Is that not what you've been doing these past few years?"

"It is, and I could use a hand."

Aldridge leaned back in the chair and regarded his old friend. "If that's the second-best news you've heard, may I ask what's the best?"

"Having you as a brother," Haverstock said with great solemnity. Then he stood. "I suppose it's time for you to speak to Elizabeth. I'll have her come down."

Aldridge cleared his throat. He wanted his closest friend to know that he wasn't as debauched as he'd appeared that afternoon. "When I arrived at Aldridge House this afternoon, I received a note from Belle Evans informing me she was going to pay a call." He shrugged. "She needed the loan of a hundred quid. It was she I was expecting in my bedchamber--not your sister."

Haverstock stiffened and did not respond for a

moment. "What was my sister doing there?"

"I have no idea."

"Then I understand if you wish to retract your offer."

"No one forced me to come here tonight. It's a marriage I want." If only he could mean those words.

Haverstock nodded solemnly and left the chamber.

No matter how humiliated one was and no matter how mortified one was over one's scandalous situation, one simply had to eat. Elizabeth regretted that she'd sent away the uneaten tray for she now realized how terribly hungry she actually was. She'd not eaten since she'd partaken of toast and tea that morning. Perhaps she could slip out of her bedchamber and stealthily make her way down to the kitchen.

Still wearing the same periwinkle gown she'd worn on her disastrous visit to Aldridge House, she began to creep down the stairs. When she reached the entry corridor, the door to Haverstock's library opened, and her brother came strolling out. "Oh, there you are, Lizzie. You have a visitor." He waved his arm toward the library. "Right this way."

She most particularly did not want to see a caller right now--even if she was wearing her most becoming dress. Unfortunately, she was not courageous enough to defy her commanding brother. It was one thing to turn him away from her bedchamber, but she could hardly stomp her foot and refuse to do as he bid her now. Now that she'd left the security of her locked room.

Her brow raised in query, she reluctantly

moved toward the library, opened the door, and started into the chamber. The room was dark. Its only source of light came from the fire blazing in the hearth and an oil lamp burning upon the desk. She saw that a man rose as she entered. As she moved closer, her breath caught. It was the Duke of Aldridge! Obviously, he was the most debauched man in all of England. And Italy, too, she imagined!

She was powerless to prevent the red, hot heat from rushing to her cheeks. Facing him made her recall that awkward moment when she had seen his glistening flesh. *Every inch of it.* Yet as the duke stood in her brother's library, effecting a courtly bow to a humiliated maiden, she could almost forget his wickedness.

Now he looked ever so proper dressed in well-fitted gray breeches, a fine black jacket, and snowy white cravat tied beneath a pensive face. He could have cut a dashing figure at Almack's. And this brooding-looking, dark-haired man now standing before her would undoubtedly be the most handsome man to grace its chamber in years.

Inarticulate sounds emanated from her vocal chords, then she spun back toward the door.

He raced to bar her progress. "I beg that you not go away before I have the chance to apologize to you for . . ." Setting a gentle hand to her arm, he swallowed. "For this afternoon. All I can say in my defense is that I thought---"

"You thought I was Belle Evans." Even in her innocence, Elizabeth had heard of the most notorious courtesan in London. Once Elizabeth had leave to think on the duke's exclamation that afternoon, she realized who he had been expecting to come strolling through his bedchamber door. Which still did not diminish her disgust with his behavior. To think that a tryst with a trollop was uppermost in his mind his first day home in half a decade!

He nodded gravely. "I had reason to believe she was coming to my chamber--but not for the purpose you must imagine." He shook his head as if he had blundered. "Forgive me for introducing so delicate a subject. I am deeply sorry."

She drew a deep breath and squared her shoulders. "I should never have gone to your house without a chaperon. I am deeply sorry." Then she shook her head as if *she* had blundered. "I assure you it was never my intention to accuse you of compromising my virtue, never my intention to wrangle a marriage proposal from my brother's dearest friend."

"Nevertheless, I feel I *have* compromised your virtue."

Suddenly, she realized why he was here. Her brother *had* forced him into marriage with her--a marriage neither of them wanted. She had thought she couldn't be more humiliated than she'd been that afternoon.

She'd been wrong. "No, no, no!" She held up a hand. "If you mean to offer for me, I mean to refuse."

His dark brows quirked. "Haverstock did not force me to come here tonight."

"You can say nothing to persuade me that you favor a marriage with me."

"I may not be able to make you see the truth, but I shall try. Why do you think I came back to England?"

She felt his dark gaze boring into hers but was

powerless to speak.

"I wished to find a suitable wife, and you must know how agreeable I find an alliance between our two families."

Her spine stiffened, and she put hands to hips. "But, your grace, I do not wish to be married."

"Are your affections engaged?"

"No. I mean to be a spinster."

"May I inquire as to why a . . . confirmed spinster wished to call on me this afternoon?"

"I intended to ask you to offer your house on Trent Square for the use of war widows and their children."

He didn't say anything for a moment. Then it looked as if a weight had been lifted from his (ever so broad) shoulders. "How very commendable. I have heard of the good works your sister Charlotte and her clergyman husband are doing--as well as the sewing school Lady Haverstock established to teach a trade to the lowest sort of woman. I should be delighted to offer my house on Trent Square for so noble a purpose. I'll instruct my man of business to see to it." He shrugged. "I hadn't even remembered that I owned Trent Square."

The man was sinfully rich. "Then that's all I ask of you--not that it's insignificant. It's very generous of you."

He drew her hand into his. "Now I have something to ask of you."

She had never before been alone with a man, never had a man hold her hand so intimately. Her pulse skittered, and she thought if she were asked to speak, she would be incapable of summoning her voice.

Surely he wasn't going to ask her to marry him! Hadn't she done her best to exonerate him from blame for the afternoon's fiasco? Hadn't she made it clear she had no intentions of marrying?

Nevertheless as they stood there facing one another in the semi-darkness, the ticking of the chimneypiece clock and the hiss of coals the only sounds to be heard, she unaccountably began to tremble.

His voice was low and husky when he spoke. "Will you do me the honor of becoming my duchess?"

"You don't have to do this," she managed in a shaky voice.

"It's time that I see to the succession, and there is no woman I'd rather have for the mother of my children."

If he'd thought to woo her with such a declaration, nothing could have been further from reality. All his declaration accomplished was her total mortification. Being the mother of his children entailed the very thing that had so embarrassed her that very afternoon.

Yet as she stood there contemplating it, she did not find him so very profligate. The man's intentions were honorable!

"It's very kind of you, your grace, but I assure you, it's not necessary. Once my brother is apprised of the facts, he won't expect you to offer me marriage."

"Your brother knows I had no intention of compromising you. He knows about. . . Belle Evans. And I assure you, both your brother and I could never have hoped for a happier alliance than for you to become my bride."

Despite that he'd left England rather than duel

a jealous husband, despite that he'd broken the faro bank at Whites with unconscionable wagering, despite that he'd been conducting a very public intrigue with the married Contessa Savatini these past four years, Elizabeth had to give the Duke of Aldridge credit for a nobility few aristocratic men possessed.

Noble or not, she refused to marry this man. “I am deeply appreciative of your offer, your grace, but my resolve to stay unwed is unwavering.” Then, feigning a defiant manner, she said, “I bid you goodnight.”

Once again, he barred her progress, this time firmly coiling his hand around her arm. "I am accustomed to getting what I want, Elizabeth."

Chapter 3

She raced up the stairs, her heartbeat hammering, her hands trembling. She could still feel the heat of where his hand had touched, still hear him huskily addressing her by her Christian name. No man had ever called her just *Elizabeth.* It was unbearably intimate!

In her bedchamber, she shakily closed the door behind her and commenced to pacing. Her hunger had been snuffed out like a candle. Had a feast been spread before her, she would have been unable to eat. That insufferable rake! What could possibly have possessed him to seek her for a wife--other than guilt about subjecting her to such an improper spectacle that afternoon?

Did the officious man not realize that now--in the nineteenth century--men and women married for love? (Except for her greedy sister Kate.) The Duke of Aldridge did not love her, and she most certainly did not love him.

She collapsed on to her bed. She'd spoken the truth when she told Anna she was incapable of loving any man except the one who did not return her affections. *Captain Smythe.* She wanted to hate the handsome officer for stealing her heart with his exclusive attentions that did not culminate in a marriage offer.

He'd led her to believe he was in love with her

before he returned to the Peninsula, but nary a letter had she received from him in the ensuing year. She had learned, too, that he was dallying with a Spanish noblewoman. *The rake!*

As her thoughts wandered to her conversation with Anna earlier that day, she was stunned to realize that had occurred less than twelve hours previously. It seemed as if days had passed since her well-publicized fiasco at Aldridge House. It certainly seemed like days had passed since she'd last eaten.

She did feel weak from hunger, but her insides were far too jittery to welcome nourishment.

A knock sounded upon her door. She expected Haverstock. No doubt he was prepared to congratulate her for snaring a duke. She dreaded telling him the truth. He was bound to be deeply disappointed. Not only would it have been prestigious to have a duchess for a sister, but Haverstock would enjoy deepening the connection with his oldest friend. Were she to marry Aldridge, her brother's two best friends would also be his brothers-in-law.

"Come in."

It wasn't Haverstock who came strolling into her room. It was Anna. A smile brightened her lovely face as she strolled straight to Elizabeth. "I've come to offer my felicitations. Charles told me the duke's offered for you."

"He did." Her pale eyes connected with Anna's large brown ones. "I turned him down."

Anna dropped onto the bed. "Oh, dear."

"I am not like Kate. I cannot marry where there is no love--and I most especially don't want to trap the duke into marriage where there's no love." She drew in a breath. "He's apparently possessed of more nobility than I'd given him credit for."

"Having never met the man, I will own that I too thought he was a profligate, but it seems I was wrong." Anna sighed. "I hope you're not closing the door on this opportunity because of Captain Smythe. He doesn't deserve your regard."

Elizabeth spoke as if she were thinking aloud. "When he left England without offering for me, I thought my heart would break. Every time the post arrived, I hoped for his letter which never came. Every time I saw an officer whose build or hair colour was similar to his, my pulse would explode with anticipation. But a year has passed now, and with it, so too the pain. I no longer look for a letter, no longer think of him every hour of the day." But no man except Captain Smythe was capable of eliciting such profound feelings in her.

"Not all marriages begin with a passionate love like you once felt for Captain Smythe. Take mine and Charles.'"

Elizabeth's eyes narrowed. "You cannot tell me you two weren't passionately in love when you married. I know better. I was here. I saw the hunger in your eyes whenever you looked at one another."

Anna gave a soft smile. "Did you really believe we married for love?"

"Of course!"

"I swear on Mama's grave, neither of us was in love when we married."

Elizabeth's mouth gaped open. "I cannot believe that!"

Anna shrugged. "Ask Haverstock."

"But he worships you!"

"I think he may--as I adore him."

"I've never seen two people so much in love."

"I will own that a very short time after I plighted my life to his, I was deeply in love with him. Later, I learned he felt the same, but for a long time I didn't know he loved me. I thought. . . oh, I can't speak of such to a maiden!"

"You thought he only desired to make love to you. Because he's a man. Come, Anna, I know *something* about men and their cravings!" And that afternoon she'd learned something altogether new about the opposite sex--though she'd as lief she hadn't. Elizabeth started to shake her head, a gleeful look upon her face. "We all knew why you and Haverstock spent so much time in your bedchamber those early months of your marriage!"

A secretive smile spread slowly across Anna's face. "There are so many kinds of foundations upon which a good marriage can be built. I will own that physical ... compatibility was crucial to ours. There's also the very sense that in the eyes of God and man, you belong to your husband until death. And him to you. From the very start, even though he did not love me, Charles held respect for my position as his wife and saw to it that others respected me. That brought us closer."

Elizabeth was still stunned. She had never suspected that Anna's and Haverstock's marriage was not a great love match. "I was serious earlier today when I told you I would not marry."

"But earlier today your innocence had not been compromised. Now it has. You must know how the Aldridge servants talk! It will be all over London that you were seen running from his bedchamber."

"If I turn my back on Society as Charlotte has done—concentrating on doing good works—it won't matter if I'm shunned by the *ton*."

"It will matter to your brothers."

"I'm sorry. I know how Haverstock would have liked for me to marry Aldridge."

"All of your loved ones would be happy for the connection, but more than that, it would be good for you. Don't forget how very wealthy he is. With his money, you could do more good works than ever you dreamed."

She had not thought of that.

Anna rose. "I beg that you sleep on it. Please, consider the duke's proposal in light of the many good things that can result from it. Please?"

Elizabeth nodded solemnly. How could Anna have known the duke had vowed to make her reconsider? She could still recall the very expression on his simmering countenance when he'd said, "I am accustomed to getting what I want, Elizabeth."

Why was the man under the misapprehension that *she* was what he wanted?

During the next several days, Aldridge set about getting all his affairs in order. He delivered the hundred pounds personally to Belle Evans. He knew the "loan" would never be returned. Even though her anticipated visit had resulted in the debacle with young Lady Elizabeth Upton, he was not angry. For the more he contemplated marriage, the more he thought marriage to Lady Elizabeth might suit him.

He did not delude himself that he was in love with her. But the attributes she possessed were exactly what was required for his potential duchess. And it was time. He must see to the succession.

Once Aldridge had seen Belle, his next order of business was to have his solicitor see about the house on Trent Square. What a capital idea to allow officers' widows to use it!

It was really quite admirable of Lady Elizabeth to concern herself so much with the plight of the less fortunate. Though it did not surprise him. Haverstock had always been possessed of an acute sense of duty. Few men of his rank worked as hard or for as many hours as he did for the Crown.

Taking a cue from Haverstock, Aldridge's next action was showing up at the Foreign Office and offering his services. He learned that Haverstock had greased his path, and his duties in cryptology had already been assigned.

At Brooks later that night, he announced to all his titled friends that he fully intended to sit in the House of Lords when the next session began.

After meeting with his chief steward, Aldridge was temporarily free of obligations. Save one. Or make that two. He showed up at Haverstock House on Half Moon Street early enough in the day that Lady Elizabeth would still be at home. "Pray," he said to the butler, "the Duke of Aldridge to see Lady Elizabeth." He handed a note to the stiff man. "I beg that you give this to her. It explains why I've come."

When the duke's note was delivered to Elizabeth, she was sitting at her dressing table peering into the looking glass as Anna's skillful French maid saw to the arrangement of her hair. Elizabeth's eyes ran over the seal that was stamped with the symbol of a sword, then she opened it.

My Dear Lady Elizabeth,

I thought you and I could ride over to Trent Square so I can show you the house, and we can discuss what must be done to prepare it for your war widows. I will wait in your drawing room.

Aldridge

He hadn't forgotten! Though she did not fancy traveling with the notorious rake, she was decidedly thrilled to set into motion her scheme.

Filled with a sense of exhilaration, she could not wait. "That's perfectly good enough, Colette. I'm anxious to dress and meet my caller who awaits downstairs."

Elizabeth was quite sure Colette had peered at the signature on her letter, and the old woman's comment soon confirmed her suspicions. "What shall you wear to see the duke?"

It was Elizabeth's great misfortune that all the servants knew of her indiscretions in the duke's bedchamber three days previously. She knew the periwinkle was her most flattering dress, but that's what she had worn the last time she'd seen him, the night he proposed--the night he'd murmured her first name so intimately. "The pale yellow, I think," Elizabeth managed in a shaky voice.

"An excellent choice. So pretty with Mademoiselle's pale yellow hair."

Aldridge regarded her with his dark, pensive eyes as she moved gracefully into the drawing room. She looked a bit younger than her one and twenty years—and she looked prettier than she had that day in his bedchamber as her widened eyes perused his nakedness. How in the blazes had the girl not been snatched up before now? She was in possession of gentle beauty, as soft as the buttery colour of her hair. Pale periwinkle eyes, a perfectly formed nose, and sweet pink lips combined to produce a most agreeable face. Were all the young men in London fools?

He knew nothing about women's fashions, but he thought her muslin morning dress would be considered fashionable. It would do little to keep her warm in a chill. Its sleeves terminated well above her elbows, and its neck scooped just low enough to display the slight swell of her delectable breasts. Her bearing was as graceful as a swan's, her figure completely without flaw.

Standing, he moved to her and bowed. "I am bereft of words to describe your loveliness today, Lady Elizabeth."

She held out her hand, and he brought it to his lips for a mock kiss. "Your grace is too kind."

"I am many things, but too kind has never been used to describe me."

"I beg to differ. With all you must deal with after a five-year absence, I am shocked you remembered my little scheme."

"Your scheme is not insignificant. It's one of the most important things I've been considering." He crooked his arm, offering it to her. "Shall we carry on to Trent Square?"

She tucked her arm within his, and they moved to the entry corridor. "I'll fetch my pelisse and bonnet."

A moment later—after she donned her blue pelisse—she and he were climbing into his awaiting carriage. "It's good that you put on the pelisse. It doesn't feel like spring at all today."

She settled on the seat across from him. "It was a bitterly cold winter, and I fear it's being followed by an unseasonably cool spring. I wonder if that means we will miss summer altogether."

"It's happened before."

They both peered at the gray skies and the congested streets filled with carts of potatoes, loads of hay, and hackneys hurriedly weaving in and out of the other conveyances. Because of all the vehicles clogging the streets, it took them almost an hour to reach Trent Square. A bird could have been there in less than ten minutes. As much as he liked walking, he was enough of a gentleman not to expect his companion to slog along in this mist. Ladies objected to exposing their hair to such treatment.

When the coach pulled to a stop in front of Number 7 Trent Square, he gave the place a long look. He wasn't sure he had ever before seen the narrow, five-story terrace house. It was constructed of a red brick that had been popular a century earlier.

Once the coachman let down the step and Elizabeth and Aldridge alighted from the conveyance, Aldridge peered around the square. His was the only vehicle in sight. Which was to be expected in this non-aristocratic neighborhood. Keeping horses and carriages was beyond the means of most of those in the middle classes.

At first he and she just stood on the pavement looking up at the house, assessing its condition. "I daresay it could use fresh paint," he finally said. The white paint framing the casements was flaking in spots.

"I think it has a very solid look." She began to

move toward the three steps that led to the front door. "How does it look on the inside?"

He shrugged. "I wouldn't know. I've never before seen the house."

She stopped and looked up at him. The tip of her head came just past his shoulder. How could this lovely, *petite* creature be the sister of tall, homely, sensible Lydia? "Do not tell me this is the first time you've ever looked at the house!"

He shrugged again. "Then I won't tell you."

"It is almost incomprehensible to me that one has so much property one doesn't have time to examine every last acre."

"You forget I've been away. And I succeeded just a year before I left the country. I have an excellent steward as well as solicitor, both of whom look after my interests exceptionally well."

She paused after the first step. "Someone's in there!"

"Oh, yes. I neglected to tell you that I sent my housekeeper over yesterday. She's assembled a corps of maids to give the place a proper cleaning."

Elizabeth tried the door, and it opened freely. They walked into a small, rather dark entry hall. Its only feature was a narrow wooden staircase. "Apparently, I own all the contents, but I daresay that's not much. Not even a proper table in the entry corridor."

He was not used to stairways without family portraits painted by the great masters. To the left of the staircase, he stepped into the morning room. A parlor maid stopped dusting the wall sconces and curtseyed when she saw him.

"Do carry on," he said, smiling at the youthful maid.

"The light is good here," Elizabeth said. "Would this not be a lovely place for the children's schoolroom?"

"I see nothing lovely about it," he mumbled.

She was hurrying into an adjoining room, then moving back into the entry hall, where he met her.

"Shall we take a look at the basement?" he asked.

They descended a still-darker stairway into the dreary, damp basement where the kitchen was located. She led the way as if this were her own house. To their left was a dark cell. "A wine cellar?" she asked.

"It appears the previous occupants were not Quakers."

"Do you know anything about the home's original owners?"

"As a matter of fact, I had my solicitor look into the home's history. It was built by one Jonas White for his family which included fourteen offspring."

"Then it will be just what we need for our widows!"

He lifted a single brow. "*Our* widows?"

"Yes, ours. By so generously offering your property, you've become a major supporter of *our* war widows."

"You give me more credit than is my due. I am merely being accommodating in order to woo the mother of the next Duke of Aldridge." Why in the devil had he uttered such words?

Her eyes widened, and a most becoming blush stole into her cheeks. She spun away from him and continued along the corridor, poking her head into each small, dark room they passed.

Choosing to ignore his words, she asked, "How can we re-purpose the wine cellar?"

"Perhaps it can be an auxiliary larder."

She looked up at him in dismay. "I am surprised a duke knows about larders. I shouldn't have thought you'd have any occasion to descend into the servant's domain."

"But you see, as a lad, I was possessed of an insatiable craving for plum pudding and sweetmeats."

Her pale blue eyes sparkled with mirth. "Therefore, you had to sneak down to the kitchens for extra portions?"

"Indeed. Miss Bull Face would most certainly have objected."

"Miss Bull Face?"

He nodded gravely. "The governess who taught me my letters before I went off to Eton. Her actual name was Bullfinch, but I assure you our moniker suited her far better."

She laughed. "I perceive you've always been naughty."

He moved toward her, and she inched back, away from him, until her shoulders butted into the wall. A sliver of light highlighted her face almost as if she were a celestial being. He came even closer, and his voice grew husky. "Being naughty is much more fun than being nice, Elizabeth."

Then his face lowered, his breath became labored, and his lips settled on hers as his arms entrapped her.

Chapter 4

When she realized he was going to kiss her, she was terrified. Her heart pounded. Fear spiked through her like a rapier's point. She wanted to get away from this dark man whose mouth was crushing hers. Indeed, she tried to push him away, but her paltry strength was nothing against his.

As the kiss deepened, her entire being was cast into a sensory whirlwind. She felt as if she were spinning faster than Scottish gales. How could a kiss affect one so profoundly? Oddly stirred by his light sandalwood scent, she experienced a comforting feeling of security from the way his large body cocooned her own.

The kiss went from passionate to incredibly tender, the touch of his lips as soft as down. Like his gossamer touch, her eyelids drifted downward, and she stopped trying to push him away.

In the span of a few seconds, she came to understand how so intimate an act could blend two such diverse beings.

Then she realized how scandalous her behavior was. It was bad enough that she'd come alone with him to an unoccupied house, but now she was behaving like a strumpet.

She jerked away and spoke with rebuke. "You

mean to completely ruin me!"

His lids heavy, he shook his head and spoke in a husky voice. "No, Elizabeth, I want you for my wife."

Why did he persist with such a ridiculous notion? She stalked away, and this time he didn't try to stop her. She began to climb the stairs. Seconds later, she heard the click of his boot heels behind her.

Her hand on the banister trembled, but she schooled herself to act calm. "I wonder how many bedchambers there are." Her cheeks stung. The mention of bedchambers so soon after their intimacy embarrassed her.

"Something tells me we're going to find that out."

She watched him through narrowed eyes. "Don't expect me to be stupid enough to enter a bedchamber with you." He was entirely too virile.

His only response was a quirked brow and half smile.

She went straight to the second story where she strolled casually through a drawing room, dinner room, and small library. "Perhaps the library would make a better school room," she said.

He came into the chamber. "And may I ask who's going to instruct the children?"

"The mothers--most of whom are officers' wives--can take turns. One can teach French, another reading, another can work with sums."

His dark eyes flashed. "I can see you've given this a lot of thought."

Afraid he would try to steal another kiss, she merely nodded as she swept from the room and began to mount the wooden stairs to the next level, which was the first to feature bedchambers.

The first bedchamber they came to was furnished with two narrow beds that appeared to have been made up with fresh linens. "Oh, this will be perfect for Mrs. Hudson and her little girl!" She spun around to face him, unable to suppress her gleeful expression. "Oh, your grace, do you think she can come live here straight away?"

"Before the house is in order?"

She nodded. "You see, she had nowhere to sleep, so I used the last of my pin money to procure temporary lodgings for her, but my money has run out. I won't have another farthing until the next quarter."

His gaze softened. "That was very generous of you to use your last farthing to help the unfortunate woman."

She shrugged. "It brought me a great deal more happiness than purchasing a hat for myself."

"Well, Lady Do Gooder, have you considered how much you could assist these poor creatures if you had my fortune at your disposal?"

At least he wasn't trying to smash her against another wall to force kisses on her! "I declare, your grace, I believe you're trying to bribe me."

His dark eyes smoldered as he peered into hers. "Bribe. Purchase. Whatever it takes. I mean to have you, Elizabeth."

There he went--using that low, provocative voice--and causing wild fluctuations in her pulse. "You know I am not in love with you?"

"As I said, I always get what I want. You'll fall in love with me. After we're wed."

"You are positively insufferable!" She scurried from the chamber before he had the opportunity to corner her.

"To belatedly answer your question," he said, "I have no objection to allowing this Mrs. Hudson of yours to move in straight away."

She could have flung her grateful self into his arms. "Thank you, your grace."

For the rest of the tour, she would only enter rooms where chamber maids were cleaning. She hoped the duke was gentlemanly enough to avoid putting on a scandalous display in front of the servants.

After she had seen every room--some of them only from the doorway--her sparkling eyes looked up into his face. "This house is perfect! You are ever so kind to lend it for this purpose."

"It's not as if it's *my* house; it's merely a lease property that happens to have been inherited by me."

"Still, it's a wonderful thing you're doing."

A solemn expression on his face, he offered an arm. "Allow me to escort you to the coach."

She tucked her arm into the proffered crook of his. "Pray, your grace, could I impose on you to take me to Mrs. Hudson's so I can give her the good news?"

"Certainly." When they came to the first floor, he asked, "How is it the plight of Mrs. Hudson came to your attention?"

"My brother, James, served with her husband, and when the man died, James wrote and asked me to look in on her. He had great admiration for her husband."

"How many widows have you?"

"Personally, I have had communication with seven. They're all desperate. My brother has a contact at the War Office who can put me in touch with others."

"I think there will be room enough for thirteen families," he said, "--provided none of them have the progeny of Mr. Jonas White."

She giggled as they returned to his carriage.

"Where do we find your Mrs. Hudson?" he asked.

"Actually, not too far from here. In the Covent Garden area."

"Then, if she's respectable, we need to get her out of there."

"It was all I could afford."

"I don't like your being there at all." Hunched over, he moved to sit beside her, taking her hand into his. Her heartbeat quickened.

"We shall have to see that your pin money is replaced."

She stiffened. "I have no intentions of accepting any money from you."

"As a maiden, you are right to refuse pecuniary imbursement from any man." Then, drawing her into his arms, he spoke in that husky voice that frightened her with its intimacy. "But as my wife, Elizabeth, you'll have a very generous settlement."

Drawing in her breath, she placed both hands upon his chest and pushed away. "I shall tell my brother what a beast you're being."

He began to laugh. "I shall tell him myself."

Once he and Lady Elizabeth shared his carriage with girlish Mrs. Hudson and her three-year-old daughter, Aldridge felt inordinately satisfied with himself and the manner in which he was spending his day. Mrs. Hudson was the same age as Elizabeth. So young to be widowed, so young to be a mother. There was an incredible sweetness about her fair appearance and her simple muslin dress that showed signs of having been patched. There was also melancholy. Her eyes sparkled only when she peered at her little Louisa. He saw that the woman still wore a simple gold wedding band. Offering his property for her and others like her made him feel uncommonly good.

"My Harry always said Captain Upton was the finest officer in the Peninsula," Mrs. Hudson said, referring to Elizabeth's brother. "I should like to write to him and thank him for his concern for me and my Louisa."

"I will be happy to post it for you. My brother is always happy to receive letters. I know he will want to know how you're doing since he thought so highly of your husband."

The young window's eyes moistened. "There was never a finer man than my Harry."

After depositing Mrs. Hudson and her little Louisa to Number 7 Trent Square, he explained he would send a servant to fill the pantry, then he settled back in his luxurious carriage, eying Elizabeth. Elizabeth remained on his side of the carriage. He couldn't have been happier with any woman than he was with Lady Elizabeth. Her genuine goodness was more than he'd ever hoped to find in a wife.

He meant to make her his duchess.

Even if it meant going to Almack's. He shuddered.

Haverstock rarely put his foot down with Elizabeth, but this night he had insisted that she accompany him and Anna to Almack's Assembly

Rooms. "Even Lydia will be there," he had said.

"Pray, I know how much she dislikes dancing," Elizabeth said. "Why is she going?"

"It's something to do with Morgie's cousin being in town."

Elizabeth could not refuse her brother's request. She had previously told Anna that since she had no intentions of seeking a husband at Almack's, she had no desire to go there. Nothing that ever occurred at Almack's could give her half so much pleasure as she'd gotten that afternoon when she'd shown Mrs. Hudson her new home.

Even though she meant to avoid Society, Elizabeth quite vainly was excited to have the opportunity to wear the new ivory gown she'd gotten a few weeks earlier. It was the prettiest she'd ever owned, and she knew Anna had not flattered when she'd told Elizabeth that no dress had ever looked lovelier on her.

Anna even insisted that Elizabeth borrow her diamonds to wear with it. As she stood before her looking glass, she could not have been happier with her appearance. She had not felt so lovely even the night of her presentation ball.

But as lovely as she knew she looked, when she entered the ballroom of Almack's, she felt as if a second nose protruded from her face. Matrons stopped in mid-sentence and turned to stare at her. The drone of voices lifted, and she heard words which humiliated her. *Naked. Aldridge. Scandalous.*

Her eyes watered. Her misguided visit to Aldridge House earlier in the week had apparently been widely publicized. She had not only brought shame upon herself, she had shamed her brother. And he did not deserve it. Especially with his important post at the Foreign Office.

Her face prickling from embarrassment, she followed Anna and Haverstock, and sat in a section reserved for peers.

When the first set started, she experienced something that had not occurred a single time in the three years since she'd come out: not a single man asked her to stand up with him.

She had never been so mortified.

As she sat there trying to make small talk with Anna but speaking nonsensically, she was aware that others continued to stare at her. When the set ended, she hoped someone would rescue her from complete humiliation the next set. But when it started, no one crossed the ballroom to seek her for a partner.

Thank God her brother had gone to the card room. His humiliation would have been more painful than her own. "Oh, Anna, I've disgraced our whole family."

"You've hurt no one except yourself."

Elizabeth gave a bitter laugh. "It's a good thing I've chosen not to wed. I daresay no one would have me."

Anna's large eyes, the colour of mahogany, regarded her. "That's not so. The Duke of Aldridge wishes to make you his duchess."

As if conjured by her words, the Duke of Aldridge entered the ballroom at that very moment. All conversation ceased. All eyes riveted to the tall, handsome man who was moving toward Elizabeth. He towered over the other men and was impeccably turned out with his stylishly cut dark hair and his well-fitted jet black coat and dove breeches. She held her breath, praying he would honor her with a dance invitation. Her bruised pride needed it.

When he bowed in front of her and begged her to stand up with him, the drone of voices renewed.

She hated to admit her vanity, but she was ever so happy to set her hand into his and allow him to sweep her off her feet. Her satisfaction with him was in proportion to the depth of her humiliation. For the second time that day, she felt like throwing her arms around his neck.

The country set did not afford them the opportunity for conversation, but it allowed all the dancers--and onlookers--the opportunity to gape at the sinfully rich, sinfully handsome, purportedly wicked Duke of Aldridge.

When the set was over, he led her from the chamber and procured ratafia for her. Then to her mortification, he said in a clear voice. "Do you think, my love, we should announce our forthcoming nuptials tonight?"

It was all she could do not to sling the liquid into his smug face. She glared at him.

"I suppose that announcement ought to come from your brother."

The last thing she needed was another scene in front of all these people. "But, your grace," she finally managed, "I have not yet consented to become your duchess."

"But, my love, I always get what I want."

She moved closer and spoke in a whisper. "Does your grace want a slap in the face?"

He threw his head back, laughing. "Your sense of humor is so delightful, my darling."

She came close again. "I. Am. Not. Your. Darling."

He drew her hand into his. "Soon, love. Soon."

She lowered her voice to a whisper again. "You know I'm not in love with you, and I know you're not in love with me."

His dark eyes went solemn. "Talk to your brother. I believe he'll tell you that love follows the most reluctant spouses."

Did everyone but her know that Haverstock's and Anna's marriage had not begun as a love match? It would be hard to fathom now. No two people were could be more in love. Except for Morgie and Lydia.

And theirs had been a love match--even if it was a lifetime in coming.

As they stood there, stiffly observing one another, Morgie strolled up. "I say, Aldridge, it's devilishly good to have you back."

"My God, Morgie, but it's good to see you! Felicitations on your marriage. You chose very well."

"Did you know we have a son?"

Aldridge nodded. "It seems more felicitations are in order. I shall have to see this fine son of yours and Lady Lydia's."

Morgie's voice lowered. "Pray, don't tell Lyddie. . ." He shook his head. "He doesn't look . . . like a small lad--a very small lad. He's. . ." Morgie's brows lowered with concern, and the gap he made with hands indicated the babe's size to be a little over a foot. "Looks like me grandfather, he does. Not a hair on his head."

Elizabeth chuckled. "That's common in infants! I assure you," she said to the duke, "my nephew is a perfect little fellow."

Relief washed over Morgie's face. "You really think he's all right? That's what Lyddie keeps saying, but you know how she dotes on him."

"I would think," the duke said, "you can always rely on what Lady Lydia says. She's possessed of uncommon good sense."

The three of them returned to the ballroom. The rest of the night, the duke stayed by her side, and the rest of the night Elizabeth could not purge from her thoughts the knowledge that Lydia had come to love Morgie after years of friendship, that Anna and Haverstock's forced marriage had turned into a great love worthy of a Keats' poem.

As skeptical as she was over forced marriages, she found herself wondering if she *could* grow to love the duke--were she to consent to marrying him.

They danced with each other the last dance--a waltz, and when it ended, he bid her goodnight. "I shall call on you tomorrow."

She was so lost in her thoughts on the way home from Almack's that she never heard her brother addressing her. Then later, after she shed her lovely gown, donned her night shift, and climbed upon her bed, her thoughts returned to the Duke of Aldridge. She found herself enumerating all the reasons why she should marry him.

1. She would be able to use his money for her charitable works.

2. She could redeem her tarnished reputation.

3. She could make her brother happy, not only by achieving number 2, but also by uniting their family with that of his oldest friend.

4. And she would be an idiot to turn down so spectacular a match.

5. The fierce attraction she had once held for him could return.

And last, she kept thinking about how truly

and deeply her brother, Anna, Morgie, and Lydia were loved. Could she ever be so blessed?

She was unable to sleep. He was going to call on her the next day. She knew he would once more ask for her hand. She sensed this would be her last chance to accept his kind offer.

Could she? Would she?

Chapter 5

Throughout the night Elizabeth was possessed by a strong desire to see Captain Smythe. If only she could gaze upon a miniature of him. Perhaps that would help make up her mind. Could she risk marrying another and lose all hope of ever being loved by him?

She thought perhaps she no longer loved him, but how could that be? She had once loved him so potently she'd thought she would perish of melancholy when he sailed away. Even months after he left, the joy seemed to have been stripped from her life. Many a night she had lain in her dark room weeping for the handsome officer who had pretended to love her.

Why could she not feel toward the Duke of Aldridge as she had felt toward the Captain? That would have made her decision so easy.

Why could the duke not have come back two years ago? Then, his attentions would have made her the belle of London. Then, she would easily have rekindled her former adoration of him. Then, she would not have lost her heart to Captain Smythe.

Everything happens for a reason. That's what her aunt, the Duchess of Steffington, always said over her own sad life. Had it been preordained that Elizabeth would disgrace herself at Aldridge

House? That one imprudent act of hers could significantly affect the rest of her life.

And that of the Duke of Aldridge.

Was that one imprudent act to be a curse? Or would she one day look upon it as a Godsend? If only she knew. If only a gypsy's crystal ball could truly allow her to glimpse into the future.

One night of Almack's ostracism had changed everything. The previous morning she would not have considered the duke's proposal. But now she knew she could neither subject herself nor her family to such scandal. Even if she were resolved to stay away from Society and direct her life at doing good works, she was incapable of inflicting such shame on her family--especially upon Haverstock, whose career could be significantly hindered by her disgrace. He did so thrive in his important government position.

As murky dawn settled into another cold, gray spring day, she made her decision.

At least it was no longer misting that afternoon when Aldridge and Elizabeth drove through Hyde Park in his open barouche. He told himself this was his chance--as last night too had been--to repair Lady Elizabeth's reputation in the eyes of the *ton*. It was beastly how so innocent an act could be twisted and carried throughout the Capital like polluted autumn leaves on the briskest day. His lips folded into a grim line. His servants! Unfortunately they were given to gossip, and there did not seem to be anything he could do to prevent it.

It was beastly too that all would be forgotten were a duke to offer for the lady in question. No one dared speak ill of a duchess--and most especially a duchess who was the daughter of and sister to a marquess. Were she to become Aldridge's wife, her attendance at balls and soirees would be in fervent demand, no matter what wicked things she'd been accused of before her marriage.

He owed it to her and to her brother to beg for her hand one last time. If she refused him this afternoon, he would acquit himself of any further responsibility toward her.

It would pain him that her good name was being tarnished merely because she'd gone to his home to beg assistance for the less fortunate. He rather wished he could ring out the bells of Westminster and proclaim her innocence to all of London.

What in the blazes would he do if she refused him this afternoon? Though he knew he should settle down, there was not another woman who would fit into his life as neatly as she.

If she turned him down, he would likely continue on in his rakish pursuits. There were the races at Newmarket, faro at Brooks, and he might even pluck a comely dancer away from the opera to keep his bed warm at night.

But after seeing how content Haverstock and Morgie were in matrimony, those rakish pursuits held no allure for Aldridge. Over the past few days, he'd come to relish the notion of sharing his life with a woman whom he would value. A good woman like Lady Elizabeth Upton.

He never deluded himself that he loved her, but he thought in time, he might. Especially if she proved to be sensible as was her eldest sister.

He had enjoyed seeing Lydia briefly at Almack's the previous night. She always amused.

Though she did not mention anything so indelicate, Morgie had lowered his voice to explain to Aldridge why his wife could stay at Almack's only for half an hour: "Refuses to have a wet nurse, and upon my word, the lad's a greedy little bugger! Poor Lyddie!" Morgie had shaken his head in dismay. "Don't know where all that milk goes. He's hardly bigger than me hand."

After Morgie and Lydia Morgan left, Aldridge could not free his mind of the notion of an aristocratic lady like Lydia nursing her own babe. It raised Lydia even higher in his opinion, if that were possible.

Then quite naturally, his thoughts moved on to Lydia's younger sister. Two sisters could not have been more disparate in appearance. Elizabeth was petite, fair, and pretty; Lydia was tall, large of bone, and dark. At thirty, she'd been a confirmed spinster because men had never been able separate her unpleasing appearance from her cleverness and worthiness. Morgie, who was not particularly clever but who had always had an excellent eye for aesthetics, was the last man in the kingdom Aldridge would have expected to fall in love with Lydia. He wondered exactly how that had come about.

Why in the deuce was Aldridge concerning himself so much with love and marriage? In his two and thirty years he had never concerned himself with domesticity. Good lord, did he have one foot in the grave? His father had died suddenly in his early forties. Was the same malady going to strike down the son before he reached forty? Is that why Aldridge was so bloody hell bent on siring a son that he'd offered for Elizabeth on his first day back in England?

Or was it Elizabeth herself who was responsible for this uncharacteristic obsession of his over marriage?

Would she consent to be his wife? Would she present him with an heir? Would she suckle their son at her breast as Lydia was doing with her son? His glance surreptitiously flicked to her modest bosom, and his heartbeat unaccountably quickened. Clearing his throat, he drew her hand into his. "You must realize why I wanted to be alone with you today."

Without looking at him, she nodded.

"Say it, Elizabeth," he said, his voice like that of a stern father.

"You're going to do me the honor of asking me to become your wife."

Stunned, he regarded her from her lowered lashes to her slender hand tucked within his own. And a smile tugged at the corners of his mouth. "My, this is a departure! You suddenly find my offer an *honor*?"

She nodded shyly. "Yes, your grace."

"By Jove! Does that mean you will accept?"

She finally met his gaze with incredibly solemn eyes. He'd never actually looked at them before from this close a distance. They were so pale a shade of lavender he wondered why they were not translucent. Everything about her was pale and delicate, like a fragile spring rose. "I would feel wretched for depriving you of a love match."

He bit back his first response. He'd almost made the blunder of telling her the Dukes of Aldridge never married for love. Dukes had other obligations. One of his present obligations was seeing to the restoration of this fine young lady's reputation.

But he wasn't so noble he'd sacrifice his future for benefit of another. Since he dare not admit he had no intentions of marrying for love--what girl did not cling to the romantic notion of a love match?--he decided to be flippant. "If you must know, I mean to have the dowry your heiress sister-in-law will bestow on you. Everyone knows of the marchioness's generosity with Haverstock's sisters."

"And here I was suffering under the misapprehension you were isolated from English Society these five years past."

So she tossed flippancy back at him. He brought her hand to his lips and pressed a kiss to her gloves, just above her delicate knuckles. "Ah, my love, there is so much I have missed, so many gaps that need to be filled."

"Perhaps I can be of service."

Lamentably, his mind was so derelict that when she uttered the word *service*, his prurient thoughts arrowed to women like Belle Evans. Yet, he had no taste for women of that sort. He now wanted Lady Elizabeth Upton.

He was not in love with her, but oh, how he wanted her!

He turned to her and gave a devilish smile. "Morgie and Lydia? How did that come about?"

A soft laugh rose from her chest. "You did not credit Morgie with having such good sense?"

"You must know I count Morgie as my second-best friend in all the world. I will own he's uncommonly adept at discussing what is fashionable or where to place one's money on the Exchange."

"I think they grew close when Anna started her sewing school in the East End, and Haverstock--

unable to leave his duties at the Foreign Office--asked Morgie to look out for her and Lydia for Lydia was just as committed to the school as Anna. Morgie may never have acted upon his growing affections for Lydia if the squire from near Haymore hadn't come to London to beg Lydia's hand in marriage because he needed a mother for his large progeny."

"But Lydia could not consider such a marriage."

"My sister was persuaded that was her one and only chance of having a family and home of her own. She accepted the squire's offer."

"I think I see where this is going. Morgie began to realize what he was about to lose."

"I did not know you were so romantic, your grace."

He glared. "Continue."

"Morgie was very jealous of the squire, but it took a bit of manipulation on Lydia's part to pry a declaration from him."

"So she had actually fallen in love with Morgie during all those jaunts to the East End?"

"Indeed. They were ever so comfortable with one another."

"Ah, like you and me!"

She gave him a queer look. "Perhaps now I am more comfortable with you. Now that I no longer think of you as a wicked predator."

"I am many things, but I give you my word, I am not a wicked predator."

Her voice softened. "I know."

"To answer your initial question," he said hesitantly, "I want an heir."

Her lashes lowered. "I hope you were teasing when you spoke of my dowry? I daresay it's not *that* large."

"I was teasing."

"I thought you were. After all, you've tried to bribe my compliance by promising me not only generous pin money but also by agreeing to indulge my little scheme for the war widows. If I consented to marry you."

"A small price to pay to secure the lovely Lady Elizabeth Upton for my bride." The more he was around her, the more puzzled he became over her failure to secure a husband. How could she have gone through three seasons and still remain unwed? He understood there would have been a certain number of men who knew they were not of sufficient rank to snare a marquess's daughter.

Then another thought struck him. Could she have fancied herself in love with a man who had not come up to scratch? She *had* denied that her affections were engaged. If she had fancied herself in love previously, it should be nothing to him.

But it did matter. He did not understand why it should.

He cleared his throat again. "Are you being honest with me about. . . not holding another man in your affections?"

"There is no one."

"Some will say you've held out for a duke, but I know better."

"I was being honest earlier this week when I told you I had decided to stay a spinster and dedicate my life to good works."

"Sounds rather nunnery to me."

She giggled.

He squeezed her hand. "I am waiting for your answer, Elizabeth." His heartbeat accelerated. It wasn't every day a man asked for a woman's hand in marriage. In fact, this was the first woman to whom he had ever offered.

"Yes, your grace. I will become your wife."

He almost sighed, but he did not want her to know how insecure he'd been. "I shall see that you never regret it. Now, dearest, I have a request to make of you."

Her brows elevated.

"You are not to ever refer to me as *your grace*. We will be equals."

"What shall I call you?"

Everyone--even his siblings--called him Aldridge, but he found the notion of his wife calling him by his Christian name held far greater appeal.

When he'd finally met the Marchioness Haverstock the night before--and thought she was perhaps even more beautiful than he'd been led to expect--he was charmed that she referred to Haverstock as *Charles*. Addressing her husband by his first name was as tender as lover's caress.

"Philip," he finally said.

"Philip," she murmured.

Damn, but it sounded seductive on her sweet lips! He wanted to taste her lips again, but Hyde Park at the fashionable hour was not the place or the time. He looked forward to seeing just how seductive his bride-to-be would be.

"I shall procure a special license so we can wed straight away."

She whirled toward him. "I assure you, my sister-in-law will want to ensure I have a trousseau fit for a duchess."

"You need not ever feel beholden to your brother's heiress--no matter how delightful she is. You will be a duchess, and as my wife, it will be my pleasure to provide the funds for your trousseau." He brought the back of her hand to his nibbling lips. "I'm honored that you've consented to be my wife."

"You're saying you want to marry *before* I procure a trousseau?"

He nodded. "Why do you not run along and do your fittings, having the bills sent to me. They can all be ready by the time we return from our wedding trip to Glenmont Hall." Which could not come soon enough for him.

"It doesn't seem right to marry a duke in an old dress."

He shrugged. "Do me the goodness of wearing the ivory you wore last night."

She nodded shyly. She had to have known how lovely she looked in it. "I should like to marry at Haverstock House, in the same room where Lydia married Morgie."

"A good plan." He instructed the driver to return to Haverstock House.

He could not voice his reservations, nor his guilt that she was having to marry where there was no love.

There was something between them. Not love. He could not understand what it was, but whatever it was, it was compelling.

Chapter 6

Somehow Elizabeth had managed to get through the wedding ceremony without once picturing the handsomeness of Captain Smythe's tall form. A pity she couldn't rid her mind of how happy Morgie and Lydia had been in that very room on their wedding day less than a year earlier. Elizabeth had never dreamed she would ever marry without being madly in love.

In some ways that made her no better than Kate. But Kate's hand had *not* been rather forced to marry because she had gotten herself in a scandalous situation as had Elizabeth. Kate had barreled into a loveless marriage with her eyes wide open. All because she wanted more than anything to be a duchess. Then Mr. Reeves' elderly ducal uncle went and married a young woman, putting an end to Mrs. Kate Reeve's hopes of succeeding to a dukedom.

Unlike Kate, Elizabeth was at least being wed to a man she had come to respect. The Duke of Aldridge wasn't the disreputable rake she had initially thought him to be. She was still shocked that he had so readily agreed to the marriage once he realized she had ruined herself that day at Aldridge House. It was exceedingly noble of him.

Now she had to brace herself for the only repayment he sought: she must bear his heir.

The wedding and the wedding breakfast had been attended by most of their siblings. Her brother in the Peninsula and sister in Cornwall were missing, as were Philip's siblings who did not live close to London. Elizabeth was delighted that Margaret and Caroline Ponsby, his sisters closest to her own age, had come from Glenmont. The dowager Marchioness of Haverstock came from Haymore for her daughter's wedding, and the last one making up their party was Elizabeth's cousin, Richard Rothcomb-Smedley (whom they all called Richie), who had become something important in the House of Commons.

Throughout the wedding breakfast, she tried to keep uncharitable thoughts at bay, but it was difficult. Kate glared at the bride as if Elizabeth were a blatant husband stealer while openly flirting with Elizabeth's new husband! Kate was flagrantly shameless. And even if she was Elizabeth's sister, Elizabeth wished her in Coventry.

While Elizabeth and Caroline were gushing over their pleasure at now being sisters, Elizabeth was vaguely aware of her mother's voice. "Will your grace be traveling to Glenmont Hall today?" the dowager asked.

Elizabeth quietly sipped at her champagne, exceedingly puzzled over her mother's query. There was no duchess at the long breakfast table.

"My love," Philip said to Elizabeth, "I believe you're being addressed by your mother."

Elizabeth could have groaned over her mother's uncontrollable glee that her daughter had snared a duke. (One did not have to look far to see who Kate had taken after.) As Elizabeth's embarrassed glance flicked to her mother, she caught the menacing glare in Kate's gaze and knew her sister could not corral her jealousy.

It was beastly that it wasn't Kate who had become a duchess when she had wanted such a title her entire life. Unlike Elizabeth, who would have been perfectly happy wed to an army captain.

But that was neither here nor there. She no longer wished to be married to that wretched Captain Smythe. She was now the wife of an honorable man, and she meant to make the best of it.

Even if it was not a love match for either of them.

She turned to her mother. "Yes, Mother. We plan to leave immediately after the breakfast."

"So we can reach Glenmont by dark," the duke added.

"Do I understand that you'll be back for next week's vote in the House of Lords on the tax increase?" Richie asked the duke.

Before her new husband had the opportunity to answer, Elizabeth addressed him. "Cousin Richie thinks of nothing but his Parliamentary duties."

Philip nodded. "I am well aware of your cousin's parliamentary activities." His eyes met Richie's. "To answer your question, I am interested in doing anything that will help the British win this war, and if this tax plan will help—as I'm told it should—I shall favor it."

Richie smiled upon him. "When will you sit in Parliament?"

"I hope that I can emulate you when I take up my duties week after next. I've obtained a copy of the tax bill and plan to study it during our wedding trip."

Richie raised a brow. "Were I marrying a beauty like Lizzie, reading a tax bill would be the last thing I'd be doing on my honeymoon."

Those assembled around the table all laughed.

Except for Elizabeth. She knew what they were thinking. She and the duke would lie in bed the next several days whilst he took pleasure—which in some way would involve that, that . . . protrusion she had witnessed by mistake. Scarlet rushed to her cheeks.

Unfortunately, the image of Philip's bare, wet flesh and that. . . *dangling thing* of his also surged to her memory.

"I assure you," she said, flashing her gaze from Richie to Philip, "I shan't mind. I shall be very proud of my husband for serving his country in such a manner." She smiled up at Philip.

"And how, my dear Lizzie, would you feel about assisting your favorite cousin with his duties for the House of Commons?" Richie asked.

Her brows lowered. "Whatever could I do to help you?"

"As a married woman, you could serve as my official hostess without drawing censure."

She fleetingly wondered why this bachelor had never asked his other married cousins, Lydia or Kate, to serve as his hostess, but she must own that he *had* always been closer to her than to her sisters. Then, too, he might wish to host Parliamentary discussions or dinners at sumptuous Aldridge House, which was undisputedly one of the grandest of London's houses. "If his grace doesn't object," she said, peering up at Aldridge.

Her husband lifted her chin with a gentle

knuckle. "What are you to call me now, dearest?"

Their eyes met and held. "Philip." She could not have felt more embarrassed had she just stripped off her wedding dress in front of all these people. Not since she was a young girl had she called any male other than her brothers and cousins by their Christian name.

It was just another manifestation of this intimacy she had not been prepared for as recently as a week earlier.

"My darling, you shall be free to use our home in any manner you wish." Philip's gaze flicked to Richie. "I have no objections to allowing Mr. Rothcomb-Smedley to assemble his supporters at Aldridge House."

"How very kind you are, your grace," Richie said. "That's a most generous offer."

While far from being poor, Richie had no residence of his own in the Capital and had been leasing chambers at Albany. She supposed being able to hold dinners at Aldridge House would be advantageous to Richie's promising Parliamentary career, and she would be happy to help her favorite cousin.

The mantel clock chimed. Twelve times.

"It's time we go, love," Philip murmured.

Philip sat beside her in his coach and four and set about throwing the rug across their laps as it had become chilly. Despite that his carriage was as fine as could be purchased, it was not a comfortable place to be on a blustery day like this.

"Thank you." She looked up at him with smiling eyes. Very fine pale bluish eyes. "Will it take us very long to reach Glenmont? I've never been there before."

"That's because when I left England you were a little girl."

"I was not! I was fifteen, almost sixteen."

"And I would not have given you a second look--even though you must have been very pretty."

"As I recall, you were enamored of older, married women."

He frowned. "I only accommodated already-corrupted women."

"So you're saying you draw the line at being a woman's first seducer?"

"I have neither been a maiden's nor a matron's first seducer." He was deuced uncomfortable discussing this business with anyone, much less an innocent like Elizabeth.

She arched a brow. "Then I'll be your first . . ." She was too modest to continue.

Virgin. He swallowed. Not even as a lad at Eton had Philip discussed such intimacies. He'd be damned if he would discuss them with this girl he had married! His only response to her query was a stiff nod. "Oblige me by changing the topic of this conversation. I had forgotten your cousin is Richard Rothcomb-Smedley. I expect by the time he's thirty he'll be Chancellor of the Exchequer. He's possessed of a singular purpose."

"He is indeed, and I think he wants that position *before* he reaches thirty."

"How old is he?"

"Five and twenty." Her gaze flitted to the case he'd brought with his papers. "I have no objections if you'd like to begin reading your tax bill, though I can't credit anything with being more boring. I shall be happy to peer from the carriage window."

"Even on a gray day like this?"

"I always enjoy the country, and my. . . dear Philip, you did not answer my question about how long it will take us to arrive at Glenmont."

"I hope to reach by dark, but even though the days are getting longer it still can be dark before five at this time of year."

"It can be dark by four in the afternoon."

"Since there's been no rain in the past several days, the roads should be good. With no impediments, we should arrive in about four hours."

"I'm glad it's not dark yet so you'll be able to see Glenmont Hall." Philip set aside the papers he'd been perusing throughout the journey. "If you'll look to the right, beyond the glen, you can see it."

She edged closer to the window and pressed her face into its coolness as her gaze swept across the glen's tall grasses rippling in the wind. And just beyond, she saw it. The nearly breathtaking sight of Glenmont Hall recalled Haverstock's praise. Her brother had said no other country home in the kingdom could match Glenmont. At the time, country homes had held no allure for her.

Now she realized Haverstock had not exaggerated.

Even had Glenmont not been so vast--stretching as far as the window would allow her to see--it would have impressed. The pale, ivory-stoned building featured the elements of classical architecture: the central pediment, Corinthian columns, perfect symmetry, and statuary of mythological beings. From this distance she could not tell if the ivory statues lined up along the roofline were Grecian maidens or warriors.

As the carriage clattered along the gravel lane toward the house, she saw they were maidens. A shimmering lake dipping in front caught the reflection of the house and maidens. The place was sheer perfection.

Her throat went dry. *I will be mistress of all of this.* This was now her home and would be until the day she died.

Philip would expect some kind of response from her. "It's so beautiful! Can the interiors possibly be worthy of so fine a home?"

He shrugged. "You'll have to judge for yourself. I do prefer the loveliness of the countryside, but I think the interiors will not offend."

"I'm sure they won't." She had been unable to remove her mesmerized gaze from the perfection of Glenmont. "I see the influence of Capability Brown in your parkland."

"Not just his influence. His complete direction. He worked on this for a decade."

"How fortunate you are."

"Yes, my grandfather came back from his Grand Tour and immediately tore down the old house that had stood on this property since the thirteenth century."

"What a terrible loss."

"I'm told it was falling down in disrepair." He shrugged. "Difficult to know which camp to believe, especially since my grandfather returned from Italy so enamored of Andrea Palladio's architecture."

"Your grandfather must have been an exceedingly patient man. This is so massive an undertaking."

"Indeed it was. He never saw what you're now looking at. Only the central block had been completed before his death--and that took more than ten years to build."

"How many years did it take to build what we see today?"

"One and twenty. My father honored his father's vision--and plans conceived by my grandfather and carried out by Robert Adam."

The Scottish architect's name was one she easily recognized. It would be difficult to find a noble family in Britain which had not worked with Robert Adam or his brother at some time. "I would wager you could not tell me how many rooms you have at Glenmont."

His face screwed up in thought. "You'd win the wager."

"Can you approximate?"

He shrugged. "It's somewhere just short of three hundred."

How utterly daunting! She felt so unfit to be anyone's wife—much less a duke's! She had never even spoken to the Haverstock housekeeper on matters of . . . housekeeping, nor had she ever contemplated the protocol for seating guests at the dinner table.

When the coach pulled up in front of the portico, a footman swung open the door and hurried down the steps to open the carriage door for his master. Philip, in turn, offered Elizabeth his hand as she disembarked.

Inside, a skeleton staff of about two dozen lined up to welcome the new duchess. Elizabeth found it excessively intimidating to think she would be thought the matriarch by each and every one of them. She was but one and twenty! She was not yet old enough to inherit the legacy left her by her grandmother.

Philip had sent ahead his most valued servants--as well as the new lady's maid whose services Elizabeth had procured in accordance with her new status. He had instructed his staff to see that dinner should be ready when the master arrived.

"It's been five and thirty years since there's been a new Duchess of Aldridge," he told her, even though she knew as much.

The first servant to step forward was a tall, middle-aged butler who was possessed of thick, dark hair. "Dearest, I should like to present to you Vale, who's been butler for the Aldridges since I was a lad."

Vale bowed, deeply inclining his head.

Next, the housekeeper came to face Elizabeth, curtseying. This woman was likely in her early to mid-forties. The years had taken away her waist, but her limbs were still lean, and her whispy brown hair was only slightly threaded with gray.

"My darling, I should like to present Mrs. Plumley to you."

"And, Mrs. Plumley," Elizabeth said, meeting the housekeeper's gaze, "how long have you been in service to the Aldridges?"

"His grace was kind enough to offer me employment shortly after he succeeded." Mrs. Plumley favored Elizabeth with a friendly smile devoid of artifice.

Since Philip had succeeded whilst in his twenties, Elizabeth was struck at the maturity he must have demonstrated. She would have thought he'd have deferred to his mother for guidance in domestic decisions.

Elizabeth mirrored the housekeeper's smile. "That you are still here competently running Glenmont is testament to your capabilities."

"Thank you, your grace. Whenever during the next several days you are sufficiently rested, I should be happy to give you a tour of Glenmont."

Elizabeth's gaze lifted to Philip's. She had not realized how much taller than her he was. The tip of her head barely came to his shoulders. "Would tomorrow be agreeable for you?"

Philip nodded. "Excellent. You and Mrs. Plumley can explore the thrilling linen closets whilst I continue my study of the tax bill--after I have the pleasure of showing you the grounds early in the day."

"Very good," Mrs. Plumley said. "The dinner will be served as soon as you and the duchess change clothing, if that meets with your grace's approval."

"I am most gratified to learn that," Philip replied.

Mrs. Plumley curtseyed, then the Duke and Duchess of Aldridge strolled along the grand marble entry foyer, nodding to each freshly cleaned and starched employee before climbing the curving staircase to the bedchambers.

More massive paintings by old Italian masters adorned the walls all the way up the gilt-banistered staircase to the third floor. Turkey carpets dominated with vivid reds covered the time-worn wooden floors there.

"I am sorry the duchess's chambers haven't been done up for you. They are as they were left five years ago."

"When your mother died," she said solemnly.

He gave a morose nod. "You shall have to modernize them." At the second door they came to, he paused and opened it. "These will be your chambers."

Everything in the room was ivory: the silken draperies and bed curtains, the brocade settee, the plastered walls, and even the carpet. All the furnishings were gilt. It looked far too formal for Elizabeth's taste. She would never feel comfortable here.

Fortunately, she did not have to convey her dissatisfaction.

"It looks nothing like you, now that I think on it. My mother was entirely too . . . stilted. She had been with the French court for a brief time and spent the rest of her life emulating Versailles."

She nodded. "I should like the warmth of wood and a bit more colour."

"My duchess shall have it."

Her maid had placed her hairbrush and hand mirror on the opulent dressing table that was lit by slender silver candlesticks. She supposed her clothing, too, had already been unpacked. "Shall you collect me once I've dressed for dinner?"

"I shall. Will half an hour give you enough time?"

A quick glance in the looking glass told her that Fanny's artistry with Elizabeth's hair that morning had held well enough. Otherwise, a half hour would not do for re-dresssing herself and her hair. "I think so."

He leaned into her and brushed a kiss across her cheek. "Good. I'm starving. I'll knock at your door in thirty minutes."

Instead of returning by the door they had entered, he disappeared into a door on the same wall as the headboard of her bed. *To his chambers.* Of course they would adjoin one another! The impending intimacy sent her pulse racing.

Fanny seemed most capable as she helped Elizabeth out of her wedding dress and into one of red velvet which exposed her bare, milk white shoulders. When Philip collected her--coming directly from his bedchamber without using the corridor--his eyes widened when he gazed upon her. "How beautiful you look." There was something in his hand. A silken box.

"I've brought you some of the family jewels. I had hoped to see you wear the Aldridge rubies tonight." He swallowed hard as his simmering gaze raked over her.

"How amazing that I chose to wear the red tonight!" She moved to him as he began to open the box. When she saw the scalloped necklace of large rubies and diamonds set in gold she froze. "Oh, your grace! I shall be afraid to wear anything so beautiful and so valuable!"

His gaze still simmering, he moved to place the necklace on her, and he spoke in a low, husky voice. "Oblige me by not calling me- - -"

"Your grace. Sorry. . .Philip." Her eyes could not leave the looking glass as he clasped the opulent necklace at the back of her neck. Then his head dipped to give her a nibbling kiss in the hollow of her neck.

Goosebumps covered her exposed flesh.

By the time they reached the dinner room, it was quite dark beyond the tall casements, but the three chandeliers above the table glittered with the light of more than a hundred candles.

"I've requested that your place be beside me

since there's just the two of us," he said.

A smile played at her lips. "I am happy, indeed, that I shan't have to shout down the table at you."

A footman poured wine into their glasses as another footman came from the kitchen to spoon clear turtle soup into their bowls. While Philip was consuming his soup, she took the opportunity to peer at him.

What power he emanated! There was an air about him that bespoke authority, and his very solidness in stature and personality commanded respect from male and female alike.

The fire at his back danced in his dark hair as her gaze pored over his nearly black eyes, strong jaw line, and handsome face. She came to realize that even were he not a duke, he could have had any woman in the kingdom.

Why me?

She should be flattered, but she was not. Everything about their so-called courtship had happened so rapidly, she felt as if she'd been tossed into a cyclone. Would she ever feel normal again?

For most of the dinner, they ate in silence. After the sweetmeats were eaten, he placed his hand on hers and spoke in a gentle voice. "I thought you and I could sit before the fire in the library and enjoy a glass of Madeira before going to bed."

Anything that would delay the bed business held vast appeal. She nodded.

Chapter 7

He had selected the library for two reasons. First, it was his favorite room at Glenmont, and secondly, on a blustery night like this, it was the warmest chamber in this chilly house. That was the trouble with all this bloody marble: when it was cold outside, it was cold inside.

As he strolled into the chamber and began to pour the Madeira, Elizabeth stood statue-still in the room's doorway.

Was something the matter? He spun around to peer at her just as a smile lifted her fair face, and a sparkle glittered in her eyes. "It's a wonderful library! I had expected something massive--like the rest of Glenmont--but this is a most comforting chamber."

Her comments oddly satisfied him. She obviously shared his good opinion of the Glenmont library. "I thought it clever of my grandfather to run the books vertically rather than horizontally to keep the chamber's intimacy." Despite that a second story of fine, leather-bound books in dark wood bookcases soared to lofty heights, the library managed to retain its coziness. The square room owed its intimacy to the red-hued Turkey carpets and the fireplaces on each of the four walls, all of them ablaze tonight.

"Won't you sit at the sofa?" he asked. A pair of blue velvet sofas faced each other in front of the room's largest fireplace.

A moment later he set the two full glasses on the table in front of her and came to sit at her left, offering her the glass of Madeira. They sat there sipping in silence for a moment, both watching the fire blaze as winds howled outside. Could anything be better than being here on a cold night with this fine woman who was now his wife?

He had damn near lost his breath when he had strolled into her bedchamber earlier and saw her standing there, the rich red velvet accentuating the milky white of her delicate shoulders and the sweet swell of her breasts. Her pale blonde hair had been swept up, but a few loose strands escaped.

It was the carelessness of those few delicate strands that almost undid him. How he wanted to touch them, to loosen her silken hair, to loosen the scarlet dress until it pooled on the carpet beneath her feet. He had tried not to even glance at the bed for fear of acting on his seductive thoughts.

Now, as they sat in the library, the silence between them was like the glare of an unwelcome guest. Sadly, conversation was hindered by their lack of familiarity. What did he *really* know about her? Of course he knew things like her age and lineage. He knew that she possessed a kind heart. He now knew she shared his good opinion of his favorite room. "Tell me," he finally managed, "are you fond of dancing?" Was that the best he could do?

"Only slightly more than Lydia. Why do you

ask? Surely, you're not planning an assembly here?"

He laughed. How ridiculous she must think him. "No, these next few days will be devoted to two activities and only those two activities."

She raised a brow. "And they are?"

"First, I desire to get to know you better."

She offered him a sweet smile. "And second?"

"I'm going to finish reading that blasted tax bill. I have a great deal to learn."

"I wonder how many members of the House of Lords are taking their duties as seriously as you? Do you think others are slaving over the lengthy bill?"

He shrugged. "My father never did."

"Nor did mine."

He refrained from speaking ill of the man who was her father. It was best to avoid mention of the disagreeable man. Finding something complimentary to say about him was impossible. Philip thanked God the man's offspring did not take after him.

Tender-hearted Elizabeth was as unlike her father as white to black. And Haverstock, too, was as honorable a man as there was.

"Since you desire to take this time to further our acquaintance," she said, "I think it was most kind of your unmarried sisters to leave Glenmont to us."

"Indeed it was. I knew if they were here, you'd ignore me."

Her eyes widened. "So you asked them to go to London?"

He chuckled. "I was teasing you. My sisters are clever enough to understand that a honeymoon calls for privacy."

The fire once more held her attention. Was she embarrassed to think of their impending intimacy? A pity he could not offer her assurances, but he was incapable of speaking of intimacies even to a Cyprian. Some things just weren't discussed.

He watched as she brought the glass to her lips and sipped. Soon, he would possess those lips.

"I will own," she said, still gazing at the fireplace, "that it seems terribly unnatural to be alone with a man. I keep looking over my shoulder for a chaperon."

"You must start thinking of me as your husband. Then our being together will seem completely natural." He hoped.

She took another sip as her head dipped in assent.

He'd encouraged her to drink the Madeira. It should serve to relax her--perhaps even encourage her to be more amorous. He finished his own drink, and a moment later rose and refilled both their glasses.

As she sipped at the second glass, he could almost see the tension uncoil from her. A smile began to play upon her lips, and her eyes met his with increasing regularity and with more warmth. "Was it difficult for you to leave the Contessa Savatini?"

He stiffened. "You are never to speak of . . . of women I am supposed to have bedded." He gave her an icy stare. "One cannot believe everything one hears."

"I'm sorry. I thought you wished for you and me to become better acquainted."

"The subject you initiated is taboo."

Her lashes lowered, and she was silent for a moment. "It shan't be repeated," she said apologetically.

He chastised himself for spoiling the mood. She was mellowing, and he'd gone and spoken to her with no more tenderness than he'd speak to a dishonest servant. He pressed her slim hand between both of his. "Forgive me, dearest. It may have sounded like I was angry with you, but I assure you, I am not."

She nervously sipped at the Madeira, then began to giggle.

"Pray, what amuses you so?" he asked.

"Your ineptitude in initiating conversation. *Do you enjoy dancing?*" she mimicked.

His hopes were dashed. She *did* notice the stupidity of his question. He could not avoid adding his hearty laugh to her melodious giggle.

"Now it is my turn," she finally said, meeting his gaze with laughing eyes. "Allow me to make an elucidating inquiry about you. Tell me, your grace, do you prefer the index finger or the ring finger?" The serious look she directed at him belied her levity.

"Oh, definitely the ring finger."

"But can you point with it?"

"A most serious consideration, to be sure." He lowered his brows in mock thought.

She began stabbing him--most inelegantly--with her finger which wore the Aldridge ruby he'd placed there that morning.

His deep laugh bellowed. "Not bloody well, I see."

"You're not 'posed to say bloody in the presence of a lady. 'Tis bloody indecent."

Once again, she had him laughing. By Jove, if

a man had to be shackled, he could do much worse. There was something utterly satisfying about being married to one who made you laugh.

The wine had relaxed her enough to allow her to say things she would never say were she perfectly sober. He fancied this fanciful bride of his.

Especially when she used the word *indecent.* For being indecent with her was exactly what he wished most. Being with this woman not only made him laugh, but the very scent of her fragrant rose water, the melodious trill of her laughter, the delicacy of her graceful neck, the milkiness of her bare shoulders--all of these things had come to intoxicate him.

Whether she knew it or not, Elizabeth was unexpectedly sensuous.

His throat went dry, and he was unable to peel his gaze away from her seductive loveliness. He moved closer, so close that their thighs touched, so close that the softness of her breast brushed against his upper arm. "But, my love," he murmured huskily, "I am indecent."

In the seconds when their eyes locked, hers went from sparkling to darkly smoldering.

He drew closer. His breath grew short. His head lowered until his mouth hungrily captured hers. When he drew her into his arms, he was nearly devastated by the whimpering noise she made, by the feel of her arms encircling him, and by the thorough manner in which she returned his ardor. Her mouth opened needily for his wet, swirling kiss.

When at last he pulled away, their sultry gazes locked, then his gaze traveled to the heavy rise and fall of her chest, the enticing tops of her creamy breasts, and he was suddenly compelled to taste them. His head dipped to the bodice of her dress, his open mouth suckling at her.

Her breath shuddered, but she did not demand that he stop. She gave a satisfied moan that nearly unhinged him. She wanted this as much as he! Somehow he managed to free one breast and draw its rosy nipple into his mouth. The inhale and exhale of her whimpering breath--along with the pleasure of tasting her--nearly drove him mad.

In a lifetime of vagrant passions, he'd never experienced anything like this. For this woman was *his*. His wife. An element of purity pervaded everything that occurred between their two bodies.

As satisfied as he was holding her, he wanted more. Were she completely foxed, he would not have been able to consummate this marriage. But since the wine had merely rendered her . . . compliant, he thought perhaps this was the perfect time to complete their union.

Once again their hungry gazes locked as his hand cupped her breast. He spoke in a husky voice. "Will my duchess come to bed now?"

Desire burned in her smoky eyes when she nodded.

Chapter 8

When she awakened the next morning—exactly one full day after taking her marital vows—Philip stood beside her bed, a large silver tray in his hand. Though he was unshaven, he was fully dressed.

Unlike her. To her very great surprise, she realized she was thankful it was her husband, and not her maid, who witnessed her nakedness (even though most of said nakedness lay beneath the bed coverings). After everything that occurred between her and Philip on their wedding night, her maidenly modesty had vanished with the same finality as her chaperons.

Her pulse sped up as she gazed upon him. Even were he not a duke, he would have conveyed power with his towering physical presence. This dark knight she had married exuded masculinity from his black hair to the dark line of stubble on his square jaw, and along the sinewy muscles of his body. And what a magnificent body it was!

He spoke with levity and not without a devilish glint in his eye. "I took the liberty of getting the tray from your maid."

She scooted away from the bed's edge so he could place the tray there. "I am ever so grateful. I would have died of mortification had Fanny seen me like this." Clutching the sheet over her breasts, she added, "Now, my dear husband, I beg that you find my night shift. It must be tangled in the sheets."

His caressing gaze then traveled to the floor. "No, my love. It's actually here on the carpet." He stooped to pick it up, then handed it to her. "Shall you need assistance?" His brow quirked, his mischievous smile returned.

"I can manage quite well on my own, thank you." She did not fancy him staring at her breasts under the light of day. Night was quite another matter.

"Good because I cannot guarantee my proper conduct." His lazy gaze traveled from her face downward.

Her universe was confusingly skewed this morning. Everything that she had once deemed *improper* now seemed proper. Because their union had been sanctified by a sacrament. Yet in the light of day she was having a great deal of difficulty owning her wanton behavior of the night before. Dear lord, would Philip think her brazen?

She flicked a furtive glance at him, and the tenderness she saw on his face indicated he was pleased with her.

It suddenly occurred to Elizabeth that such intimacies as they had partaken of the previous night could also be performed in the daytime. The very memory of those intimacies sent her heartbeat racing, sent a molten heat to her core.

It was as if she looked at him with new eyes. He was no longer the powerful Duke of Aldridge over whom maidens swooned and men cowered. This gentle lover was her husband. She would never know the feel of any other man's hands on her body for she belonged to him. And he to her.

No longer could she call him Aldridge, or even your grace. He was now simply *Philip*. The name on her lips sounded like a lover's whisper. And perhaps that's what it was.

She may not have entered into this marriage as a woman in love. She may not possess his love. But she was now his in every way. Until death.

She took the soft chambray shift and eyed him. "Oblige me by turning your back whilst I slip this on."

He chuckled, but did as she requested, moving to her tall casements and beginning to draw open the draperies to reveal a gray day that was not overly dreary. Then he came to sit on the side of her bed. "How long before you'll be ready to ride?"

"Three quarters of an hour should be enough." She smiled at him. "I am ever so grateful that it isn't raining."

"As am I." He stood and peered down at her. "I shall just have Lawford shave me, then I'll run along to the mews and get our horses. If I recall, all of Haverstock's sisters are excellent riders."

"I fear you have me mixed up with Lydia. She rides as well as any man. I am merely competent—owing to the fact that for some peculiar reason I was terrified of horses as a child. My stern father despised my weakness." She had often wondered if her father had despised her. A colder man never existed.

"But you're not terrified any longer?"

She shook her head. "I conquered my fear. James was ever so good about helping me reason through my irrational thinking. He saw to it, too, that I had my very own mount—one which was gentle. As long as my brother was with me, I thoroughly adored galloping over every inch of Haymore."

"I shall be almost as happy about having James for a brother as I am to have Haverstock."

She nodded. "My brothers have both grown up to be fine men—which is a wonder considering my father." She stopped. She did not want to malign her father. Even if he deserved it.

Philip shrugged. "He must have done some things right. Look at his offspring."

Except for Kate, they all had turned out to be admirable adults.

Atop his mount, Philip faced the portico and awaited his wife. He did not have to wait long. Elizabeth, dressed in a dark green velvet riding habit, hurried from the house, a smile flashing when she saw the youthful groom holding the reins to her mount. Jacob assisted her in mounting, then she and Philip began to canter toward the north.

"She's a lovely horse," Elizabeth said.

He chuckled. "The gelding is not a she."

"Oh." Her gaze remained straight ahead.

Maidenly modesty. Then, with a deep, spiraling satisfaction, he realized she was no longer a maiden.

He knew he should probably save the best for last, but after a nearly five-year absence, he hungered to feast his eyes on the one place on earth that he held most dear. He was also impatient to see Elizabeth's reaction to the parkland north of Glenmont. Would she--like most people glimpsing the fine property for the first time--find the landscape magnificent?

Emblazoned on Philip's mind's eye as

distinctly as his mother's angelic face was Capability Brown's crowning achievement—a natural-looking lake spanned by a humpbacked stone bridge. It could be viewed from every window on the north side of the house. Like a sparkling jewel, the lake was framed by evergreen trees in every conceivable shade of green. Beyond them rose a gentle hill, just beginning to turn green after being stripped of its colour by winter's stark hand.

Once he and his bride rounded the west end of Glenmont's main house, her mount slowed as she took in the mesmerizing scene that stretched before them as far as the eye could see. Then she exclaimed. "Oh, Philip, this must be the loveliest spot in all of England."

It was all he could do to tamp down his swelling pride. "I am glad you think so. It's now your home, more so even than Haymore."

She nodded knowingly and spoke softly. "Because I shall probably live for more years here than ever I did in the home where I was born."

"It's very likely, my love."

It seemed inconceivable that just two generations ago, this land had been flat, dry and barren. Old Capability was a genius. And Philip's grandfather's pockets had been very deep. It had taken several hundred workmen a year to dig out the lake, and the excavated earth had made a very fine hill. But since Capability never did anything the easy way, he had insisted the hill be located off in the distance. Which necessitated massive transport headaches. Or backaches.

As if pulled to a magnet, their horses went straight to the glistening water, and when they neared it, she said, "I should love to stroll alongside the lake."

"Then we shall tether our mounts."

A moment later they were walking toward the bridge. "What is there about those ornamental bridges that seem to beckon us to walk along them?" she asked.

He shrugged. "They are inviting." Especially his. He'd been too young, too irresponsible to enjoy all that he had inherited when he succeeded to the dukedom. Now, he could not believe he'd been able to turn his back on all this. For now he had a strong desire to never leave.

As good as it was to be home again and as much as he appreciated all that he saw, he lamented that it was not a sunny day, lamented that spring's full carpet of green had yet to cover this land he loved so much. How he wished the lawns were a verdant, velvety green with yellow daffodils springing up willy nilly as they tended to do. He wanted, too, for her to see the blood-red rhododendron that bloomed so profusely here. They were said to be the most glorious in all of England.

Even though the calendar said it was spring, neither the weather nor the blooms were yet to give evidence of it. Still, without spring's heady scents and splashes of colour, there was something elementally pleasing about this cold, almost wintery day. Here. This deep satisfaction with Glenmont's landscape intrinsically tied to its isolation. For miles ahead, it was only the two of them. Only he and his duchess.

It was perplexing to him that while he was not accustomed to being married, he was rapidly growing accustomed to wanting to share everything with this woman he had wed. It felt so novel after two and thirty years of bachelorhood to suddenly have a life's partner. Novel but not entirely unwelcome.

He remembered the night he'd asked Haverstock for her hand in marriage. Then, as now, he'd experienced a feeling of bliss at the very notion of having a son. A son to whom he could leave Glenmont and all the other ducal properties. A son born of the union between Philip and Elizabeth. His mouth went dry. His thoughts flitted to the previous night. To Elizabeth's bed.

And he was nearly overwhelmed with strong emotions unlike anything he'd ever before experienced.

Wind hissed and chilled, and gravel crunched beneath their feet as they followed the path to the bridge. "I hope you're not too cold," he said.

"I shouldn't mind if I were for I love it here." She looked up at him. "Now I know why you told me last night that you preferred the outdoors here at Glenmont."

He took her hand and sighed. "I find I don't want to return to London. Even though my duties call." For too long he had shirked his duties. He had to do whatever he could to stop Napoleon. He had to use his leadership capabilities--and he hoped, intelligence--to help pass legislation to benefit their kingdom. And he had young sisters to launch into society.

Had he only himself to consider, he thought he could exist here alone with sweet Elizabeth for the rest of his days.

"I know," she said softly. "I feel the same. Even though I have duties too."

They came to a complete stop at the bridge's summit, and he peered into her fair face. He'd never before noticed the faint sprinkle of freckles on her nose. Stray strands of flaxen hair trickled along her cheek. Damn, but she looked incredibly young! Was that why she elicited in him a deep sense of protectiveness?

He stroked her face, sweeping away the errant locks. "Oh yes, Number 7 Trent Square."

"It's good to have purpose. Long before she ever met Haverstock, Anna carried out her charities in the East End. It's in her nature to be benevolent and caring, and I pray that I have been influenced by her goodness."

Haverstock had married very well. His wife was possessed of a kind heart, large purse, and stunning beauty. The Marchioness of Haverstock was certainly more beautiful than the new Duchess of Aldridge.

But since the marchioness was already taken, the duke thought he'd done very well for himself with Elizabeth. She was good breeding stock. That's what the Dukes of Aldridge looked for in a wife. Earlier dukes, of course, had married for fortune, too, but he did not have to seek a woman with a fortune. All the cumulative holdings brought to the dukedom by earlier advantageous marriages had left him exceedingly well off.

"I think you are very good." Even the bedchamber aspects of this marriage were far more satisfying than he had dreamed they could be. This wife of his was surprisingly more affectionate than he'd expected. He must remember to give the lady Madeira every night.

"I hope I never disappoint. If I do, you must tell me," she said. "I think I should like us to be open with one another. Do you not think that honesty is a good foundation for a marriage?"

"Pray, I hope that does not mean that you wish to pry away confessions about my *former* wicked ways!"

She giggled, then turned toward the lake beneath them, and leaned into the bridge's stone balustrade. "I should like to think of the rest of our life as beginning on the day we married."

"Whew!"

Their laughing eyes met, then he came to sit beside her upon the bridge's rock wall, his legs dangling toward the water below. How refreshingly naive the poor girl was! He could never be completely honest with her. A man simply did not tell his wife about his mistress. All the Dukes of Aldridge took mistresses.

At the present, he would not seek a mistress. Not when his duchess's lovemaking was proving to be so satisfactory. He drew in a breath. He must direct his thoughts away from such arousing thoughts. But he dare not bring up the topic of dancing. Or finger preferences.

What did females like to discuss? Love. Social activities. Clothing. None of these subjects remotely interested him, but he must make the effort to establish as easy an intimacy in their conversations as there had been . . . No, he couldn't allow himself to remember the feel of her silken flesh. He suddenly blurted out, "You must help me ensure that my unmarried sisters get suitable mates. I will own that I was disappointed when Clair didn't take."

Elizabeth nodded. "I was surprised."

"I know she's not considered pretty though she certainly is to those of us who love her. Do you remember how old she is now?"

"She's three and twenty. Almost exactly two

years older than me."

"Everyone will believe she's on the shelf. So men won't seek her."

"It's difficult to seek someone who's not there. You know that she no longer attends balls?"

He frowned. "I did not."

"Her appearance is not offensive. It's just that she exercises a careless disregard for . . . the things that other young ladies care about."

"Like fashion, attending balls, and falling in love?"

"Exactly. I had thought that despite her lack of effort, any number of men would want her for a wife because she's the daughter of a duke."

"It seems you were mistaken."

"I should love to tell her what to wear and how to dress her hair."

"Perhaps if I -- as head of the household now -- asked her to heed your advice, it would send a message that I want her to marry."

"Pray, Philip, don't. It might wound her deeply. I'm afraid she would think you don't want to be burdened with an old maid sister, even though I know that's not what you mean. You love her and want what's best for her."

"Was not Lydia exactly like Clair?"

She nodded. "I had come to believe that if she had not received an offer in thirty years, she never would. I thought she was happy with spinsterhood. Later, I learned that she had loved Morgie always and didn't think a fashionable man like him would ever lose his heart to her. She is less attractive than Clair."

He did not know if he should nod in affirmation or ignore the comment. He chose the latter.

"I never even suspected she held a tendre for Morgie," Elizabeth said, "but Haverstock said she was very clever in the manner in which she coaxed a declaration of affection from him." She looked up at him and smiled. "They adore each other."

He had even learned that Morgie was so besotted over his own wife that he had failed to take a mistress. Haverstock was besotted in the same way. Philip was incapable of loving as those two did. No woman had ever besotted him.

More's the pity.

The next week was the happiest in her life. How difficult it was to feign acceptance when her husband announced his intentions of returning to London. She never wanted to leave Glenmont. It wasn't the magnificence of the home and its land that held her heart. It was so much more.

To her complete amazement, she realized on the third day of their marriage that she had fallen totally, blindingly, madly in love with Philip. How difficult it had been during their lovemaking not to whisper words of love. How she longed to say *I love you* to the man who lay beside her at night, the man who captured her heart.

But she could not make such a declaration without forcing a similar--insincere--one from him. Hearing those words upon his lips would make her the happiest woman in the three kingdoms, but she only wanted to hear them if they truly came from his heart.

Would that day ever come, she wondered morosely.

The discovery that she loved Philip uncovered memories buried beneath the years of time. She now recalled with the clarity of clear spring water the first time she saw him. She remembered distinctly that she was four, and she had blurted out, "I'm going to marry Charles's friend. He's so handsome, he must be a prince."

Mama had told her he wasn't a prince but would be the closest thing to it when he became a duke. As a little girl, she fancied herself growing up to be the Duchess of Aldridge. But as he grew into manhood, the gap between him and the little girl she had been grew wider.

Because she was far too drab to entice a rake like him and because he was gone from England by the time she came out, all her girlish affections for him had been suppressed. Until now.

Now that old flame had ignited with more potency than she had ever dreamed possible.

She knew they were utterly compatible. Their backgrounds were similar. They held each other in high regard. And their physical intimacy brought each of them to quivering masses of pleasure.

A pity man did not have to be in love in order to slake his physical needs, needs she'd been told that men experienced much more acutely than women.

Though she certainly held Philip's affection now, she knew he was not in love with her. Fortunately, she had a lifetime in which to do everything in her power to secure his love.

If only she could. If only she were a more patient person. Or a more beautiful woman.

She had thought her wantonness that first night in his arms was due to the Madeira she was unaccustomed to drinking. But under the light of day whilst cold sober, she longed to feel his arms around her, to feel him stroking her intimately, to feel herself writhing beneath her husband's glorious body.

During those blissful days she could forget there was a world outside the boundaries of Glenmont. It was only she and the man she loved. During those days they had seldom spent a moment apart.

All of that would end when they returned to London. Duty, friends, perhaps even other women (she thought, a rent to her heart) would claim him. Was there anything she could do to prevent that from happening?

She would be an exemplary wife. His needs, his interests would always come first. It would be difficult not to cling to him, but she knew that clinging vines destroyed their sustenance.

During the carriage ride back to London, he ignored her as he read through the thick pages of the tax bill. She must not be jealous of his duty. He had set it all aside during their honeymoon to shower her with attention.

Such attentions were sure to stop now that they were returning to the capital.

Once the foul skies of London came into view, she interrupted his reading. "Pray, my dearest, before we arrive at Aldridge House you must tell me about the servants there."

He put the bill aside. "You only need to concern yourself with Barrow, who must be in his eighties. I am the third Duke of Aldridge he has served."

"Surely you're wealthy enough to pension him off."

He shook his head as if in exasperation. "I tried. The Aldridges are like his own family. He wouldn't have anything to live for were he not to serve us. He told me as long as he could walk, he wanted to keep serving."

"If I recall correctly, he can only barely walk," she said with levity.

"Right you are! He's quite elderly."

"And his hearing?"

"I think perhaps it is not very good--nor is his sight, but you understand I've been from England for five years."

She nodded. "So you haven't been able to observe."

"I know, kind soul that you are, you will be patient with him."

"Of course."

He puckered his lips in thought. "Our housekeeper in town is quite a bit older than Mrs. Plumley. Her name is Mrs. Harrigan, and I'm her second Duke of Aldridge."

She peered from the carriage window and recognized that they were on Piccadilly. "I shall be making their acquaintances momentarily."

Chapter 9

There was no greeting party to welcome the new duchess. It had been understood that the newly wedded couple would be returning the following day. Therefore, Margaret and Caroline were paying morning calls, and Mrs. Harrigan must be below stairs. Only white-haired Barrow met them as they came into the wide entry corridor that was lined with priceless portraits of Ponsby family members over the last two centuries.

"My dearest duchess," Philip said, "allow me to present Barrow to you. He is treasured by every member of the Ponsby family."

"I am delighted," she said as the servant executed a shaky bow. She sincerely hoped he did not remember her from that *other day* (which she now thought the luckiest day of her life).

"Certainly, your grace," Barrow said to her, then he proceeded to turn his back on them and shuffle along the corridor.

Her gaze met Philip's, her brows lowered.

"Daresay," he whispered, "he *is* hard of hearing. Must have thought you requested the candles be lighted."

Her husband was right. Seconds later, Barrow and a strapping young footman came to stand in front of the towering mirror, and the footman began to light the sconces which flanked it--even though it was but two in the afternoon, and the soaring ceiling of domed glass filled the entry chamber with daylight.

She gave her husband a querying look, but he shook his head almost imperceptibly. "Come, my darling, allow me to show you the duchess's chambers."

While Elizabeth was unfamiliar with Aldridge House, she had spent some time in other palatial ducal residences. Her aunt had been the Duchess of Steffington, and her maternal grandfather was the Duke of Fane. But since Elizabeth had neither fortune nor great beauty, she had not (at least not since she had come from the school room) thought it possible she would ever be mistress of anything so grand as Glenmont Hall. Or even Aldridge House. Only one house in all of London could rival its grandeur: the Regent's own Carlton House.

As they mounted the broad marble staircase side by side, she concentrated on acting duchessy. This necessitated that she refrain from gushing. Everywhere she looked, everything she saw from the gilt banister to the massive crystal chandeliers was gush-worthy. But she could not underscore to Philip how unworthy she was to be his duchess.

She had not felt so inadequate at Glenmont. There, it had just been the two of them, and he had been ever so solicitous of her. But here in London she would be held up to scrutiny from every lady who had ever hoped to snare the Duke of Aldridge for herself. The servants too might resent a new mistress. Even his sisters of whom she had always been excessively fond might think her an intruder in a domain they had ruled during his long absence from England.

And what would happen when he invited friends from Parliament? Would they think her stupid? She would have to offset the disadvantage of her youth by educating herself about government.

Perhaps Richie could be helpful in that.

There was nothing she would not do to try to earn Philip's love.

When they reached the third level where the bedchambers were located, he said, "You will not only find my mother's former chambers outdated, you will also find they're not at all to your taste. I beg that you seek a clever person to redo them for you. A pity I didn't think of it before we left London. I daresay they might have been redecorated by now."

"But I daresay the chambers would be permeated by those noxious paint odors which aggravate my stomach so terribly." She moved closer to him, slipping her arm into his. "I should have to move into your chambers."

A slow smile eased across his dark face, and he spoke huskily. "I'll summon the painters today." He winked.

At least in the bedchamber activities, she must please him. Now she must set about to become the perfect wife.

They walked past the door to his bedchamber--that place where she had first seen her husband undressed. To her dying day she would be able to visualize him standing there with the fire framing his glistening, beautifully sculpted body.

"The next door will be to the duchess's bedchamber," he said.

It proved to be in exactly the same ornately formal mode as the duchess's chambers at Glenmont Hall, but here the bed was exquisite. She did not think she could change a thing about it. The full tester which stood high above the bed was done totally in gilt that had been shaped like a crown. From it flowed ivory silken draperies embroidered with silken threads in the same shade of turquoise of the velvet draperies that gathered beneath the ivory. How comforting was the image of closing those velvet draperies around the bed--around her husband and her--on a cold winter night.

She forgot all about acting duchessy and let her inner *bourgeois* self be revealed. "Oh, my goodness, it looks like a magnificent state bed!"

His eyes flashed with pleasure. His pride over this bed must be greater than any scorn he could hold toward a *hausfrau* wife. "It is an exact copy of a state bed that my maternal great grandfather, the Duke of Baley, had made for Charles II. My grandmother loved it so much, he had it copied as a wedding gift for her."

"I shall feel like a queen sleeping there!" Her sparkling eyes met his, and her breath hitched when she saw the way he stared at her. Hunger heated his dark, smoldering eyes.

She moved into his arms as his crushing kisses ignited her searing passions. As they always did.

That night at dinner they were joined by Margaret and Caroline. The sisters were separated by the same age difference as she and Kate but were so much closer than she and Kate. (It was some consolation that no one--not even the man she had married the previous year--was close to exasperating Kate.) Seeing how affectionate these sisters were with each other made Elizabeth lament that Charlotte, her youngest sister and the one to whom she was closest in temperament, had married.

She and Charlotte would always be close, but their relationship had changed almost as dramatically as had Charlotte's station when she chose to marry a Methodist clergyman of modest means. The two stayed so busy with their ministry in the East End that Elizabeth seldom saw Charlotte, and when they were together, Elizabeth had come to understand that Charlotte's husband had supplanted her as the one with whom Charlotte now shared all her confidences, all her innermost thoughts.

Would Elizabeth and Philip ever be that close? She could wish away all his riches in order to toil alongside him day in and day out as did Charlotte and her Mr. Hogart.

How Elizabeth hoped that these new sisters would take her into their family circle in the same way she and her sisters had welcomed Anna.

"When does Clair return from Aunt Hopkins-Feversham's?" Philip queried his sisters as he poured Bordeaux into his wife's glass.

Caro, the youngest, rolled her eyes. "I daresay he's using aunt's proper name for your benefit, Elizabeth. We've always just called her Auntie Hop-Sham."

"Owing to the fact that as young children Hopkins-Feversham was far too difficult for us to pronounce," Margaret explained in her soft voice.

"But to answer your question, Aldridge," Caro said, setting down her fork and regarding him in much the same manner as an authoritative governess, "Clair said she hoped to return around the same time as you and your bride. She was utterly vexed that you had the wedding conducted before her return."

Margaret favored Elizabeth with a smile. "She was, of course, delighted with Aldridge's selection of a bride."

"Indeed," Caro continued, "She said you were always her favorite of Haverstock's sisters . . . well, except for Lady Lydia."

"I believe she phrased it that you were her favorite among Haverstock's *pretty sisters* because while everyone adores Lady Lydia, everyone knows she is not in possession of beauty," Margaret clarified.

Elizabeth was grateful her new sisters felt comfortable enough with her to speak with perfect honesty. "Fortunately, Lydia is everyone's favorite of Haverstock's sisters. Being in possession of others' good opinion is far better than being in possession of a loveliness that will fade. Do you not agree?"

"My wife is quite the philosopher."

"I think she phrased that beautifully," Margaret said.

Caro nodded. "Speaking of dear Lady Lydia, we must have the Morgans to dinner."

It struck Elizabeth that though Lady Caroline was the youngest in the family, she had taken on rather an matriarchal role, almost as if she were a firstborn.

"And the marquess too," Margaret added.

The duke nodded readily. "A very good plan." Then his expression became pensive, and he hesitated before he directed his next comment to his duchess. "Um, do you think Lady Lydia can get away long enough for dinner?" He then averted his gaze and began to push his peas around the crested porcelain plate.

Both sisters' brows shot up. "What could possibly prevent Lady Lydia from getting away?" Caro demanded.

Philip swallowed. He appeared reluctant to answer his sister's question. Then he cleared his throat and finally spoke. "She has not obtained . . . ahem, certain services for her infant son."

It was all Elizabeth could do not to burst out laughing. Her husband was embarrassed to mention suckling--or even the words *wet nurse*--in front of his sisters! How could so virile a man be so modest?

Both sisters looked puzzled.

Elizabeth cleared up the mystery. "My sister has no wet nurse."

"Do you mean to say she does not leave her house?" an incredulous Caro asked.

Elizabeth answered. "I will own, my sister dislikes leaving her little angel, but since this is so close I believe he could manage without her for a few hours."

The sisters went suddenly, glaringly silent. They, too, were embarrassed to speak of such a matter. At least in front of their brother. Margaret made a great fuss about cutting up her veal whilst Caroline gulped down her wine.

"It would be delightful to have your family members. Will you invite them?" Margaret finally managed. Gentle Margaret had always been the family's peacekeeper. It was she who had the ability to speak graciously to everyone, she who could smooth the wrinkles from the messiest situations.

Elizabeth's glance flicked to the duke. "Is that agreeable to you, dearest?"

"It would make me very happy. But not tomorrow night. We will go to the theatre then for new staging of *School for Scandal.*"

"We're greatly looking forward to it," Caro said.

"And, my love, since I'm going to be a fixture in politics, I thought we'd start dining with Lord and Lady Holland."

Finally, a topic of which she knew something. Though Whigs, the Hollands' dinners were legendary for attracting a lively assortment of interesting people. She had met his lordship, but never his lady, owing to the fact that as a divorced woman, she was not welcome in houses of the *ton* and never around unmarried ladies. Now that Elizabeth herself was a married lady, there was no longer an impediment to their meeting. "I should enjoy that excessively--and I shall sit there like a mute sponge."

He smiled at her, then put down his napkin and rose. "I am sure you ladies can amuse yourselves while I run along to my club."

I must conceal my disappointment. "But, dearest, do you not need to ring and have your gig brought around?"

He shook his head. "I can walk there much faster. It's less than five minutes from Berkeley Square to White's."

"Pray," Elizabeth pleaded, "Do. Not. Walk. Home. I wouldn't at all like for a cut-throat footpad to leave me a widow a week after my marriage."

Caro whirled to her brother. "She's absolutely right, Aldridge. You must give us your word that under no circumstances will you walk home."

He chuckled. "Ladies, I give you my word. I'm not so great a fool." He strode to Elizabeth and brushed a kiss across her cheek. "Don't wait up for me."

His first night back in London, and already he was slipping away from her.

Damn, he'd not been at White's in nearly five years. Where had all these bloody strangers come from? Not one of his friends was there. Is that what marriage did to one? Thinking back on it, marriage had never previously affected his acquaintances a whit. If they wanted to dine at their club and gamble the night away, their wives accepted it.

Were Haverstock and Morgie so besotted over their wives that they were squashed beneath their ladies' thumbs?

He nodded to Palmer, whom he'd known most of his life, though the two had never been close. The nod opened him to a series of questions about his return to England and queries regarding his marriage.

He attempted to give the appearance he was looking for a specific person, and when he did not find him, promptly took his leave. He would try Brook's just down the street.

He'd more often gone to White's because that's where his father and his uncles had always congregated. But now that he was going to take an active part in government, he thought perhaps the Brook's crowd might be more to his liking.

His father would roll over in his grave if he knew his son was considering aligning himself with the Whigs. The old duke had been a Tory through and through. All of the Dukes of Aldridge had been Tories.

It wasn't that Philip was actually a Whig. It was just that he preferred to be open minded and wanted to adopt the best features of each of the political camps. His guiding principle would be to do what was best for Britain.

At Brook's he was pleased there was at least one person he knew: Elizabeth's cousin, Richard Rothcomb-Smedley. The fellow leapt to his feet, offered Philip his hand, and begged him to join his table.

"I'm surprised to see your grace back so soon from your wedding trip. Did the weather in Middlesex turn bad?" The man's dark blond eyebrows lowered.

Philip directed a cold stare at the young man. There was a faint resemblance between him and Elizabeth. Perhaps it was just that he was blond. He supposed Rothcomb-Smedley's better-than-average height and broad shoulders would appeal to women. No matter how important the fellow was in government, Philip could not warm to him. Not when the only two times Philip had been in his presence he had the audacity to intimate that Philip did not properly appreciate the woman he had married.

By Jove! Philip--not this youthful upstart--had asked for her hand. Wasn't that enough to prove his commitment to her? It was not in the duke's nature to dance attendance upon any woman.

"The weather in Middlesex is the same as it is in London. But after being from England for five years, I have many calls upon my attention." He sat down, and Rothcomb-Smedley introduced him to his companion, Lord Dessington who served with Elizabeth's cousin in the House of Commons.

"I believe I know your father, the Earl of Lancer," Philip said.

Dessington nodded. "I understand you will be serving in the House of Lords with my father."

"I begin this week."

"Tell me, your grace," Rothcomb-Smedley said, "did you finish reading the tax bill?"

"I did. As a matter of fact," Philip peered at the viscount Dessington, "your father was kind enough to furnish me his copy--one of only three, I'm told."

"My father means to butter you up in the hopes that you will support the Whigs."

"I will support whatever faction I believe is right. As it happens, I think the tax bill is damned good, and I mean to support it."

"Then we are gratified to have you as an ally," Rothcomb-Smedley said. "I still find it incredible that you chose to spend your honeymoon reading a tax bill."

Philip glared. "What I did on my honeymoon is no concern of yours." Especially those other, intimate activities which rather dominated their very satisfactory wedding trip.

Rothcomb-Smedley sighed. "You're a fortunate man. Were I not a second son who needed to marry an heiress, I would have offered for Elizabeth."

Was the man telling him he was in love with Philip's wife? *What cheek!* To refrain from glaring once more at his arrogant companion, his gaze fanned over the cozy chamber with an air of boredom only a duke could get away with. "Does Haverstock no longer come to his club?"

"My cousin is the only man I know who's even more serious than I over his duties to his country," Rothcomb-Smedley said.

Philip stood. "A year from now I hope you say that about me."

"Then you'll be in the House of Lords tomorrow?"

He nodded. And at the Foreign Office--but he needn't have that be widely known.

"Will I see you at the Holland's Thursday night?"

"Yes."

Rothcomb-Smedley lifted a brow. "With the duchess?"

Was the damned ass obsessed over Elizabeth? Philip had a good mind to go without her just to disappoint her cousin. But he had already invited her.

Chapter 10

He'd told her not to wait up. Did that mean he had no plans to come home? Would he be visiting Belle Evans or a woman like her? The very thought nearly brought her to her knees. As much as she wanted to push such torturing thoughts from her mind, she far too keenly felt her first separation from her husband. It stung that he wanted to be away from her for she treasured every minute they spent together.

After she and the sisters returned from a visit to Almack's assembly rooms, Fanny assisted her in dressing for bed, then Elizabeth went through her dressing room which connected to his. She stood before the door to his dressing room, fighting with herself. She wanted to stroll into his bedchamber on the odd chance that he had returned. But how would that look?

It would look as if she were forcing herself on her husband.

She also considered leaving the connecting door ajar so she would hear him when he returned, but were she to do that, he would believe her a nosy, meddling wife. A clinger. She did not fancy doing anything that would drive them apart. Husbands found such actions distasteful.

She stormed to her lonely bed.

The honeymoon was over. She must accept that and not force herself into her husband's pocket. That would be sure to chase him into the arms of a woman like Belle Evans. Why did men of their class consider mistresses as necessary as a fine equipage? It was such a despicable practice.

She knew with certainty neither Haverstock nor Morgie had taken a mistress since they married. But, then, the demands on Haverstock's time barely allowed him to be with his adored wife.

Elizabeth smiled to herself. She must welcome Philip's plan to take seriously his duties for that could keep him from other women's beds.

Those very duties of his could work in her favor in another way. Were she to share his interests, that would bring them even closer together. She remembered how Lord Wickshire practiced all his Parliamentary speeches on his lady, who was vastly interested in matters of government. It was said that Lady Wickshire's suggestions made her husband's stellar speeches even more memorable.

It was no accident, Elizabeth thought, that Lord and Lady Wickshire were one of the most devoted couples she'd ever seen.

At least until Haverstock wed Anna.

As soon as she could, Elizabeth planned to cultivate Richie's absorption with Parliament. He was just the person to school her!

As she lay there in the darkness she attempted to direct her thoughts away from her absent husband. Number 7 Trent Square would give her purpose. In fact, the only good thing about returning to London was that it would allow her to proceed with her plans for the widows. Her last waking thoughts were of the many things she needed to do the following day to give the neediest of the widows a new home.

He'd been mildly disappointed upon returning from Brook's to learn that his wife and sisters had gone to Almack's. When he'd left a few hours earlier, he'd thought he would be away several hours. But he had not considered that the men and diversions that had occupied him so fully five years previously no longer held allure.

Much had changed. Especially his two closest friends. Philip found he did not enjoy his club without Haverstock and Morgie, both of whom had changed vastly. He was still trying to determine if they had changed for the better. As young men, their hedonistic ways barely kept them on the fringe of respectability. But, oh, the fun they had!

Now Haverstock certainly had earned the admiration of a great many men in exalted positions in government. That change, Philip must grudgingly admit, was for the better.

But what of Haverstock's total capitulation to that lovely wife of his? Was it not a sign of weakness for a man to be ruled by a wife? Not that the marchioness actually ordered Haverstock about. It was more that he seemed incapable of things that would separate him from her.

As these thoughts drifted through his mind, Philip realized he had initiated the present separation from Elizabeth. It struck him that this was the first time they had parted since the day they had spoken their wedding vows. He found himself wishing she were lying there in his bed beside him. A sudden void came over him. Though it was an unfamiliar feeling, he attributed it to acute desire.

For he could not deny his desire for her had nearly become an obsession.

Good lord, was he becoming Haverstock?

The following morning, she carried the breakfast tray into her husband's chamber. She would not have exercised so assertive a measure had he not told her the previous day that his full schedule of activities would take up all of the day.

Upon hearing his chamber door squeak open, he rose up onto his elbows and regarded her with a devilish grin. "How did you know I would not bite off your head for awakening me at so ungodly an hour?"

She set the tray beside him on the bed. "Because you told me yourself yesterday that you had a full day of activities planned." She sat there and tried to speak casually. "Were you very late coming home, my dearest?" There! It was out, and she thought perhaps she hadn't sounded too much the meddlesome shrew. In fact, one hearing her remark would think she found nothing whatsoever troublesome about her husband staying away most of the night.

What a good actress she was!

He chuckled. "Actually, I was home before you."

Her mouth opened into a perfect O. "I shall be offended that you didn't wait up for me." So much for being a good actress.

"I thought I owed it to you to give you a rest from my bothersome self."

Without thinking on what she was doing, her

hand stroked the lean plains of his face. "You're never bothersome." As soon as she'd said the tenderly spoken words, she wished she had them back. He was sure to think her the most clinging vine imaginable.

She had all but confessed that she never tired of making love to him. He was sure to think he'd married a doxy!

He took her hand, pressed a nibbly kiss into her palm, then diverted his attention from her as he began to slather marmalade onto his toast.

Taking a cue from him, she poured his strong coffee into a delicate porcelain cup and began to add the sugar just as he liked it.

"What plans have you today--other than sitting in the House of Lords?"

"Can I trust you with a confidence?"

"Of course!"

"I shall be working at the Foreign Office, but I'd as lief not own up to it."

"Then you'll be doing what Haverstock does?"

His eyes widened. "I thought your brother's activities were clandestine."

She shrugged. "They are, but give me credit for not being a complete moron. I daresay it's difficult to hide those kinds of activities from those with whom one lives--not that Haverstock hasn't tried!"

"No one, save you, is to know what I'll be doing there," he said in a stern voice.

"I perceive you're good at ciphers."

"I am grateful I have not wed an imbecile; now, you must prove your trustworthiness."

He bit into his toast. "Tell me about your day."

"I am ever so anxious to get started at Number 7 Trent Square."

"I'm sorry I won't be able to spend as much

time there as I'd like, but you must inform me if there's anything your widows need."

"I don't know myself yet. By the way, your sisters are most enthusiastic about the Trent Square project and begged to accompany me there today. They have vowed to assist in any way needed. Dearest Margaret even insisted I accept some of her own pin money to give to the widows."

"I'm very proud of the Ponsby women. And that includes you." He threw his bare legs over the side of the bed. "I can't linger. I told Haverstock I'd meet him in Whitehall this morning."

"Are you still planning on the theatre tonight?"

"I am indeed." He brushed his lips across her cheek.

Mrs. Hudson and her little girl were not the only ones at Number 7 Trent Square when the sisters arrived there that morning.

"Oh, Lady Elizabeth," Mrs. Hudson began, "I hope you don't object, but I took the liberty of inviting Mrs. Leander to come here when she and her five children were thrown out on the street."

Elizabeth had never before met Mrs. Leander, but she sounded as if she was in need of any assistance they could provide. "You did the right thing, Mrs. Hudson. Is Mrs. Leander also the widow of a soldier?"

"Aye. Mr. Leander served with my Harry."

Elizabeth turned to her sisters. "Allow me to present to you Mrs. Hudson." Then turning back to the youthful widow, she said, "These are my new sisters-in-law, Lady Margaret on the left, Lady Caroline on the right."

Caro inclined her head. "A pleasure to meet you, Mrs. Hudson, and pray, dear lady, you must now refer to my sister-in-law as *your grace*."

Mrs. Hudson's eyes rounded as she peered at Elizabeth. "You married a duke?"

Pride surged within Elizabeth, and she nodded. "The Duke of Aldridge. You met him a couple of weeks ago."

Mrs. Hudson dipped into a pronounced curtsey. "I offer my felicitations on your marriage. I believe the duke has chosen well."

"It's I who am the fortunate one," Elizabeth said.

"Would it be excessively rude of me to say how handsome is your duke?" Mrs. Hudson asked.

All three of the Ponsby women giggled.

"We are accustomed to women swooning over our brother," Caro said, a trickle of laughter ringing in her voice. "People expect dukes to be stooped over with age and possessed of white hair."

Another slender woman carrying a babe edged up behind Mrs. Hudson. She was older than Mrs. Hudson—perhaps thirty. Dark hair framed her pale face in which were set large brown eyes that were as solemn as she.

Mrs. Hudson introduced Mrs. Leander, who curtsied when she addressed the duchess.

"I told Mrs. Leander she and her little ones could take the bedchamber beside mine. Is that all right?" Mrs. Hudson asked.

"It matters not to me. I think, though, that chamber's too small for five children," Elizabeth said. "Please, Mrs. Leander, feel free to select a larger one. Unfortunately, the children will have to stay in their mother's bedchamber so we can make the home available to more families in need."

Tears began to stream down Mrs. Leander's pallid cheeks. "I don't know what me and my children would have done had you not made this wonderful house available to us."

Elizabeth was powerless not to tear up herself. "We are all happy to help, but it will be up to you widows to devise a division of labor."

Mrs. Leander's face brightened. "I am accounted a fair cook."

The Ponsby sisters nodded, and Margaret said, "That's wonderful."

"My brother, who is serving in the Peninsula, has furnished me a list of widows from his regiment. He narrowed it to those who reside in London. I shall see if I can find them and invite them to make their home here." Elizabeth addressed Philip's sisters. "Whilst I go off looking for the other widows, I shall need you two to draw up a list of needed items."

Caro nodded. "Things like candles, bed linens, coal . . . items that must be acquired."

"Oh, goodness, I forgot about coal!" Elizabeth turned to Mrs. Hudson. "Were you warm enough last night?"

The widow nodded. "We were so very grateful to have a roof over our heads and blankets to cover us."

Throughout the rest of the day as Elizabeth crisscrossed London, bringing more desperate families to Number 7, she fought back tears many times. Nothing she had ever done had given her such satisfaction.

Another of the widows, a Mrs. Boyle, also had five children. Elizabeth found her living with her sister in a flat in Hackney, where twelve children slept on the floor of the flat's only room. Elizabeth had never in her life seen people live in such straightened circumstances.

At the end of the day, five families were residing at Number 7, where the air was filled with the aroma of a rich broth Mrs. Leander was cooking.

Elizabeth planned to continue locating the rest of the widows each day until the house was filled.

When she and the sisters returned to Aldridge House, they were exhausted.

"I declare," an enthusiastic Caro said, "I have never enjoyed myself as excessively as I did today."

A smile on her kindly face, Margaret nodded. "I believe I've lost my heart to Mrs. Leander's little lad."

"The babe?" Caro asked.

"Yes. He's just learned to walk, but his mother likes to hold him to keep him from falling down stairs."

"So that's why you kept holding him?"

"To protect him—and because he felt so very good in my arms."

Elizabeth smiled at tender-hearted Margaret. "Then you must wed and have a babe of your own."

There was a wistful expression on Margaret's face. "Now I know why Lady Lydia wishes to nurse her lad."

Caro's nose wrinkled with distaste. "I would never!"

"What of you?" Margaret asked Elizabeth.

It only then occurred to Elizabeth that at this moment she could be increasing with Philip's babe. Her cheeks grew hot even though the notion of breeding filled her with happiness. "I should have to defer to Philip."

Caro stiffened. "Why would you consult him? It's your body!"

At that moment Elizabeth felt as if it was no longer her body or Philip's body. They belonged to each other. How could she explain that to a maiden? "I shouldn't like to do anything to displease dear Philip."

"I think that's wonderfully admirable," Margaret said. "It's obvious you're in love with your husband."

"I hope I'm not too obvious. What man wants a smothering wife?"

As she trudged up the stairs to her chambers, she almost wished they weren't going to the theatre that night. How she would enjoy sitting by the fire in her chamber whilst the Duke and Duchess of Aldridge shared with each other an accounting of their day's events.

As it was, she needed to be ready for the theatre in an hour.

When she reached the third level, she heard Barrow's shaking voice filling the stairwell. "Has the new duchess come?"

"Aye," the footman answered. "She's just gone upstairs."

"Did I not give you the note his grace sent around for her?"

"You did not, sir."

Barrow spoke to himself. "Dear me, where did I put it?"

"I'm sure as I couldn't say, sir."

By the time poor old half-blind Barrow found the note and climbed the stairs to deliver it to her,

Philip could very well be home. She pivoted and came right back downstairs.

She could hear the elderly butler talking to himself. "Now where did I go? Let me see, I went to . . . "

The footman shouted to be heard. "I saw that you went into the library to put the duke's post on his desk."

"That must be where I left it!"

She found Barrow in the library, his gnarly hand clutching a wrinkled piece of foolscap. "You have saved me from walking upstairs," he said. "The duke sent you this."

She thanked him, took the letter, and opened it.

Dearest Elizabeth,

I regret to inform you that I won't be able to get away. Please go on to the theatre without me.

He signed it with a capital *A.*

Chapter 11

The lighting may have been dim that night at Theatre Royal Drury Lane, but not so dim that Elizabeth was not aware that all eyes were directed at the Duke of Aldridge's box. Even those in the pit lifted their gazes to gawk at the new duchess. She held her shoulders high and attempted to exude a satisfied countenance. Would she be able to conceal from all these people her deep humiliation? Her first trip to the theatre as the Duchess of Aldridge, and she was not accompanied by her husband. That single occurrence would not have been so embarrassing if it hadn't been preceded by her first visit to Almack's as a duchess—also without her newly wedded husband.

The Duke of Aldridge's box on this night was occupied solely by women.

She shouldn't care what others thought, but since her scandalous behavior nearly three weeks previously, she did. Philip's disinterest in being with his wife sent a signal that the duke had married her only because he was forced to do so. Had that been the case, she would never have consented to marry him. He had convinced her that he *wanted* to marry her. He wanted her for his duchess, and he wanted her for the mother of his children—a thought that melted her insides to the consistency of warm butter.

Now he no longer acted as if he were a married man.

Ever since she had come out, she had hoped for a revival of this play. She had heard so much about it. But now that she had the opportunity to see Sheridan's most-favored play, her personal woes distracted her attention from the actors on the stage.

Though the actress portraying Lady Teazdale looked nothing like Lady Melbourne, it was widely believed that Sheridan had modeled the character on her. That notorious Whig matriarch had never been on good terms with Elizabeth's mother. When in Lady Melbourne's sphere, Lady Haverstock had a propensity to drop handkerchiefs, fans, or theatre programs—anything she happened to be holding—to have a reason to stoop over and avoid having to greet the wicked Lady Melbourne.

"Do you see Lady Melbourne's in her box tonight?" whispered Lydia, who sat at Elizabeth's left.

Elizabeth nodded. "It's good that Mama's not with us since she believes all Whig women are scandalous."

"That's the Tory in her coming out. After all, Mama's blinded by her allegiance to the Tories, as was Papa, Mama's father, and all of her ancestors."

"She *is* massively resistant to new ways."

Lydia harrumphed. "I have tried and tried to persuade her not to travel about in her ancient sedan chair. People just don't use them much anymore."

"It's not unlike the way she always insisted

Papa powder his hair long after such a practice had fallen from fashion."

While she sat in their darkened box, her mind wandering, Elizabeth was startled to realize that Belle Evans sat in a box directly across the theatre from their box. Elizabeth was unable to avert her gaze from the beautiful woman. Belle Evans was taller than average and possessed of rich, dark hair which accentuated the milky white of her skin. Her well-hanging pink dress and gray plume in her hair indicated the courtesan had unerringly good taste.

Were she not so notorious, no one seeing her for the first time would ever know the lovely woman had debased herself in so profligate a manner. Why had she thrown propriety to the gutter?

It wasn't for Elizabeth to judge. She had been born to a privileged class. She knew that many young girls were forced into prostitution at a tender age to keep from starving. Perhaps Belle Evans came from so unfortunate a circumstance.

Though Belle Evans's head turned toward the stage, Elizabeth was sure the courtesan was watching her.

A pity that Philip must have at some point been on intimate terms with her.

Elizabeth prayed that was no longer the case.

The very idea of him lying with another woman put her in a bleak mood. She wondered if he might even be with another woman right now.

But as she looked over those assembled, she realized none of the men she knew to be members of the House of Lords were in attendance though many of their wives were. Relief washed over her. The House of Lords must still be in session!

Philip wasn't being an unfaithful husband. He was being a dutiful citizen. She was ever so proud of him.

During the intermission, Lydia took her leave. "Must dash off to feed my little angel."

As she was leaving, Richie was entering the Duke of Aldridge's box. He came to sit in the seat vacated by Lydia. "I see that you are once again being neglected by that husband of yours," he said playfully.

"Do you not think he might still be at the House of Lords?" she asked shyly, afraid he would refute her statement.

"Of course he is. I expect they won't quit the chamber until after midnight."

Then I shall wait up for him. One night she could be patient. On the second night, though, she would allow herself to become Philip's barnacle. "I must own I am very ignorant about government, but now I find myself wishing to learn. Will you help me? No one's more knowledgeable than you."

He smiled. "I should be happy to. May I collect you for a ride in the park tomorrow afternoon?"

If she started early in the day, she should be able to devote five or six hours to the widows, which would allow her to be available for a drive in Hyde Park at four. "That would be delightful."

After the theatre, Cook had a cold supper for them and a few of the sisters' friends who stopped by. Elizabeth ate a few bites, then excused herself. "It's been a very long day, and I'm tired."

As she climbed the stairs she heard Caro tell the others what fun they'd had that day, and she began to explain about the home for widows.

Just on the third step, Elizabeth spun around,

returned to the dinner room, and addressed Barrow. She had learned that she must elevate her voice when speaking to him. "If the duke should return whilst the food is still laid, would you offer to send him a tray to my chamber?"

"Yes, your grace."

As she was leaving the dinner room the second time, she heard Caro soliciting donations to purchase additional beds for Number 7 Trent Square.

Finally, an occurrence over which Elizabeth could smile this night.

In her room, she and Fanny selected a soft muslin night shift of snowy white, embroidered with lilacs. It was her favorite. Because she was not going directly to bed and because the room was chilly, they found her ivory Kashmir shawl to throw over her shoulders. Fanny came to set a candelabra near the settee so that Elizabeth could read. After Fanny left, Elizabeth raced to her husband's dressing room. This time she left the door to his dressing room ajar and hers open wide. She would not countenance missing him another night.

A knock sounded upon her chamber door. She was certain Philip wouldn't come that way. "Who is it?"

"I've brought your tray, your grace." It was the footman. Barrow must not have heard her correctly. She could not permit the footman to see her in her night shift! "If you will, please take it to the duke's chamber. It is for him I requested it."

"Very well, your grace."

She waited several minutes before she moved to his bedchamber to fetch the tray and bring it to her chamber. Then she settled back on the settee and returned to her book, *The Memoirs of Lord Chatham.* She had selected it because, as the first William Pitt, Lord Chatham had preceded his son—their country's leader through most of her life—as head of the government. Reading his recollections about his career in government would help inform her.

After an hour, she heard someone enter Philip's chamber, and she put down her book and went to see if her husband had returned. As she reached their connecting door, their gazes locked.

"You waited for me." Though he looked tired, he still bespoke power and masculinity. The dark stubble on his square jaw accentuated the white of the well-tied cravat beneath it. Her gaze raked over him from his crown of dark hair to the toe of his black leather shoes. And she was ever so grateful women were not permitted in the House of Lords. What woman could look at him and not fall in love?

"I shall be most gratified if you will tell me of all the things you did today," she said, offering him a shy nod. "I've had a tray of cold meats brought up for you, and I thought perhaps we each could have a glass of port."

He regarded her with affection. "This will undoubtedly be the best part of an exhausting day."

His comment was like laughter to her heart. They went to sit side by side on her settee in front of the comforting fire, and she poured each of them a glass of port. He had already attacked the plate. "It's been hours since I've eaten. How good of you to see to my needs."

"I perceived—even though your note to me was decidedly uncommunicative—that you were held up at the House of Lords."

"Indeed I was."

"I shall want to hear everything about your day. It began at the Foreign Office, did it not?"

His masculine fingers combed through his head of thick, dark hair. "It did."

"You got your own office there?"

He nodded. "Right next to your brother's. He kindly shared some of his knowledge of cryptography with me and allowed me to start on a portion of his present undertakings."

"You can't expect to be an expert on your first day, dearest. It takes time to become proficient in such an unnatural method of communication."

His eyes looked black; his countenance, though, was playful. "As it happens, I've had a bit of experience in inventing codes. My brothers and I were mad over them as lads."

Her brows raised. "You met with success on your first day?"

He nodded sheepishly. "I shouldn't like to boast, but since you are my wife and since you appear to be interested in my duties, I will tell you that your brother said I had a talent for code breaking."

"Oh, my darling, that's wonderful! And do you enjoy it?"

"I do. The knowledge that I'm helping my country defeat that mad Frenchman is perhaps the most exhilarating thing I've ever experienced."

She understood how he felt for that kind of exhilaration is exactly how she had felt earlier that day when helping the widows. "There are many of us who should be grateful that you've returned to England."

He lifted her hand and brought it to his lips.

"It's I who am grateful." He took a sip of his port. "Oblige me by not telling anyone either about my functions at the Foreign Office or about my so-called skill. Not even the Marchioness Haverstock."

"I shall be an obedient wife," she said in exaggerated fashion. "Now you must tell me about sitting in the House of Lords."

He reached for a chunk of cheese and ate it before he began. "The last five hours were perhaps the most boring I've experienced since I sat through Dr. Fyne's mumbling three-hour lecture on astronomy."

"Why was tonight so boring?"

"Lord Beavers was speaking in opposition to the tax bill."

"The Lord Beavers who is ninety?"

He nodded.

"I should think his voice was not very powerful."

"You would be correct."

"Was he lucid?"

"Shockingly so for a man of his years. He effectively quoted from Smith's *Wealth of Nations*—not at all in a way in which I could agree—but to those of a like mind with him, most convincingly."

Oh dear, another book she needed to read. She made a mental note to ask Richie about Adam Smith when they met on the morrow.

"Knowing that Lord Beaver lost heavily on the 'Change, I would guess that he's not in favor of a tax increase," she said.

"Your guess, my love, would be correct."

"And your feelings on the matter?"

A grim look on his face, he formulated his

reply before speaking. "Our country is at war. Wars are expensive. If we want to be victorious, we must not consider individual needs but must look to what's for the greater good."

She knew a bit about Jeremy Bentham's political philosophy. "Then my dukely husband is a Benthamite?"

"I will own, not many dukes would agree with me, and I would not necessarily call myself a Benthamite, but I will do everything in my power to see that this tax bill passes for I do believe in the *greater good.*"

"You make me very proud," she said, her voice only barely above a whisper.

"That's because you dedicate yourself to helping others, and *you* make me very proud."

"When do you deliver your maiden address?"

He shrugged. "I would prefer to work behind the scenes rather that standing in front of everyone."

"What about before Lord Beavers spoke? Were you welcomed in the chamber?"

"I will own I felt . . . like I'd come home."

"I suppose many of your lifelong acquaintances were in the chamber with you."

He nodded. "A handful of them I was at Oxford with." He leaned back into the soft upholstery. "Even if it was an exhausting day, I know this is what I am meant to do. Speaking of which. . . how did *your* day go with the widows?" He popped another cube of cold mutton into his mouth.

She filled him in on what had occurred. "Your sisters are just as excited about this as I am. Margaret even offered a generous donation from her own pin money. It was enough to purchase food for a week. And Mrs. Leander is a talented cook."

"Mrs. Leander? Is that the one with five children?"

"The first one with five children! There's another. Now Caro has determined each child shall have his or her own bed, and she's on a quest to get beds donated because we won't have nearly enough."

"Good. Hopefully, that will keep my sister out of mischief."

"The only people under this roof who get into mischief are sitting in this room right now, your grace!"

He chuckled, then regarded her with stormy dark eyes. "Permit me to ask that you nevermore speak ill of my duchess." Her drew closer to her, setting his arm around her.

She flowed into his embrace and lifted her face to his. The sound of his heavy breathing and the faint scent of his sandalwood made her feel even more intoxicated than the port.

His head lowered. Their lips joined for a hungry kiss. She gloried in the feel of being swathed within his strong embrace, in the feel of his tongue touching hers, in the needy way in which they clung to one another.

He must want to be here with her as much as she wanted him to be there. . .

Chapter 12

As Elizabeth and her sisters-in-law hurried in the following afternoon, Richie awaited her in the porter's hall at Aldridge House. It had been a hectic day for her, locating widows of the men who had served with James. "Oh dear," she said, eying her cousin as she untied her bonnet. "I'd forgotten I was to ride in the park with you today. I beg that you allow me to freshen my appearance."

Her cousin's eye lazily ran along the length of her, and a smile curved his lips. "You cannot improve upon perfection."

He himself, she noted, dressed impeccably in fine leather Hessians, well-cut breeches, snowy linen shirt with freshly starched cravat. His fine woolen coat of warm brown perfectly harmonized with his stylishly cut hair. Though he was considerably shorter than her husband, he was considerably taller than she.

She offered him a mock scowl. "I daresay my cousin needs spectacles."

He shook his head emphatically. "Please, Elizabeth, come just as you are. Nothing could be more pleasing."

She eyed the bonnet that was still in her hands. "I perceive your time is tightly allotted, and you merely do not want me squandering something so vastly important." She began to put the bonnet back on her head.

A moment later they were in his curricle on the way to Hyde Park. "What is it you're doing with Aldridge's sisters all day?" he asked.

"They are kind enough to assist me with our home for officers' widows. His grace has donated a large house on Trent Square for their home, and we're busy seeing that each chamber is put to the best possible use."

He pulled on the ribbons, lurching to a stop to allow a laden cart of potatoes to pass on the intersecting street. "How is it you even know of the plight of these widows?"

"It all began when James asked me to look in on Mrs. Hudson, whose husband had been a great favorite of his in the Peninsula."

"And what with the Marchioness Haverstock setting an inspiring example of charitable works, it's only natural you have your own."

"There's also Charlotte and Mr. Hogart's wonderful philanthropy to emulate."

"Oh yes, the bloody Methodist."

They had reached the park's main gate and had gotten in the queue behind a large, open barouche in which two couples faced each other. She nodded to Miss Shelton, the only one in the barouche she knew.

It only then occurred to her that this was the first time she had been to Hyde Park since her marriage. And she was not accompanied by her husband. Another disappointment. First, Almack's, then the theatre, and now, this. It stung that others would know Philip was not in love with the woman he had married.

Yet were she to choose between him being with her or him doing his duty to his country, she would not hesitate to encourage him to serve in Parliament and at the Foreign Office.

"I must ask something of you," Richie said.

Her brows shot up.

"Next Friday I should like to host a political dinner at Aldridge House. With you as my official hostess, of course."

His request was not unexpected. "Is there a purpose to this?" she asked.

"I plan to invite Members who are currently opposed to the tax increase."

"With the hope of changing their minds?"

He nodded. "I wouldn't ask you if I didn't believe I can count on your husband's support."

"I cannot speak for Philip, but I do believe he favors the increase."

"It's an uphill battle, you know."

"I know."

"But wars are costly."

She sighed. "I should like Parliament to pass a bill providing a generous pension to war widows."

"It is a pity that these men give their lives to our country, but our country turns its back on the dead men's families."

"Indeed."

"Are you endeavoring to sway your husband to your way of thinking?"

"Such a measure only just occurred to me, but you can depend on it that I will bring up the topic with my husband."

"When you see Aldridge—which it has been my observation is not often."

She stiffened. "In public, yes, we are not seen much together, but be assured we have private time with each other every day." Her heart fluttered at the memories of their intimacies.

They entered the park, and Richie doffed his cap at Lord Elsworth. A much younger, fair-haired girl was seated beside him in the barouche. Elizabeth wondered if she were the man's daughter.

"I will be happy to serve as your hostess next Friday, but don't forget what I'm asking of you."

He paused and turned to her. "You want me to educate you on political thought and how Parliament works?"

She nodded. "I am desirous of learning everything I can about government."

"It will be my pleasure to teach you." He smiled down at her. "Now I shall have a very good excuse for spending time every day with one of the loveliest ladies in London. I shall be the envy of all the bachelors."

A frown creased her forehead. She was not comfortable with the way Richie had been acting with her, almost as if he wanted others to think he was her lover. He must understand at the outset that she would never be unfaithful to her husband. Ever. And if he even tried to be too familiar with her, she would terminate her relationship with her cousin immediately. "I fail to see how you could be envied for spending time with another man's devoted wife."

"You must know there are many men who are attracted to neglected wives."

She whirled at him and spoke sharply. "I am *not* a neglected wife."

"It just appears that you are."

"If I must continue to be subjected to your ridiculous assumptions regarding my marriage, I will never ride with you again. The reason my husband is not in my pocket is because he and I both choose duty first."

He looked contrite. "Forgive me."

"Philip's chief reason for returning to England was to do everything in his power to crush Napoleon."

"I never meant to malign your husband." He turned his rig toward the Serpentine.

It was then that she noticed the vivid green buds dotting along barren tree branches. "Finally, a sign of spring."

"Still much chill, though."

"But fortunately not too cold for open carriages." The beginning of spring accounted for the never-ending conveyances winding their way like a giant ribbon through London's largest park.

"Why are you so eager to learn about the workings of government?" he asked.

She spun to glare at him. "Can you not understand?"

He shrugged.

"I mean to be the perfect wife. Philip is keenly interested in Parliament."

He pulled back his mare and eyed her, a look of wonderment upon his face. "Are you telling me this marriage of yours is a love match? You're in love with your husband?"

"Of course."

When she returned to Aldridge House, she was met with great excitement. All smiles, Margaret greeted her. "Clair's home!"

Elizabeth quickly raced up the stairs with Margaret to Clair's bedchamber. There, the two sisters were sitting upon the window seat, and

Caroline was telling Clair about Number 7 Trent Square.

When Clair looked up and saw Elizabeth, she sprang from her seat and raced across the room to hug her new sister. "If anything could make me happier than having Aldridge back after so long an absence, it's his selection of a wife. He could not have done better." Were the hug not enough to convey her approval, Clair then took Elizabeth's hand and pressed it between hers. "I was unaware that my brother was possessed of such excellent judgment. Now do come and tell me all about this scheme that you are carrying out at Trent Square. It sounds terribly like something I should love to participate in above all things!"

Elizabeth sat on a French chair, facing the window seat where the three sisters sat shoulder to shoulder. It seemed almost inconceivable that Clair could be sisters to the other two. No ladies in the *ton* dressed more beautifully than Margaret and Caroline. The perusing of the fashion prints in *Ackermann's* occupied much of their time, and the pair of them—or their maid—went to great pains with the styling of their hair every day. Almack's, to them, was the center of the universe; capturing young men's attention was the force that guided all their actions—except for their desire to help with Elizabeth's charitable project.

Poor Clair. Seeing her side-by-side with these two sisters plainly illustrated how shortchanged she had been with her physical appearance. The three shared just one single physical trait. They each had hair the colour of tree bark. While her sisters were rounded in the very areas where a man liked to see a woman rounded, Clair was almost hideously thin. And where the other sisters were possessed of delicate, creamy complexions, Clair was covered from head to foot with freckles. Still, if she cared a whit about her appearance, she might convey a more flattering look.

Sadly, Lady Clair Ponsby's interest in being fashionable was as absent as the meaty bits other ladies liked to flaunt.

Whether Clair knew it or not, marriage could enrich her life immeasurably. And Elizabeth vowed to assist in such an endeavor, whether or not Clair was aware of her meddling.

Elizabeth sketched out her plans for Trent Square, filling her in on what had heretofore been done.

Clair's brows lowered. "You've done all this in a matter of weeks?"

"With Philip's help," Elizabeth answered. "And now with most able assistance from the Ponsby sisters."

"Have you filled all the bedchambers?" Clair asked.

"Yes and no," Elizabeth responded.

"How can it not be either yes or no?"

"Because," Caroline said authoritatively, "we've selected all the needy families, but we have yet to locate all of them."

Clair, who was highly intelligent and well read, mumbled almost to herself. "Yes, I can see where the difficulties arise when one has no home at which they can be reached."

Elizabeth smiled. "I shall be delighted to have you working with us."

"It is ever so much fun," Margaret said. "The children are such dears, and the mothers are all a pleasure to be near."

"Whilst I was riding in the park with my cousin Richie today, I had what I think a brilliant idea."

"Pray, you must share with us!" Caroline's always-ready interest in Elizabeth's project secured the lady's firm position in Elizabeth's affections.

"As brilliant as it is, I shall need help from every member of this family," Elizabeth said.

"Enlighten us, please," Clair commanded.

"Would it not be wonderful if Parliament granted a comfortable pension to the widows of our soldiers?"

Clair nodded thoughtfully. "It is so obvious one wonders why it hasn't already been done."

"I've asked for Richie's support, and I plan to make a convincing case to my dear Philip. . ." Elizabeth's face brightened as she eyed Clair. "Did you know your brother is sitting in the House of Lords?"

"If I get any prouder of my eldest brother," Clair said, "I am sure I will explode. We must owe our gratitude for his transformation to you, my dear Elizabeth."

"You underestimate your brother. Compulsion to duty is why he returned to England."

Clair lifted a brow. "And his marriage to you? To what do we owe this splendid addition to our family?"

She could not admit her very own mistake resulted in his offer of marriage. For one reason, she could no longer look upon her rash action that day as a mistake. Not when it yielded such blissful results.

Instead, Elizabeth spoke only for herself when

she answered. "Love."

God, but the sight of his home filled him with satisfaction. In his exhausted state, he could sink into his bed and sleep for four and twenty hours. He began to trudge up the stairs which were lit only by a single sconce at this hour. His wife and sisters would long be asleep. He frowned to himself. This would be the first day since they had wed that he had not at least spoken to his wife.

He wished like the devil he could have come home early enough to see her, to speak with her, to. . . hold her in his arms. His need for her rather startled him. Not being with his Elizabeth left a gnawing void in his existence.

He had told Lawford not to wait up for him. He'd told Elizabeth the same thing, and now he wished he hadn't. At the third floor, he began to creak along the long wooden corridor, regretfully past his wife's chamber, then to his own.

Why in the devil had Lawford left so many candles burning?

Then he saw her. She was in her night shift with the creamy shawl draped around her shoulders, sitting in front of the fire reading.

No sight had ever been lovelier.

How had she known how badly he craved being with her? Did marriage establish a magical connection between two beings? A connection where one intrinsically sensed the other's needs?

"You shouldn't have waited up."

She put down her book and favored him with a sweet smile. "I shouldn't like to establish the practice of either of us going to bed without sharing the day's activities with one another." Her gaze flicked to the book. "Besides, I'm fascinated with Smith's work."

"Adam Smith?"

She nodded.

He came to press a kiss to her cheek, then to sit beside his wife. "I did not know women were interested in such things."

"This woman must educate herself to be her husband's perfect helpmate."

Had he not spent most of his life schooling himself to always be unwaveringly strong, her words could have choked him with emotion. Dear God! If one must be shackled, one could do no better than to have Elizabeth for a wife. "You bring to mind Lady Wickshire."

"I mean to. She is my model. Is she not a perfect wife?"

His arm settled around her, and he spoke huskily. "The Wickshires' marriage is well known for being one of the strongest, most loving unions ever." Why in the blazes should Elizabeth wish to emulate that?

"That is, until my brother wed Anna. No two people are more devoted to each other than they."

His brows lowered, he smiled. "Not Morgie and Lydia?"

She shrugged. "Their marriage is altogether different. They do not sweet talk to one another in public, and I always get the impression that Lydia has reversed the marital roles."

"You mean she wears the pants in the family?"

"I suppose that *is* what I mean, but please don't disparage such a marriage. For them, it is the perfect marriage, and it would be impossible to be more devoted to one another."

"I wish my own sisters could have so strong a

union."

"Oh! Clair is home."

"And you took her to Almack's tonight?"

She shook her head. "She refused to go. Said she had nothing suitable to wear. So I firmly told her I will be taking her to the dressmakers."

"Good."

"She's awfully eager to help out at Trent Square."

"I knew she would be. How did things go there today?"

"I was only there a few minutes. I am still trying to locate some of the widows whose husbands James wrote me about."

It suddenly occurred to him that it was not likely these widows lived in Mayfair. His brows lowered. "Do not tell me you've been going to unsavory neighborhoods without a man to protect you!"

"Then I will not tell you."

He scowled. "Now I understand how Haverstock felt about his wife traipsing off to the East End without proper protection!"

"Quite frankly, I never worried about facing danger because the coachman was with me."

"The man is hardly bigger than you! Some protector he would be! I don't like you going off like that. Tomorrow, you'll take our biggest, strongest footman, and I'll fit him with a sword. That should repel any threat."

"Oh, my dearest Philip, I am so touched that you worry about me."

He did not like speaking of his emotions. He had never been capable of demonstrating his feelings. But, God, how he wanted this woman! His simmering gaze raked over her, slowly, lingeringly, then he hauled her into his arms, crushing her against him while they hungrily kissed.

Her breath was as ragged as his. Who would ever have thought this daughter of a stiff marquess could unleash such passions? And how in the hell had that cold father of hers sired a woman as gentle and loving as Elizabeth?

He slung away her book, gathered her up into his arms as if she were a small child, and strode to his bed.

Chapter 13

Philip was deciphering at his desk next to a tall casement that overlooked the Horse Guards when Haverstock walked into his office.

"I promised my wife I would personally seek you out with an invitation for a family dinner at our house tonight. She is at present imploring your wife to join us, along with Morgie and Lydia." Haverstock shrugged. "We thought it would be a good time since there's no House of Lords tonight, no assemblies at Almack's."

"Sounds most agreeable to me. Even though I see you every day, we seldom get to really converse with one another." How fortunate Philip was to have married the sister of his best friend in the world. Even as lads who pledged a lifelong friendship, they had not ever considered that one day they would, through marriage, become family to one another. Lads were not likely to visualize themselves as husbands, he thought, smiling, especially when defending castles and riding fast horses held far more allure.

"May I bring my most sensible sister?" Philip asked. "She's just down from the country, and I haven't seen her in five years."

"Yes, of course. Allow me to guess. You are referring to Clair?"

"Indeed."

Haverstock came to sit in a chair in front of his brother-in-law's desk. "I keep hearing that Elizabeth is seen every day in the park with our cousin Richie." His eyes narrowed. "Do you not object?"

Every day? He most certainly *did* object! Especially since that damned Richie acted as if he was in love with Philip's wife. Yet Philip could not betray his emotions to Haverstock. Or to anyone. "My dear wife is merely using her cousin to educate her on the ways of government."

"Why in the blazes does she want to know about the bloody government?"

"She claims she wants to be the perfect wife. Am I not the most fortunate man?"

Haverstock's face gentled. "That is very commendable."

"She's quite the prize. I count my good fortune every day. I will own, I am puzzled as to how one possessed of her beauty and many other attributes could still be unmarried three years after coming out."

"It's that damned Smythe's- - -" Haverstock clamped shut his mouth.

Philip felt as if he'd just been struck down by a thoroughbred on the turf at Newmarket. "Are you saying my wife was previously betrothed?"

"She was never betrothed," Haverstock snapped, bitterness in his voice.

What man who had engaged her affections would not to wish to marry Elizabeth? God, just being the daughter of a marquess was enough to ensure she was highly sought after. Philip's brows squeezed together. "She fell in love with a man who did not return her ardor?"

Haverstock stood. "You will have to ask her. I

do not know the nature of the feelings she may have held for Captain Smythe."

A military man? "My wife and I have decided that our lives began on the day we married. Anything that came before our wedding is no longer of consequence." Yet it *did* concern him if she had come into their marriage while being in love with another man.

"That is an excellent plan." Haverstock moved toward the door.

"Wait."

His brother-in-law turned back.

"This. . . this captain. . . did he want to marry Elizabeth?"

Haverstock did not respond immediately. "I believe he did, but he didn't think it right until after the war. It wouldn't be right to leave her a widow."

While that sounded like a noble gesture—denying one's own strongest desires to protect the one he loved—Philip took no consolation in it. His stomach turned. "We shall see you tonight."

When he walked into his wife's bedchamber that night, she sat before her dressing table as her maid finished pinning up her hair. She wore a pale blue gown of nearly sheer fabric. "I cannot believe you have once again worn a dress that corresponds in colour to the gems I've brought."

Her glittering gaze followed him through his reflection in her mirror. "Sapphires?"

"Indeed."

"Thank you, Fanny," she said, dismissing her servant.

He removed the necklace from the velvet box and moved to fasten it around her elegant neck, which he seemed incapable of doing without availing himself of the opportunity to nibble on her neck. When he finished, he stood back, and he too peered into the looking glass. "Beautiful."

She came to her feet and flung her arms gratefully about his neck. "Thank you, my dearest. The necklace is lovely."

He kissed her softly. "Not nearly as lovely as you."

She linked her arm with his, and they left. "I cannot tell you how thrilled I am to have you home tonight," she said.

He chuckled. "I cannot convey to you how deuced good it is to be home tonight. Or, allow me to rephrase. To be with my family tonight."

Clair awaited them in the porter's hall, and as good as it was to see her again, he lamented that she had taken no pains to make herself look more attractive. They hugged. They told each other they looked wonderful. They said how good it was to see one another again.

Then the three of them got into the carriage for the short ride to Haverstock House. "And Auntie Hop-sham?" he asked.

"She is well. She sent a family heirloom to give to you and Elizabeth as a wedding gift. It's a small, but very exquisite, piece of silver. She called it a bon bon dish."

"Very thoughtful of her," he said.

At Haverstock House, he was pleased to see the gathering would be just the three couples and his sister. Then the marchioness announced that they were awaiting her husband's cousin.

Not that damn Rothcomb-Smedley! From what Haverstock had said to him earlier that day, Philip thought perhaps Haverstock was a bit out of charity with his cousin.

"I had the good fortune," Lady Haverstock continued, "of nearly bumping into Richie at the bookseller's today, and I thought how delightful it would be if he could join us tonight."

It would make the numbers even, Philip consoled himself.

Haverstock's gaze connected to Philip's, but their expressions remained unreadable.

Soon Rothcomb-Smedley came strolling into the saloon as if it were his own bloody house. A more confident upstart Philip had never seen.

The marchioness turned to the Duke of Aldridge. "Will you show me into the dinner room, your grace?"

Then, as precedent demanded, Haverstock turned to his duchess sister and escorted her, while the four others paired up to enter the dining chamber. As the daughter of a duke, Clair outranked Lady Lydia, a marquess's daughter, who would be the last to enter the dinner chamber.

He overheard Rothcomb-Smedley greeting Clair. "We missed you at the big wedding."

"I was at Auntie Hop-sham's—never dreaming that my wayward brother was on his way back to England—and totally surprised, but delighted, over his choice of a wife."

Philip had no desire to hear Rothcomb-Smedley gush over his wife. He turned his attention to his hostess. It was difficult not to stare at Lady Haverstock. She was possessed of extraordinary beauty. Now that he thought about it, he realized she rather resembled the Contessa Savatini, who was said to be the most beautiful woman in all of Italy. Yet, Haverstock's marchioness was even prettier, likely because this dark-haired beauty radiated a sweetness that was far more admirable than the seductive qualities exuded by the Contessa.

"I did not think my husband could have been happier than he was when he learned of your return to England," the marchioness said, "but that joy was eclipsed by the wedding of his sister to his dearest friend."

"The joy is mine." Philip held out the chair for the marchioness, then sat to her right. Elizabeth sat to Haverstock's right, and Lydia sat next to her, with Rothcomb-Smedley directly across from Philip. As much as he did not want to converse with the man, he was pleased that Rothcomb-Smedley would not be seated near his wife.

Morgie sat beside Philip and turned to address him. "You did know I have a son?"

Philip chuckled. "Yes, my wife is excessively fond of her little nephew."

Morgie's voice lowered. "Don't tell Lyddie—she's uncommonly attached to the little fellow—but I'm alarmed. He don't talk. He don't sit up. He doesn't even have a single tooth!"

"You mustn't be concerned. Elizabeth says he's perfect."

Morgie's countenance brightened. "Me mother said the same thing. You'd think the babe was hers the way she dotes on him. (First grandchild, you know.) Though no one is as fond of the fellow as Lyddie."

"You're most fortunate. What man doesn't want a son?"

"I will own, I was exceedingly happy when I found out we were going to be parents—except for worrying about Lyddie, but I imagined having a lad to ride with and shoot with and – well, you know, do all the manly things with."

"Give him time."

As Philip began to serve himself from the wide array of offerings ranging from roasted hare and buttered lobster to steaming bowls heaped with vegetables, he listened as his sister and Rothcomb-Smedley conversed with one another. "Elizabeth tells me you are in the process of educating her about Parliament," Clair said.

"I hope I can be helpful in that regard."

Clair took the plate of roasted pheasant that he handed her. "I've always been vastly interested in government."

"I shouldn't like for you to supplant me with Elizabeth." Rothcomb-Smedley gave her a mock glare.

Philip found his hands fisting with anger toward his wife's cousin. Right in front of her husband's nose, he was flaunting his affection for Elizabeth!

"Oh, I'm not *that* knowledgeable—not like a sitting member of Parliament, especially one such as you who has so many responsibilities."

Philip wished to God the man had never stood for Parliament.

"Most young women," Rothcomb-Smedley said, "would have no idea of the offices I hold."

She shrugged. "As I said. I have a strong interest in Parliament, and I daresay it will grow now that my brother has taken his seat in the House of Lords."

He nodded across the table to Philip. "By the way, your grace, I shall be most indebted to you and Elizabeth for allowing me to host a dinner at Aldridge House next Friday."

Philip seethed. Why did Rothcomb-Smedley persist in calling *his* wife by her first name when he should have used *her grace*? He flicked an impatient glance at his wife, who was talking to Lydia about the baby. "My wife has failed to tell me about this."

Rothcomb-Smedley lifted a brow. "I pray I am not the source of a conflict between you and the duchess."

"Not at all. My wife and I—even when there is a gap in communication—are always in harmony with the other's plans. Speaking of my wife's plans," he said to his sister, "Elizabeth says you are eager to help with her widows."

"I started today! There is much to be done. Currently living under that roof are three and twenty children—with more expected. That is far too many for a single school room."

"You're concerning yourself also with the children's education?" Philip asked.

"Of course. I've taken it upon myself to start setting up various chambers for the teaching of different subjects. I've even apportioned the former wine cellar."

Clair had always been his favorite sister. He thought one of the reasons he preferred her was because she was the most intelligent. She would be a fine teacher. He recalled how she used to play "governess" to Margaret and Caro. "Allow me to guess which subject you will provide instruction in."

She smiled at him. "You cannot possibly know where my current preferences lie. You've been away five years. "

"I would wager you're still excessively adept at mathematics."

A dismayed expression on her face, she nodded. "You remembered. . ."

"How could I forget? It was so novel for a girl to be passionate about mathematics."

Rothcomb-Smedley turned an admiring eye upon her. "You truly fancy mathematics? As well as the study of Parliamentary law? A girl after my own heart."

Then why in the devil did the man have such a compulsion to be with Philip's wife every day?

"I say," Morgie said to Clair, "that's jolly good that you fancy mathematics. It was always my favorite field of study."

Philip looked good naturedly upon his lifelong friend. "I vow, Morgie, I was at school with you every year and have no recollection of you enjoying any aspect of study."

"Bloody well hated the lot of learning. Except for maths. Comes from being from a long line of bankers. We get off to percents and sums and the like—especially when they pertain to money."

"I will own that no one of our acquaintance knows more about the acquisition of money than you," Philip said.

Morgie frowned. "Except Father wouldn't hear of me taking my place on the 'Change. Said he'd worked hard all his life so his son can be an idle gentleman."

Philip knew that if Morgie's father was still alive he'd be filled with pride, especially in the promise of a new generation. What would it be like to have a son, and later a grandson to carry on? Philip was oddly envious.

His wife's voice rang out, but it was not to him she spoke, but to her cousin. "Will you be at the Hollands for dinner on Thursday, Richie?"

"Indeed I will."

"Wonderful!" she said. "Then I'll know someone besides Philip." Her laughing eyes met her husband's, and he was powerless not to smile.

"Wouldn't want me wife to go there," Morgie mumbled.

"Why not?" the marchioness asked.

"Divorced woman and all that," he replied.

Clair glared at Morgie but kept her disapproval to herself.

Even though he had been gone these five years, Philip had kept informed about his sister's progressive ideas. It was good that he'd come home to keep a watchful eye over the lot of them. It really wouldn't do for them to start cavorting with divorced women. Or prostitutes.

Just last year his eldest sister had been forced to take time away from her three children to intercede with Clair when she developed a plan to help destitute prostitutes. This intercession necessitated that Sarah leave her beloved countryside and come to London. Much to the consternation of Clair, who had befriended the most unsavory sort of common streetwalker with the firm intention of reforming her. There was almost no end to the tireless, worrisome letters Sarah had dispatched to him in Italy.

How ironic, Philip had thought, that Sarah had turned out to be the ever-so-proper wife and mother. The year she was presented she had given him more grief than all the other siblings had in these eight ensuing years.

Sarah had been far too polite to beg him to come home, but he knew it was time.

Just another reason compelling him to return.

He chatted amiably with Lady Haverstock

while half way listening to his wife discuss Smith's *Wealth of Nations* with her brother. Philip expected Elizabeth—having just finished reading the book—to remember all those economic theories down to the smallest details. But Haverstock not only held his own with his sister, but he spoke of Smith's work with great intelligence. Had Haverstock just finished rereading the work?

Philip swelled with pride over the intelligent woman he had wed. She was good stock. Just like her fine brother.

After the meal the men stayed in the dinner room, drinking port and discussing Parliament. "Me father's last request was that I stand for the Liversham seat in the House of Commons," Morgie said, frowning.

Rothcomb-Smedley grinned. "What an excellent plan! Of course you'll win with the Morgan fortune behind you." His expression went from happy to troubled. He faced Philip. "As we speak, Lord Hervey is gathering a large group of lords at White's with the express purpose of rallying opposition to the tax bill,"

Even though Philip was not fond of Rothcomb-Smedley, he knew the two had to work together for the good of the country. For, unlike most of the peers with whom the Duke of Aldridge served, his wife's cousin—like Philip—wanted what was best for their country rather than what was best for their purses. He eyed Rothcomb-Smedley, while leaping to his feet. "Then why in the hell are you here?"

Rothcomb-Smedley stood. "You're right. We need to go."

With the duke leading the way, the four of them reentered the drawing room. His face somber, his gaze connected with Elizabeth's. "It appears we are not to have the pleasure of an evening away from duty."

All expression drained from her face. "You're leaving?"

He nodded solemnly.

Her gaze flicked to her cousin. "You're going with him?"

Rothcomb-Smedley nodded. "We have fires to put out."

Before he left, Philip moved to his wife and brushed a kiss across her cheek. She stiffened.

As he and Rothcomb-Smedley rode to St. James, Philip could not purge from his troubled thoughts the sorrowful look on his wife's face.

Chapter 14

After sweeping past White's porter and entering the club's largest chamber, Philip's gaze swung from the front of the room where Alvanley was seated at the bow window with three other men, all of them talking loudly and drinking large quantities of brandy. Philip's attention settled on the gathering of white and silver-headed peers who were seated and standing around Lord Knolles. At least a dozen fellow members of the House of Lords were intently listening to the Lord Chancellor, who looked like a monarch holding court right in the center of London's most prestigious club.

"I presently control four and twenty seats in the House of Commons," Lord Knolles said. "Together, we—those of you with me tonight—can exert our authority over these men who owe their offices to us." His gaze fanned over those encircling him. "I daresay those of us here account for nearly half the members of the House of Commons."

"And if we don't stand up against this unjust tax increase," Lord Highsmith said, a grim expression upon his face, "every man here will lose his lands."

"That's not true!" Philip moved closer, glaring at the knot of powerful peers.

Lord Knolles' eyes narrowed. "The Right Honorable Duke of Aldridge disagrees?"

"Aldridge's father must be turning in his grave," Lord Clapington mumbled.

"Who'd have thought the duke would turn out to be a bloody Whig?" another said.

"I am neither Whig, nor Tory," Philip said, his voice powerful yet respectful. "I am an Englishman, and I will always vote for what I feel is best for my country."

Lord Knolles heaved an audible sigh. "You cannot be expected to know about the workings of *English* government. You've sat in our chamber for merely a week—after spending several *years* away from this country you profess to love so thoroughly."

The aging peer was still in possession of a strong voice, even though advancing years had left his shoulders sagging, his nose bulbous, and his hands shaking.

Rothcomb-Smedley stepped closer to the Lord Chancellor. "Now see here, Lord Knolles, you cannot know how deeply the Duke of Aldridge is committed to crushing France." His gaze flared to Philip.

Philip cautioned himself to speak without rancor, to be respectful. "Because I have been in Italy, my lord, I was able to observe what happens to a grand old kingdom, like the Kingdom of Naples and Sicily, when that Corsican monster usurps some of the most noble families in all of Europe to place his corrupt siblings upon the throne."

"We cannot allow that to happen in England," Rothcomb-Smedley said. "Like you men, I was born to a noble old English family. My mother was a sister of the old Marquess of Haverstock, and my father was a younger son of the Earl of Sutton. No one could wish to preserve these old properties more than I."

The aristocrats being addressed listened without interrupting. Was that because Philip and Rothcomb-Smedley had spoken rationally and with courtesy?

"The proposed tax will increase the present rate by just ten percent," Philip said. "I understand for those of us with extensive properties, a ten percent reduction of income is a great deal of money, but it takes vast amounts to man and equip a competitive navy and an army large enough to defeat the enemy on all fronts. We cannot be *as good as,* we must be *better than.*"

"We have not the advantage of the French who are beefing up their ranks with soldiers from lands they've conquered," Rothcomb-Smedley added, bracing his palms on the long table Knolles headed, his intense gaze circling around those gathered. "And I give you my word that once we've won this bloody war, we will restore the tax rate to its current level."

"We will be victorious," Philip said, his voice firm.

The Lord Chancellor addressed Rothcomb-Smedley. "What is the sentiment in the House of Commons toward the tax bill?"

"It's too close to call."

"You must admit, the members in the House of Commons do not have as much to lose as those of us in the House of Lords," Lord Clapington said.

Philip stood tall, his expression serious, his eyes cold as they connected with each man there.

"I should not have to remind you," Philip said, his voice deliberate, his eyes cold, "that our personal losses and gains should never motivate a member of the House of Lords. One concern and one concern only—what is best for Britain—should guide all our decisions."

"He sounds like a bloody Benthamite!" Lord Highsmith snapped.

"He's no more a Benthamite than he's a Tory or a Whig," Rothcomb-Smedley defended.

Lord Knolles' brows lowered. "Where, may I ask, your grace, is Lord Haverstock? Why did he not accompany you two here? I'm curious to see how he stands on the matter of increasing taxes."

"Yes," Lord Highsmith added, "We all appreciate the many contributions Haverstock has made to our country. Why does he not support your extravagant scheme?"

"My cousin does not make up his mind until he's apprised of all the facts," Rothcomb-Smedley said.

"But," Philip said, "my brother-in-law is presently studying it."

Highsmith regarded Philip with antagonism sparking in his mossy eyes, a sneer upon his lips. "Our chamber was better off when the Duke of Aldridge was making his way through Italy in the beds of married women."

Anger surged within Philip. He wanted to call the man out. The two men faced one another, the sharp opposition between them as palpable as a sword. How he wanted to throw down the gauntlet and take his satisfaction on Highsmith's body. But nothing could be gained by such an action, and much could be lost. His responsibilities had to take precedence over personal affront.

Rothcomb-Smedley whirled at Highsmith. "That was a bloody ungentlemanly thing to say!"

"He's right, Highsmith," the Lord Chancellor said in a calm voice. "I must ask that you beg his grace's pardon."

Philip's black eyes locked with Highsmith's smoldering gaze. The other man swallowed, then in a weak voice said, "Forgive me, your grace. My comments were unpardonable."

A firm nod in Highsmith's direction was Philip's only response.

Then he nodded to Lord Knolles, gratified that the Lord Chancellor would conduct himself nobly. Because of that, Philip knew there was hope, hope that he could change the silver-headed leader's opposition to the tax increase.

He had stayed at White's only long enough to lay the foundation for his war against opponents to the tax measure. Just as the war with France had not begun in a single day, its end would take time. Philip was prepared to wear down his opponents' resistance. He was prepared to hammer at their resistance day in and day out until he wore them down. He was prepared to compliment, mollify, and even bribe every last one of them to achieve his aim. He was even prepared to do something he'd never before done. He was prepared to humble himself.

It had been a tiring day, a tiring week. He had looked forward to this family night tonight. It was deuced good to see Clair again. Even if she spent no more time on her appearance than a scullery maid.

He hoped his wife was not asleep when he

returned. It was good to have someone to tell about his ideals and others' resistance to those ideals. It was good to be wed to someone who was possessed of the same quest for noble purpose as he.

Neither Philip nor Elizabeth had entered this marriage with a commitment to love one another. He had certainly grown to admire her, even to crave being with her.

Especially in bed, he thought a little breathlessly.

After dropping off Rothcomb-Smedley, Philip's coach drew up in front of his house on Berkeley Square as he disembarked, his gaze lifting to Elizabeth's windows. His spirits buoyed when he saw light filling the tall casements. She had waited up for him.

When he entered her bedchamber a moment later, she smiled. "Allow me to get you a glass of brandy, dearest, and then you must tell me all about your night."

After they settled back on her settee near the fire, he told her why he had felt compelled to leave Haverstock House immediately after dinner, told her of the confrontation with the aging lords. "Rothcomb-Smedley was a rock. I think we shall work well together."

He took his wife's hand and nibbled upon the flesh between her thumb and index finger. "You forgive me for leaving?"

"You and I have always insisted that duty comes first."

"It seems I've my own Lady Wickshire."

"Indeed you do. Now, dearest, I have something to ask of you."

He continued nibbling at her hand, his brows

hiked. "What, love?"

"I have been bursting to tell you of my scheme, which only came to me today and which Richie has already agreed to champion in the House of Commons."

Just when he was beginning to see that damned cousin of hers in a more agreeable light, Philip was reminded of the man's annoying closeness to his wife. "I shall be offended."

Her lovely pale brown brows lowered. "Why?"

"You've chosen to inform your cousin of your scheme before you told your husband. I daresay Lady Wickshire would never have done something like that." He strove for levity, but there was nothing humorous about the painful truth of his words.

"I beg your forgiveness that I've not conducted myself as would Lady Wickshire." Playfulness rang in her voice. "You must believe me when I tell you the only reason Richie was the first to hear of my scheme was because it only popped into my head as we were riding in the park."

"What is this scheme which has my duchess so excited?" He tipped his glass and took a long swig.

"I implore you to champion legislation that would provide a nice pension for the widows of soldiers who died for our country."

He nodded thoughtfully. "Yes, I can see why Rothcomb-Smedley would favor such a plan. It's appalling that something like this hasn't been done before."

Her pale eyes shimmered with delight. "Then you will help in this endeavor?"

He sighed. "How can I not? The pity of it is that those opposed to any hike in taxes will brand me as a spendthrift with others' money. Their faulty logic will not take into account that as the third-largest land owner in Great Britain, I pay more taxes than any of the men who serve with me in Parliament."

"I know, love."

"I can see I'm going to have to start twisting arms."

"Oh, Lord Wickshire, you've made your lady most proud!"

He chuckled. Seeing her milky exposed shoulders shiver, he tenderly draped her Kashmir shawl around her more tightly.

"Did anything interesting occur after your cousin and I left?" he asked.

"The wind went out of our sails once you left our little gathering."

"It was beastly good to see Clair, but can you not do something about her appearance? I am incapable of knowing the slightest thing about ladies' fashions, but I do know her hair is not at all the thing. She could look a great deal better with just a bit of effort put into it."

His wife nodded. "I have told her nothing can keep us from going to the dressmaker's tomorrow. And you are right about her hair. A woman needs a bit of fluff about her face in order to distinguish her from males."

"That's it! She pulls her hair tightly back into that dull bun. By God, you've hit the nail upon the head! Her lackadaisical disregard for appearance has the effect of making her look like a lad!"

She didn't really look like a male. A dainty slenderness characterized her, and her voice was utterly feminine. "I shall do my best to try to talk her into getting that straight hair of hers shorn. That is the latest fashion rage."

"Yes, I find that look most becoming in a young woman." His voice lowered, and he moved closer to speak in a husky whisper. "But not as becoming as pale gold hair artfully swept away from a lovely face." His fingers sifted through his wife's golden curls. "Tell me what occurred with Trent Square today."

"We now have located all but one family—which is a very good thing since there is but one bedchamber unclaimed."

"And the footman I selected? Do you think he can repel would-be cutthroats?"

"But of course. Abraham is ever so tall and appears excessively strong. Then there's that menacing sword you insisted he strap on." She lovingly peered up at him and spoke softly. "It was very thoughtful of you, and I will own I do feel safer now when we are crisscrossing the more unsavory neighborhoods."

She gazed into the fire. "Caroline has really taken Trent Square to heart and has collected donations from half the families she knows to buy additional beds and coal."

"I am surprised something besides Almack's holds her attention."

"You will be very proud of her. She says, 'Every child should have his own bed.'"

His brows lowered. "Is it actually possible to crowd a half a dozen beds into a single bedchamber?"

She shrugged. "Some of them are small. Child-sized. I will own, there is very little room to move around once a chamber fills with all those beds, but there are many common areas in the house for them to gather for activities."

"Like Clair's school?"

"Yes. Oh, Caroline, bless her soul, bought a pianoforte for Trent Square, and Margaret has volunteered to begin instructing the children on the instrument. You cannot believe how popular such an activity is! The children are fighting over who gets to sit upon the bench with Lady Margaret."

"I'm proud of all of you."

"We are grateful to you for giving us the house."

He drew her to him and murmured. "Everything I have is yours, Elizabeth."

"We are as one," she whispered.

His lips greedily lowered to hers.

On Thursday night Philip and his wife dined at Holland House in Kensington. He'd been hearing about these gatherings for years but was still unprepared for the vast scale of these dinners. This night, he counted thirty-eight at the long, seemingly never-ending table. Males considerably outnumbered females, and to his dissatisfaction, it was Rothcomb-Smedley who was seated next to *his* wife—on the opposite end of the table from him.

Though he would have preferred to have Elizabeth close, he was pleased that she hadn't been cast into a sea of strangers—the fear of which she had revealed earlier that night during their coach ride there. By nature, Elizabeth had difficulty putting herself forward in these kinds of situations. Not like him. Perhaps because he had held the rank of duke since he was a fairly young man, he was accustomed to the ease with which others deferred to him in matters ranging from food preferences to comments about the magnificence of Glenmont Hall, which it seemed everyone had seen during its public days.

He supposed he should be honored that he was seated next to their hostess, but the didactic woman was excessively annoying. As the only child of an exceedingly wealthy sugar planter, she had been raised with the expectation that she could secure anything her heart desired, whether it be a piece of property or dissolving one marriage in order to embark on another with the young man she had fallen passionately in love with. That young man she had so adored now submitted to her every command.

Philip would have preferred to sit next to jolly Lord Holland, who at present was talking to Elizabeth, who as the highest ranking woman at the table, sat beside their host. Philip's chief aim in coming to this dinner was to begin laying the foundations for approval of the tax bill. Lord Knolles was not there, nor were any of the men who had been at White's the previous night. But there were other men whose support he sought.

One of them, Lord Herkness, was seated across the table from him. "I had an interesting conversation about the tax bill last night at White's with some of our colleagues," Philip began.

"Indeed?" Herkness said.

"I have made no secret that I support the increase," Philip said.

Lord Herkness raised a brow. "And our Lord Chancellor has made no secret that he opposes it."

"Napoleon keeps swelling his armies with the

conquered. To prevail over them, we must come up with the money to equip a larger army and to purchase more ships to maintain our domination of the seas."

Lord Herkness made not a single comment.

Good lord, is he simply going to ignore me?

Then the silent man across from him nodded.

"Your grace," Lady Holland said to Philip, "I beg that you not discuss this wretched war at my table. You must know how tattered my emotions are over it. I cannot deny that I have been exceedingly close to Napoleon, and simply cannot bear to defeat the dear man. He gave me his portrait, you know. I must show it to you after dinner."

It was all Philip could do not to leap to his feet, curse the woman's traitorous words, and storm from this house. But Philip must remember his single priority: passage of the tax bill. Besides, if he had any hope of the bill being approved, he would need help from Lord Holland, who was easily one of the most popular men in Parliament. "In your home, my lady, I shall respect your wishes, but I cannot help but to lament that your personal feelings are in opposition to what's best for the country your husband so faithfully serves."

"Dear Lord Holland is a far truer patriot than his wife, I must confess." She took a sip from her delicate wine glass. "So you've married Lord Haverstock's last unmarried sister. . ." Lady Holland's eyes locked with his, and he realized that she was probably the same age as he, not the old matriarch he had expected.

"Yes, my lady, it was my good fortune that Lady Elizabeth was still available when I returned from my travels."

Her gaze swept to the head of the table where her portly husband was animatedly chatting with Philip's wife. "She is lovely. This is the first time I've seen her. Though she's not as beautiful as her brother's marchioness. I do believe Lady Haverstock is the most beautiful woman I've ever seen."

He shrugged. "But she was already wed to my closest friend. I count myself fortunate that I was able to woo my lovely Elizabeth."

"Do you know that is my first name?"

"Elizabeth is a lovely name."

"Thank you. I understand that you have only recently returned from several years in Italy? Oh, to be back there! That is where Lord Holland and I met and fell in love."

"It is much changed now. None of the Bourbons or Habsburgs rule there any longer. Only Napoleon's puppets."

Her face was inscrutable. "I never did care for the King of Naples. His wife, though, was most pleasant. Like her sister, Marie Antoinette, or so the Duchess of Devonshire told me. I never knew the French queen, owing to my youth." She took the large bowl of pigeon pie—one of half a dozen identical ones—scooped more on to her plate, then passed it to him, forcing him to set down the small bowl of calf's feet jelly from which he had been serving himself.

After dinner, he was pleased to be separated from Lady Holland whilst the men stayed in the dinner room, drinking their port and talking about Parliamentary matters. He did feel beastly for poor Elizabeth when she tossed him a fearful look as she departed the chamber with a gaggle of unfamiliar matrons.

He was flattered when Lord Holland said, "Pray, your grace, will you not come sit by me?"

When Philip did, his lordship said, "We must become more well acquainted now that you're back from Italy."

"I am honored to be asked here tonight. As it happens, I am trying to gather support for passage of the tax increase bill."

Lord Holland's face collapsed. "Oh, dear. I told my wife I would not vote in favor of it."

"Then I shall have to attempt to charm your lovely wife." Philip's lightly spoken words belied his grievous disappointment. It seemed everywhere he turned he met with immovable opposition.

Chapter 15

"I still don't know why you thought it necessary I have four new dresses," Clair snapped as she and her sister-in-law climbed into the Aldridge coach. She had been subjected to more than two hours of looking through pattern books, selecting colours and fabrics, and being measured and pinned whilst standing in front of the entire staff of Madam Duvall's virtually undressed for three-quarters of an hour.

Elizabeth instructed the coachmen to take them to Trent Square, then pleasantly greeted Abraham, the tall, well-formed footman who Philip had selected to serve as their protector outside the genteel avenues of Mayfair.

In the coach, she faced Clair. "If you must know, I am being selfish."

"In what way?"

"Since I am required to serve as chaperon for Philip's unmarried sisters when they attend balls or the assemblies at Almack's, I crave a sensible woman to keep me company."

"You don't need someone to keep you company. A woman as young and as lovely as you could dance every set. You need not sit around with the gossiping matrons."

"Aw, but like you, I have no desire to dance. Except with Philip, that is."

"But I detest assemblies, and I do not fancy

dancing in the least. In fact, my dancing is most inferior."

"If your dancing is inferior, it is because you put no effort into learning to do it properly. Just as you put no effort into dressing your hair." Elizabeth had been dreading approaching the subject of Clair's hair. It was difficult to criticize one's appearance without offending, and Elizabeth had spent her life avoiding giving offense to anyone—even an incompetent servant.

"But you know I care not about what is fashionable."

"We are all well aware of that. But I must ask you—as your sister—an exceedingly personal question."

Clair's finely shaped brow rose in query.

Elizabeth had agonized for many hours over how she would approach these matters with Clair without making her feel as if they wanted to be rid of the spinster. Then it occurred to her that she need only be honest, to speak from her heart.

"First, I must tell you how grievously I miss my sister Charlotte since she's married," Elizabeth began. "I would like nothing better than for you to replace the comfortable camaraderie we shared for nearly twenty years. Of all Philip's sisters, you are the one with whom I have the most commonality."

"I am flattered. Flattered and excessively pleased, for I believe I could be closer to you than I am to any of my birth sisters."

Elizabeth favored her with a gentle smile. "For my own feelings, I would hope you never wed and go away to your own home. But I must ask what it is *you* want from life. Do you never want to fall in love? To marry? To have your own home? Your own children?"

Clair did not answer for a moment. "I will own, I've never given much thought to love. I am utterly UNlike my sisters in that regard. But, yes, it would please me to one day be mistress of my own home. I would like to have a family. And I suppose, a husband. It is just that nothing in the world bores me more than an assembly or a ball."

"There are other ways of meeting gentlemen—though now that I know you don't hate men, I shall have to insist upon you dancing, if asked."

"I am much more interested in hearing about these *other ways*."

"For example, next Friday, I shall being serving as my cousin Richie's hostess for a political dinner. You must be there. I think you, being knowledgeable about Parliament, will make contributions to the conversation."

"I will be honored to sit at *that* table!"

Elizabeth's heartbeat skidded. She needed to bring up that other matter. Now. "Before that, I think it will be good to have my maid rearrange your hair. I would suggest you allow her to cut it into the style that is so fashionable right now."

Clair's eyes narrowed. "Then how would I be able to put it into a bun?"

Elizabeth shrugged. "You won't."

"Then I'd have to wear curl papers!"

"What would that hurt? We all do."

It was a moment before Clair responded. "Only to please you, I will submit to having my hair cut and curled. I'll be the lamb to slaughter."

Elizabeth laughed.

Both ladies were happy to arrive at Trent Square. It was Abraham, tall and blond and handsome, who opened the coach door for them.

"We will need you to assist in the moving of some more furnishings," Elizabeth told him.

There was always something there that demanded their attentions. When they entered the large, rambling house, the sound of banging piano keys filled the residence. The two ladies went straight to the music room. There, surrounding Margaret were three girls and two boys—all of them roughly the same size, which Elizabeth judged to be about seven years of age. Next to Margaret on the pianoforte bench was the lad who was happily pounding upon the keys. "Why, Joseph, do you not show the others now how to do the scales?" Margaret prodded in a gentle voice.

The other children were so fascinated over the instrument they had not noticed Elizabeth and Clair enter the chamber.

After complimenting Joseph on his scales, the two women hunted down Caroline. "Your grace," she said to Elizabeth, "I should like to present to you the latest and last family to occupy Trent Square. This is Mrs. Wright, and her two daughters and two sons."

The woman stepped forward and curtseyed to Elizabeth, who thought the woman looked a great deal like Clair because she was freckled and careless with her hair and was even near the same age as Clair.

"I am pleased to meet you," Elizabeth said, lowering herself to be on level with the children. "And what are your names?" Remarkably, they all looked to be nearly the same age. If she were one to wager, she would bet no more than three years separated the youngest of the four from the oldest.

Their appreciative gazes raking over the duchess's fine lavender dress that was adorned with purple ribbands, the children stepped up and shyly whispered their names, except for Sarah, the smallest. Sarah apparently did not know how to say anything without using all the power her lungs could command to inform Elizabeth—and anyone within forty feet—that she was three.

Mrs. Hudson then swept into the chamber. Because she had been the first tenant at the Trent Square home, she had taken it upon herself to be the abbess, dowager, and headmaster, all rolled into one young woman barely twenty years of age. "Your grace, this is so exciting. We have now filled every chamber! Can you believe that among us are eight and twenty children?"

And Mrs. Hudson contributed only one small girl to that total.

Elizabeth was almost overcome by the realization that were it not for her scheme, those twenty-eight children would not have a warm comfortable home, food in their bellies, and a bed to sleep in. "I couldn't be happier. I pray all of you will get along as a single, happy family."

"I am certain we shall. Why, Mrs. Leander was just telling me today she felt as if she were one of the royal princesses."

Elizabeth and Clair laughed. "I shan't want to get your hopes up," an exhilarated Elizabeth said to Mrs. Hudson, "but I am happy to tell you that my cousin and my husband have agreed to support a new bill that would provide soldier's widows with a comfortable pension." As soon as the words were out of her mouth, Elizabeth regretted speaking them. She had been so exuberant over the measure, she had blurted without thinking. "Pray, do not place too much confidence in the plan. They are only two men in that vast body of Parliament. It will take many, many votes to approve such a measure, and as you must know, money is not something the government has in plentitude."

Tears filled the widow's eyes. "Oh, your grace, that's as wonderful as Number 7 Trent Square." She put her hands upon Elizabeth's as if to bless them. "With the Duke of Aldridge sponsoring such a bill, it must meet with approval."

"You credit my husband too much." It was a pity that Philip had been gone from England for so long. It would take time for the other Parliamentarians to trust him, time to earn their respect, time to develop those leadership skills she knew he'd been born with.

She never doubted that one day the Duke of Aldridge would be a force in Parliament. She just prayed that he could achieve that success sooner, rather than later.

"Mrs. Hudson, since Abraham has been yours to command, you must tell me if he's been helpful," Elizabeth said.

The youthful widow shyly smiled. "He has been ever so obliging."

"We have the duke to thank for insisting upon Abraham's service to us." Elizabeth's thoughts flashed back to the only day Philip had ever met Mrs. Hudson, the only day he'd ever come to Trent Square. The memory of that first stolen kiss still had the power to launch a fluttering in her heart.

When the night of Richie's dinner arrived, she

was more excited over Clair's transformation than over her own first important dinner. Even before she'd put on her jewels, she raced down the corridor to Clair's bedchamber and softly knocked upon her door. "May I come in?"

"Certainly." Clair stood in front of her vanity, gazing into her looking glass. "Can that be me?"

Elizabeth felt like one first casting her eyes upon a treasure chest filled with priceless gems. First, her gaze settled on the wisps of soft brown curls framing Clair's delicate face. Why had she never before noticed how pretty her face was? It had not a single detracting feature, unless one did not favor freckles. For her part, Elizabeth thought the freckles lent a sweet youthfulness to her sister-in-law's countenance.

She then wanted to take in every aspect of the beautiful dress that elegantly draped over the smooth curves of her sister-in-law's dainty figure. "You shall steal away my breath! Why your hair. . . it is perfection. And that dress! It's exquisite. Peach is a most becoming colour on you."

"I declare, I feel as if a stranger is staring back at me from my mirror."

"You are very lovely." Elizabeth's gaze took in the sweet pearls circling Clair's slender neck. "I cannot think of a single thing that has been omitted."

Clair's lashes lowered as she took in Elizabeth's appearance. "You're not wearing a necklace?"

"I dashed over here whilst Philip's valet was finishing with him. My dear husband insists that he always be the one to adorn me with the Aldridge jewels."

The two ladies left the chamber and leisurely

strolled to the duchess's chambers.

"Surely he's not distrustful of your maid?"

Elizabeth shook her head. "No. He's keeping all the necklaces and other jewels in his chamber at present, merely for the dramatic effect of presenting me with a new one each night. I do believe if all the Aldridge family jewels were sold, they could buy an entire country!"

"If I were you, I would feel better not having the responsibility for so valuable a collection."

Elizabeth laughed. "I agree."

They entered the chamber, where Philip stood, holding still another velvet box. When he saw his sister's stunning transformation, the seductive gaze he'd been directing at his wife instantly changed to a broad grin. "My God, Clair, you look deuced lovely!"

Clair shrugged. "You could truly recognize me?"

He chuckled. "I will own, the difference is rather like a chrysalis." He began to circle around her. "Who selected the dress? It is perfection."

"You know I'm incapable of knowing what is fashionable," Clair answered.

His gaze flicked to his wife. "You've done very well." Then he came back to peer into his sister's eyes and speak in a gentle voice. "You make me very proud."

Rothcomb-Smedley had insisted that even though this dinner was his plan and the guest invitations decided upon and personally delivered by him, he desired that Philip serve as host at the dinner table. "I could never sit at the head of the Duke of Aldridge's table." Elizabeth's cousin had requested to be seated at the center of the long table where he felt he would have the opportunity to address more of the guests.

Once they all took their places, Philip surveyed the gathering. There were eighteen members of the House of Commons, and counting his sister and wife, just six females. His gaze settled at the foot of the table where Elizabeth sat, the candlelight bathing her pretty face, her mouth curved into a smile as she chatted with Lord Highsmith's son, Richard Vickers. She was unquestionably the loveliest lady at the table. Then his eye wandered to Clair. So that she would not be surrounded completely by strangers, Elizabeth had asked Richie's permission to have Clair seated opposite him. Philip had never imagined she could look so pretty. It occurred to him that some of these bachelors dining with them could easily be attracted to his favorite sister.

Now, the only obstacle was her superior rank to most of these men. Some would understandably think that since they had no chance to court the daughter of a duke, they simply would not try. But there were always men who desired to increase their consequence.

He found himself trying to remember each man's name, trying to match the family names with their fathers, who likely served with him in the House of Lords. How truthfully Lord Knolles had spoken at White's last week when he told his followers that their group controlled the majority of the seats in the House of Commons too.

It was good that Rothcomb-Smedley had hit upon this scheme to try to break down these men's resistance, to work toward compromises that could bring about approval of the necessary tax increase.

Elizabeth had done well with the menu selection. These men would think they were dining like royalty. She had spared no expense, denied no delicacy. There was roasted pheasant, buttered lobster, roast beef with French sauce, succulent turbot, clear turtle soup. And the finest wines that could be offered.

The men drank rather greedily. Good, he thought, ply them with very good spirits, then once they were mellowed, set about to sway their opinions. "More claret, Ashworth?" he said to the man at his left, who had quickly finished his first glass of wine.

"Don't mind if I do. Excellent vintage. Very good, indeed."

"Only the best for the men who serve their country so diligently," Philip said, filling the man's glass.

"Can't imagine not serving in Parliament. I like to be in the center of things, if you know what I mean."

"Exactly why I returned from my travels. It was time I take a serious interest in this country."

Philip launched into a description of the vile things Napoleon had done in Italy and how the French armies were swelling with those who had been conquered. "It is imperative we build and equip an army superior to that of the French."

Swinnerton shook his head in dismay. "I was unaware of the extent of the French domination."

"If they're not stopped," Lorne said, "the whole world will be speaking French."

"As a strong Tory in support of our Royal Family, even though the Regent is not half the man his father once was," Vickers said, "I shouldn't like for us to be deprived of so grand a tradition as the monarchy."

"Aye, I agree," Douglass said, eying Philip. "What is it you and Rothcomb-Smedley propose?"

Philip frowned. "We must increase taxes."

"My father won't like that."

"Rothcomb-Smedley assures me that as soon as we win this war, the tax rate will revert to what it is today," Philip said.

"Can that guarantee be written into the bill?" Ashworth asked.

Philip's brows hiked. "Excellent point, Ashworth. Shall we ask Rothcomb-Smedley? He has much more experience in drafting these measures than I."

Ashworth got Rothcomb-Smedley's attention and repeated the question.

"By Jove!" A wide smile crossed Rothcomb-Smedley's face. "I will do that! Thank you for the suggestion."

"That addition should make the bill more palatable," Douglass said.

Ashworth nodded. "Indeed it should."

"You men must think of it as survival," Clair said. "Think how those in the cold climes must work hard and put away extra food and chop wood—all at some degree of sacrifice—in order to survive during the winter. The English face extermination if we don't make the sacrifice."

Philip smiled. "My sister is possessed of passionate opinions."

"A pity women cannot serve in Parliament," Rothcomb-Smedley said, eying Clair with admiration.

Philip lifted the bottle of claret. "More wine?

***

After the guests had left, he and his wife sat before the fire in the intimate library. He intended to finish off the last of the port, then take his wife to bed. He felt almost like celebrating. It had been a far more successful evening than he had ever thought it could be.

"Did you not think things went rather well?" she asked.

"I did. It was somewhat like watching ice thaw."

"A good analogy."

"I shall have to steal your cousin's plan. Will you be up to hosting another dinner next week—the next time for members of the House of Lords?"

"Of course. Remember, I wish to be your Lady Wickshire."

"As I recall, Lady Wickshire's loveliness pales when compared to that of the Duchess of Aldridge."

"Thank you, dearest. I daresay you're prejudiced, but speaking of loveliness, did you not think Clair looked most handsome?"

"I am ashamed to say that at first I did not even recognize her. She looked uncommonly fetching."

"I got so involved with the discussions I forgot to notice if any of the bachelors paid special attention to her."

"How could they not? She even expresses herself with far more intelligence than most young ladies—though my wife is sure to say I am not an impartial judge."

"Clair and I are grateful for your unfailing loyalty."

"And I am grateful for yours." He took her

hand. “How do your widows do?”

“The last family has now moved in. It is impossible to tell you how much pleasure I derive from these families. Your sisters are just as committed as I. We now have eight and twenty children. Only two of them are older than twelve.”

She went on to tell him about the children’s love of the piano and how patient Margaret was with them. As she spoke, her eyes brightened, and there was excitement in her voice. Quite naturally, she went from talk of Trent Square happenings to her enthusiasm for sponsorship of a bill to provide pensions for the soldiers’ widows and children.

God but he hated to crush her. She had never shown such exuberance over anything. “My dear, I have something disappointing to tell you.”

She stopped her animated discussions of the fatherless children and peered up at him, her brows lowered.

“I won't be able to help with the pension bill.”

Her face looked bleak. “But you agreed that it was a good plan!”

“I still agree, but I had not gauged what difficulty I would face in Parliament. Already I am being called a spendthrift. I have to weigh what is for the greater good, and clearly my efforts—feeble as they’ve been—must be channeled into defeating the French.”

“Of course, I understand that. But it shouldn’t take huge sums to help these families who’ve lost so much for their country. You said. . .”

“I bloody well know what I said, but at this time, I cannot help. I promise you that after we are victorious, I will do whatever I can for the widows.”

“But this war has already dragged on for years. So many of these families are destitute now. They may not survive until the war is won.”

“I am sorry.” He could not have felt more wretched had he just brutally struck her lovely face.

She stiffened and set down her glass, then got to her feet. “I’m going to bed now. You know I am out of charity with you.”

He nodded somberly and watched as she stormed from the room.

He had destroyed his own Lady Wickshire.

Chapter 16

It was the warmest, prettiest day of spring yet this year, and she hated to spend it indoors. But she and the Ponsby sisters had duties at Trent Square. Later, she would enjoy the fine weather when she and Richie rode in the park.

Just before leaving Aldridge House, Abraham, who had been standing attentively beside the entrance door, cleared his throat and addressed Elizabeth. No footman had ever *initiated* a conversation with her. "Your grace, I beg a private word with you."

She had come to rely upon the footman's assistance with anything that needed doing at Number 7 Trent Square. His countenance was always agreeable, and he was uncommonly good with the children. If she were not so out of charity with her husband, she would have thanked Philip for insisting that Abraham—who not just coincidentally happened to be the tallest, strongest of all the Aldridge footmen—accompany her and his sisters when they performed services relating to Trent Square.

"Certainly," she said. "Shall we step into the morning room?" She swept into that chamber, him following, then she eased the door shut and turned to him. Though he was easily twice her size, there was a youthful innocence in his well-sculpted face as he peered down at her.

"It's difficult for me to admit this, yer grace, but I never 'ad the opportunity to learn readin' and writin'."

She was astonished. All the Haverstock servants had been literate. Her severe father had required them to attend Sunday church services and Sunday school, where they were taught how to read in order to read Scripture. Her heart went out to this big, strapping, exceedingly handsome fellow who must be about the same age as her. What a very great misfortune it would be not to know how to read. She was not sure why he wanted to bring up this topic with her. . . unless he wished to be instructed. She would not hesitate to give him permission to learn reading. "Do you desire to learn?"

"More than anything, yer grace." He cleared his throat. "It occurred to me when I saw the little children at Trent Square being taught to read that I might be permitted to be instructed along with them—unless you should disapprove or need me services elsewhere."

"Of course I would never disapprove of such a thing." But the vision of those long legs of his folded into a chair beside the five-year-olds was most pitiable. "Allow me to speak to Mrs. Hudson on the subject." Mrs. Hudson was currently teaching letters and rudimentary reading skills to seven children, each of them about five years of age, give or take a year.

Not long after they arrived at Trent Square, Elizabeth begged a private word with Mrs. Hudson right after that woman had requested that Abraham go help the cook with some large sacks of flour.

Elizabeth and the youthful widow went to the morning room where the draperies were open, and sunlight filled the golden chamber. She met Mrs. Hudson's quizzing gaze. The melancholy that had defined the pretty woman when they had met for the first time a few weeks previously was fading away like a scar upon a child's knee. Elizabeth derived great satisfaction in knowing she was in some way responsible for bringing the life back into the widow's fine green eyes. Of course the credit really should go to James. Had it not been for him, none of them would be at Trent Square today.

"I should like to ask that you teach Abraham how to read."

The young mother's brows lowered. "He cannot read?"

Elizabeth solemnly shook her head.

"What a grave misfortune it must be not be able to read."

"Indeed it is. He wishes to learn so badly he asked to be permitted to learn alongside the children you're instructing, but I cannot help but be cognizant of his manliness and shouldn't want to humiliate him in any way. It took great courage for him to approach me on the subject in the first place."

"He approached you on the matter?"

"He did."

"It most certainly did take a great deal of courage. He's an admirable man. Louisa adores him." Mrs. Hudson's pensive gaze went to the window. "I would be honored to teach him how to read and write. Privately. I believe he'd learn quickly, based upon how keen his mind seems. I give him long, verbal lists of things I need him to do, and he remembers every single one. And. . . he knows the name of every child here."

"Oh, dear. He must have a remarkable memory. I must own, there are a few children whose names I still have not learned."

"But yer grace, you've had many other matters to distract your attention."

"You're too kind."

"No. Your approval of Abraham's instruction demonstrates your incredible kindness. When should you like me to begin working with him?"

Elizabeth shrugged. "Today. May I suggest that first thing every day when we arrive, you and Abraham have a private lesson? A half hour to an hour a day should suffice. I will also give him leave to study when he's not busy at Aldridge House."

Mrs. Hudson nodded. "Instead of in the school room, where the tables and chairs are so small, I thought perhaps he and I could go sit at the big table in the dinner room."

"An excellent suggestion. That way, with the two of you sitting side by side, he should learn quickly."

"I have always found that one learns best when being personally instructed."

Elizabeth nodded. "One to one. Yes, that is the best way."

That afternoon Elizabeth rode in the park with Richie. She could not remember ever seeing more conveyances in the queue to enter Hyde Park, nor had she ever seen so many couples strolling along its verdant paths.

"I must ask you," she said, "if you were serious when you told me you would support the measure regarding the widow's pensions."

"Of course I was serious. It's an excellent plan."

She nodded somberly. "Philip has changed his mind about supporting it."

Richie tipped his cap at a passing couple, then frowned. "It's probably for the best that he focus on only one bill at a time. He is meeting with a great deal of resistance on that tax bill. Because he's been out of the country for so long, it will take patience, time, and cunning in order for him to win over those set-in-their-way peers."

"But you want the tax increase as much as he, and you're willing to champion the soldiers' widows and families."

"But you forget, I have already earned the respect of my peers. I've been working with them untiringly since the day I came into my majority and won my seat. I have worked long and hard to get to where I am now. And you must know my ambitions are high."

"Everyone knows you will be Chancellor of the Exchequer before you're thirty."

A smile crossed his face. "I don't know about that, but were that to occur, I would have achieved the pinnacle of success."

She nodded at Lady Susan Robinson, who was seated beside a slender young man driving a curricle coming from the opposite direction. "Back to my education. . . Now that I can intelligently converse on Adam Smith, what book should I read next?"

"Edmund Burke makes for thoughtful reading. You've already read Paine, have you not?"

"Paine was short and sweet and rather brilliant." She wondered if her husband admired

Thomas Paine. It was difficult to fathom anyone who was not swayed by the man's ideas. "But Burke it will be next."

"I hope you'll express to Aldridge my gratitude for allowing me to host my colleagues at your house. I thought the evening a great success."

"Indeed it was. Now Philip has decided to host one for select members of the House of Lords."

"Very wise of him to do so, and might I suggest that his sister, Lady Clair, be permitted to sit at the table. She is a great contributor to the discussions. And it never hurts to have one who's pretty to look at. I didn't remember her being as lovely as she was the night of the dinner."

Elizabeth preferred not to elaborate on the measures that had been taken to render Clair more attractive. "I daresay you only notice her beauty more now that her hair has been shorn in the fashionable style."

"That's it! It becomes her."

They went on to discuss the next dinner, the one she and Philip would host. "No one, not even you or my brother, works harder than my husband." As important a function as Richie held in government, he was never too busy to take her to the park. She must own that, unlike her husband and brother, Richie's duties never began until the House of Commons assembled for the evening.

Her husband had never escorted her to Almack's or to Hyde Park since they had wed. Even Haverstock sometimes pried himself away from his duties to take Anna for a drive in the park.

Elizabeth wished Philip cherished her as Haverstock loved Anna. Ever since Anna had lost the babe and plunged into deep melancholy, her husband pampered her more than ever.

In her grave disappointment, Elizabeth was driving a wedge into the fragile bond that had united her to Philip. Since he had betrayed her by reneging on his promise to help the widows, she had avoided any intimacy with him. For the past two nights they had not slept together. For the past two mornings and late evenings, she had failed to initiate those amiable little conversations they had been conducting to apprise one another of the day's occurrences.

She felt as if she stood alone on the Salisbury Plain, watching the man she loved walking away far in the distance and knowing the separation was her fault.

How had it come to this? How foolish she was to sacrifice her marriage because of hurt feelings. He would never understand that it was not his failure to support the widows that crushed Elizabeth so; it was his failure to support his wife.

Any hope she'd had of being his Lady Wickshire had been trampled.

"While I prefer Brook's, I went to White's last night and saw your husband there."

His words were like a slap in her face. She rounded at him, her brows lowered. "At what time was that?"

"I was there at nine, and he'd been there for a good while, judging from his . . . consumption of brandy."

Her heart sank. Philip had declined to escort his sisters—and his wife—to Almack's the previous night, owing to the lateness of sessions at the House of Lords.

"Was my husband wooing his colleagues from

the House of Lords?" She strove for casualness in her voice.

"A few perhaps."

"The Lords, I take it, were sitting at the time?"

He nodded gravely.

Now added to Philip's betrayal and their subsequent estrangement was a retching disappointment. Had she imbued Philip with qualities he did not possess? She would have staked everything she possessed on her husband's nobility of character.

How could it be that he had failed to attend last night's session at the House of Lords?

"I wanted to bring up another topic with you," he said. "Your brother's refusal to take a stand on the tax increase is beginning to harm our cause. More than one member has asked me how my cousin stands on the issue, and Aldridge has also been asked about his brother-in-law's stand on the tax."

"I do wish Haverstock would voice his opinion. My brother is one of the most influential men in London."

Richie nodded. "Everyone respects Haverstock enormously."

She swelled with pride toward her brother, who'd had an uphill battle to earn respect after their father had alienated half of the *ton.* "I shall speak to him, but before I do, I'll speak to Anna. He tells her everything." *If only Philip and I were as close.*

It took two hours just to drive along the park's central lane because of the congestion of conveyances. There were two-person barouches, four-person barouches, cabriolets, curricles, and many other manners of transport. The halting progress afforded them a great many opportunities to exchange pleasantries with many of their acquaintances. She even got a glimpse of Belle Evans riding along in a grand barouche with the elderly Duke of Queensberry, who was unquestionably the most profligate man in the British Isles. Elizabeth felt compelled to stare at her. Until their eyes met, and the courtesan stiffened and looked away.

Elizabeth found herself, not for the first time, wondering if Belle had ever been in love with Philip.

When they finally left the park, Elizabeth told Richie to deposit her at Haverstock House. "I have not seen Anna much of late."

"You're not exhausted?"

"Of course I'm exhausted. My mouth feels frozen from all the forced smiling I've done the past two hours, but I miss being with Anna."

"I thought at their dinner that night she seemed to have recovered from her loss."

"That was all for my brother's benefit. She knows how frightfully he worries about her."

Richie's brows scrunched together. "You think she still mourns the lost babe?"

Elizabeth nodded. "I think, too, she despairs that she will never again find herself breeding. A year has passed, and she does not appear to be fertile."

The very idea that Elizabeth herself could be carrying Philip's babe caused a fluttering—and an altogether wondrous sensation—in Elizabeth's breast.

"I heard the babe they lost was a son." Richie's voice was somber.

Elizabeth nodded gravely. "Anna told me it

would have been less painful had it been a girl. The way it was, she felt as if she had denied her husband his heir."

"Why in the devil is she blaming herself?"

"We've all encouraged her not to. To no avail."

"I suppose it was even more painful that Lydia and Morgie bred with such ease."

"Anna vows she's happy for them. Indeed, she adores the babe."

"Aw, your grace, we have arrived at your former home."

She let herself into Haverstock House. It—far more than the opulent Aldridge House—felt like her home. But she supposed that was to be expected, given that she'd lived in this house most of her life. She greeted the servants and began to mount the stairs to the marchioness's study. When she reached it, she tapped on the door, then opened it.

Her gaze went straight to Anna, who slumped in a chair in front of her desk, her face in her hands, her shoulders heaving as she wept.

Elizabeth flew to her. "Whatever is the matter, my dearest? Dear God, has something happened to my brother?"

Anna lifted her face, shaking her head emphatically. Even with her big chocolate eyes watery and red, she was lovely. Her scarlet study was decidedly French, and in her rose-coloured frock, Anna too looked decidedly French. "No, I am just being a goose."

Relief surged through Elizabeth as she lowered herself into a slender gilt chair next to Anna's gilded escritoire, then spoke in a gentle voice. "Allow me to guess. You're dwelling on the lost babe."

Sniffing, Anna nodded solemnly. "I keep hoping to find myself breeding."

"And you will. A woman who has already carried one babe to full term can do so again." It pained Elizabeth to even mention the dead babe poor Anna had given birth to. It was one of the most harrowing experiences ever to befall their family. Anna had been nearly inconsolable, and Haverstock was more melancholy than anyone had ever seen him.

Anna shook her head. "It's been more than a year. I have failed as Charles's marchioness."

"That is *not* true! There's not another woman in the kingdom who could bring Haverstock the happiness you've brought him, not another woman in the entire world he could love as he loves and adores you."

"I will own, my dearest Charles says the same thing, but I know he's disappointed. You cannot know—as I did—how delighted he was to learn I was increasing." Her voice broke off in a sob.

"My brother would not object if his heir was James's child—whenever James settles upon a wife. And family. The brothers are exceedingly close. Believe me when I tell you that the thing Haverstock wants most is your happiness. He's utterly besotted over you. Now I beg that you think happy thoughts."

Anna dabbed at her moist eyes with a lace-edged handkerchief, forced a smile, and spoke with levity. "Don't tell Lyddie, but the little fellow doesn't say a word."

Anna's good-humored mock of Morgie sent them both laughing.

A tap sounded at the marchioness's door and

Anna bid the servant to enter.

The butler's gaze went straight to Elizabeth. "I believe you have a caller, your grace. The gentleman asked to see Lady Cynthia."

Only someone away from England last year would still call her Cynthia. Only someone away from the country would have called for her at her *former* home. Good lord, could it be the dashing officer who had broken her heart the previous year? Her stomach churned, her insides trembled. "Pray, what is the gentleman's name?"

"Captain Smythe."

Chapter 17

Her hands trembled as she clutched the banister, descending the stairway. When she reached the door of the saloon where the Captain awaited, her chest tightened.

He stood when she entered. What a striking man he was in his bright red regimental coat that stretched across his broad shoulders. Everything about him bespoke power and precision. The hilt of his sword, the epaulets, the cording and buttons—every bit of it gilded with perfection and not the slightest evidence of tarnish to be found.

She was powerless not to run her eye over him. His dark handsomeness had not diminished in the least. He was tall and well formed with a noble face and confident countenance.

It suddenly occurred to her how much the Captain resembled her husband. Since Philip had been in Italy when Elizabeth came out, it now seemed obvious she had transferred to Captain Smythe all the devotion her brother's good friend, the heir to the Duke of Aldridge, had once inspired in her,.

The Captain looked exactly as he had the last time she had seen him. She easily recalled the way her heartbeat so madly rapped every time she saw him. Whenever his deep voice had lowered when he spoke to her, his every word had sounded like a declaration of affection.

Today, though, there was one noticeable difference. The sight of him no longer sent her into a swoon of adoration. She felt nothing.

He bowed. "You are as lovely as ever, Lady Cynthia."

She curtsied in return, almost imperceptibly nodding. "I no longer use the name Cynthia. I have returned to my birth name of Elizabeth since the death of my namesake, my Aunt Elizabeth. To honor her."

"It will be difficult for me to ever stop thinking of you as Lady Cynthia."

"Actually, I am no longer referred to as *my lady*, either."

He stiffened. If she was not mistaken, his tanned face blanched. His broad fingers coiled around the hilt of his sword. "Pray, do not tell me you've married."

She nodded solemnly. "I am now known as the Duchess of Aldridge."

For the next several seconds the Captain was incapable of speech. "Yet you're here. At your old home. Does that mean Aldridge has returned to Italy?"

Why was it that everyone assumed she was a neglected wife? "Am I not permitted to visit my family?"

"Forgive me. It is just that I am suffering from shock. I knew when I last saw you that I risked losing you by not declaring myself." He sighed. "I should have been better prepared for the announcement of your nuptials and my own disappointment."

That he admitted disappointment offered her

some degree of compensation for those months of sleepless nights he had caused her. "One cannot lose something one never had, Captain," she said, her voice icy.

He grimaced. "I deserve that."

Her brows lifted. "Won't you sit?"

Still displaying a dejected manner, he dropped back into the chair he'd been sitting in when she entered. "In Venice I attended many of the same events as the Duke of Aldridge, but we were never introduced. He and a certain Contessa were quite the talk of the town."

Her stomach roiled at the mention of the Contessa Savatini. Oddly, she envied Captain Smythe. How Elizabeth longed to be able to judge whether the Contessa really was the loveliest woman in all of Italy, as everyone said. "How fortunate you were to see Venice. My dear Aldridge has pledged to take me there once we've won this beastly war. You must tell me how the war progresses."

"I came to London to get away from the war. I choose not to speak of it while I am here."

She had never seen him when he did not exude confidence. Until now.

There was no pleasure in knowing she was responsible for his melancholy, no pleasure to be taken in his suffering. "How long will you be in London?"

He shrugged. "I know not. Several weeks, most likely."

"Then we may be attending some of the same assemblies. My husband has three unmarried sisters I chaperon."

"How painful it will be for me. I had hoped. . . that is, I had reason to believe that you were strongly attached to me. I came here today to seek your hand in marriage." He stood and addressed her in a dismissive voice. "How foolish I've been to have thought you could be happy with a lowly army captain when you could become a duchess." He started for the door.

She stiffened, her fingers coiled. "If you believe that, Captain, you are mistaken."

He stopped, turned, and regarded her with flaring eyes.

"The year before last and last year," she continued, "I would have turned down the King of the World to have become Mrs. Smythe. As it was, you left England without ever giving me the slightest hope that I had a chance of winning your affections."

"My God, but I've made a mess of things." He stormed from the chamber.

She sat there in a daze. Why had she not just allowed him to leave? Why had she felt the necessity of declaring to him those affections which had once nearly crippled her, affections she thought the Captain had not returned?

Even before she had given herself—body and soul—to her husband, the intensity of her love for the Captain had been extinguished by his disregard for her.

And now he was declaring that he had loved her then and wanted to marry her now. If he spoke the truth, how could he have been incapable of expressing those feelings last year? How could he have not written a single letter to her?

She no longer had any regrets. More than anything, she felt as if she could go down on her knees and praise him for his former coldness, the coldness that had preserved her unmarried state for her ultimate lover.

More sounds were heard in the corridor, then Lydia came strolling into the saloon. "Dear lord, wasn't that Captain Smythe I saw leaving?"

Elizabeth gave a little harrumph. "Indeed it was. The arrogant man expected to find the former Lady Cynthia sitting around her brother's house pining away for him."

Lydia regarded her with pensive eyes. "From your tone I gather all that passion he once elicited in you has vanished."

"Long before I wed."

Lydia lowered herself onto the silken sofa next to her sister. "Good riddance! I never liked the Captain."

"You say that only because you know how devastated I was when he left me without offering marriage."

Lydia nodded. "I suppose now he's come to regret it."

"Apparently so."

"And you really don't fancy yourself in love with him any longer?"

"It's my belief a woman can only be in love with one man at a time."

"I can certainly not disagree with that." She regarded Elizabeth with one of those all-knowing stares she'd developed at a young age. "Does that mean you've fallen madly in love with Aldridge?"

Elizabeth's eyes moistened, and she nodded, then burst into tears.

Lydia came and drew Elizabeth into her arms. "Whatever's the matter? It's a very good thing to be in love with one's husband. It's what I prayed for when you wed Aldridge for I knew you didn't love him on the day of your wedding."

It was always Lydia to whom all the Upton sisters confided. Their mother had been—and still was—cold and reserved. Lydia was as warm as she was wise. "I'm the cause of a rift between Philip and me."

Lydia hugged her, then drew back and eyed her younger sister. "That's a very easy matter to remedy. You beg his forgiveness, beg to start anew."

The solution was so completely simple, Elizabeth chastised herself for having so stubbornly clung to her silly anger. All because her pride was bruised.

Lydia withdrew a handkerchief from her reticule and handed it to Elizabeth.

Her hurt at being betrayed by Philip had overruled her common sense. Now she clearly understood that a disagreement should never come between them. "I've been so wretchedly miserable. I will throw myself upon him and beg forgiveness."

"I thought that night we all ate together here that you showed the symptoms of having been pierced by Cupid's arrow."

Elizabeth dabbed away the tears that streaked her face. "I would prefer it if you saw those same signs in my husband."

"He will come around—if he hasn't already. Men are not quick to realize such things." Lydia's face brightened. "I'm so happy you're here today. It will save me from having to go to Aldridge House to see you."

"I'm happy to see you too. Happy and surprised. I thought you rarely left your little darling."

Lydia's face softened. "I will own, it's difficult to be away from him. I feel as if I'm missing an appendage."

Elizabeth envied her sister. How dearly she would like to have a little Philip of her very own. "So how have you managed getting away?"

"I just fed him, and he's fast asleep." Lydia's voice lowered. "I've been worried about Anna. I wanted to see her when the baby's not present. I think she's still very low about their loss."

"Indeed she is. I found her sobbing a short time ago."

Lydia's face clouded. "The poor darling. She's torturing herself. I feel it in my bones she *will* conceive again."

"I am very glad to hear that for everyone knows you're always right. Now, pray, tell me why you were coming to Aldridge House?"

"Haverstock told me you and the duke are having a political dinner next Friday."

"We had discussed that, yes. But I've seen so little of Philip that I hadn't realized he'd gone ahead and sent the invitations. I suppose his secretary took care of that." She silently grieved that Philip had not further consulted her. "Why do you mention that?"

"I should like you to invite Morgie and me."

Elizabeth raised a brow. "You know it's just dull members of the House of Lords?"

"I do, and I assure you I will be bored, but I promised my dear mother-in-law that I will encourage Morgie to enter politics. It was what his papa wanted. Morgie has finally agreed to stand for Parliament, and I thought the dinner might perk his interest. God knows he needs a diversion."

"A diversion from what?"

"Need you ask?"

"His smothering presence?"

Lydia's shoulders sagged. "The dear man was beside himself with worry when we learned I was breeding. You recall several years ago his eldest sister died in childbed?"

Elizabeth nodded somberly. "It was very sad."

"Morgie worried like the devil about me. He seemed to feel that as long as he was at my side, no harm could come to me."

How Elizabeth wished Philip loved her like that. "I think that's incredibly romantic."

"There's not another man in the kingdom I'd prefer over my dear Morgie. You did, however, perfectly describe my husband when you referred to his smothering presence. The man needs another interest."

"Then I am delighted he will stand for Parliament, and I am delighted that you and he will come to our house for the dinner."

Elizabeth supposed she needed to hurry home and work with cook on the menu and begin drawing up seating arrangements. How much more enjoyable it would have been had she and Philip discussed this together. This rift tore her apart.

Lydia was right to encourage her to swallow her pride and apologize for their chasm. Her only hope of happiness was to restore their marriage's previous harmony. She stood. "Run along to Anna. Tell her what you told me. That you're certain she will breed again. Everyone knows you're always right."

Her sister stood and took both of Elizabeth's hands. "Then believe this: Aldridge will reveal his love for you."

He wondered where his wife was, then realized she was likely gallivanting about Hyde Park with that damned cousin of hers. Philip poured himself a tall glass of Madeira and settled back in his library's desk chair. He'd not seen the room by the light of day in a very long time. He'd spent so little time here, so little time with his wife. He would have felt the guilt of a negligent husband if it weren't for the fact that love had never been a part of their relationship. Elizabeth was probably happy to spend her time with Rothcomb-Smedley instead of with the dull stick who was her own husband. This dull stick should be in the House of Lords at present, but the estrangement from his wife was eating at him like a corrosive acid. He needed to see her, needed to bridge this rupture between them.

When he was mellow from the second glass of Madeira, he heard her in the corridor. He stiffened as the door to the library came open, and his wife stood in the doorway. How lovely she looked in the aquamarine coloured frock. A pity there was hostility in her countenance. "Barrow said you wanted to see me?"

He stood. "I do. Won't you come sit on the sofa with me?"

Chapter 18

She was taken aback by his presence. Why was he not at the House of Lords? And why did he have so grave a look upon his face? For the second time in the same afternoon she found herself frightened that something terrible was going to be revealed. "Is something the matter?"

He moved to her. His face softened, his hand touched her arm. "Yes, you've made your husband a most wretched creature."

His simple act of touching her, the seriously uttered words that had tumbled from his lips almost had the power to send her into a molten heap. She peered up into his dark eyes, saw the sincerity of his words, and was incredibly moved. Her heartbeat was pounding so unnaturally, it was all she could do to look placid as she lowered herself to the sofa.

As soon as he was beside her, they both started to speak at once. They each stopped. Smiled. "You first," he said.

"I've been wretched too."

A gentle smile broke across his noble face. "Forgive me for saying I am most happy to learn you've been unhappy."

They laughed again.

He brought her hand to his lips for one of those nibbly kisses that always affected her so provocatively. "I have greatly missed our daily chats." His intense gaze bore into hers. "They were the second best part of every day."

Her lashes dropped seductively. "And what was the best part, if I might ask?"

His husky voice lowered. "When you're in my arms, in my bed, you wench."

Being called a wench in this context was an aphrodisiac. "I've missed those things too."

"I have felt like a traitorous husband, but my resolve to focus on only one new law is inflexible. Can we not agree to disagree?"

"Yes, my dearest. I was going to propose the same pact."

"You know how much I agree with you about their needs, but I must channel all my energies into accomplishing what I can for the greater good."

She was so happy that she'd read Jeremy Bentham's works, that she understood the political philosophy of the *greater good.* How proud she was of her husband for adhering to such a philosophy. Not many men like him, men in possession of vast wealth, would have embraced such thinking. "I do understand, my dearest. I truly mean to be your helpmate, not to be some didactic harpy." Without even being aware of what she was doing, she settled her hand on his muscled thigh and spoke softly. "I am sorry for causing this rift. I know that once you've accomplished the tax increase, then you will help the widows."

"Indeed I will."

"If you must know, the reason I was so angry was because I felt you'd reneged on your promise to me, that you had betrayed me."

He drew her into his arms. "I hope to God neither of us ever betrays the other."

She wanted to tell him she could never betray him, but the words stuck in her throat. She refused to be the first to make a cake of herself by declaring her love for him. The first declaration—if indeed it ever came—had to come from him.

There was a tap upon the library door, and they separated.

Barrow, holding what appeared to be a letter on a small silver tray, came shuffling into the chamber, the poor old fellow's shoulders slumped with age, his voice shaky. "The page delivering this asked that it be brought to his grace. He awaits a response."

Philip took it, tore it open, and began to read. Once Barrow had closed the door behind him, he chuckled. "I believe poor old Barrow was requested to give this to *her* grace. Here, it's from your favorite sister."

"The dear man *is* decidedly deaf." She took the note and skimmed over its contents. "You lied! This is most certainly *not* from my favorite sister." How could he have known that which she had never voiced? Kate was her *least* favorite sister.

"Of course I knew that. It's obvious to this man who has come to know you so well that you can only barely tolerate Kate."

She had never told anyone of the awkward relationship her otherwise loving family had with Kate. "How did you know?"

"Because I'm coming to know everything about this wife of mine."

Except how much she loves you. "Then I pray you never betray me."

"I will never betray you."

But like other men of their class, she fully expected him to take a mistress. Did he not realize that nothing could betray her more?

She perused the letter, then peered up at him. "Do you object to Kate and Mr. Reeves using your box at the theatre tonight?"

"Of course not. And it's not my box. It's *ours*."

Would she ever become accustomed to being the Duchess of Aldridge? This house still felt like his home. It lacked the familiarity she'd felt that afternoon at Haverstock House. She got up and went to his desk to compose her response to Kate, then rang for a servant to take it to the waiting page.

As she got up to return to the sofa, her husband stood, regarding her with a smoldering gaze. Her pulse accelerated as she went to him, as she melted into his comforting embrace.

"I need you," he said, his voice low and full of emotion.

She nodded simply. "Let us go to your bedchamber, my dearest."

"Leaving this bed is the most difficult thing I've ever done," he murmured much later. Night had turned his chamber black.

She felt the same. Their lovemaking had never been more passionate, her love for him never more potent.

He went up on one arm. "I dare not allow myself a kiss for I could never be strong enough to stop." His bare legs swung over the side of the bed, and he shimmied into his breeches then bent to scoop up her frock. Their heated encounter had not allowed for a slow disrobing. Her stays had remained, her thin shift greedily pushed up, her drawers shoved down as she'd eagerly parted her thighs to receive him.

"Allow me to help restore your dress," he said, his voice more gentle and less husky than it had been when they'd entered his chamber and slammed into each other's arms with breathless urgency.

Once her dress was on, she lit a candle and turned to regard him. "I should like to watch you dress. I believe I may even be able to tie your cravat. I used to do James's before Papa got him a valet." She knew she should be embarrassed to admit how she loved to stare at her husband's bare, lithe body in the candlelight. Even that first day—that day he'd stood in his bath, water gleaming on his bronzed torso—she had thought him magnificent.

"I shall not make eye contact with you. I cannot permit myself the pleasure for I really must be off to the House of Lords."

She frowned. "And I had hoped we would have you tonight. I promised to take the girls to Almack's."

"I'm sorry. Perhaps next time. I realize how neglectful I've been of my family."

She started to ask why he had neglected the House of Lords the previous night but decided against it. She wanted neither to introduce an inharmonious subject after such a heavenly encounter, nor to have Philip think her cousin was spying on him. "Indeed you have. I had to learn from Lydia that you've gone ahead with plans for your own political dinner here on Friday."

"I thought we'd agreed to it."

"We had, but I wasn't aware we'd set a date."

"Forgive me. Had there not been such friction between us, we would have better communicated."

"I vow to be a better wife."

He stopped adjusting his buttons and allowed himself to peer at her. "There is no better wife."

Now she understood what he'd meant about not making eye contact. As their gazes locked, she felt compelled to move to him, to fit herself to him and initiate a fresh wave of passion.

But she couldn't; they couldn't. They both had obligations.

She stayed rooted to the Turkey carpet, flooded with profound feelings of love and stunned by his declaration. "I shall try to be worthy of your praise, my dearest." Then her gaze flicked away and she tried for flippancy. "Now, I believe I'll have a go with your cravat, you handsome devil."

Before she went to Almack's she had the satisfaction of Philip placing still another lovely jeweled necklace on her. Tonight's was diamonds, and they complimented her soft white dress that was shot with silver threads.

He stayed long enough to see all of his sisters dressed in their elegant finery, and he paid particular attention to Clair's transformation and complimented her with great sincerity.

At the assembly rooms, Elizabeth took pleasure in Clair's success. She danced as much as Margaret or Caro, even though she was not as pretty as her sisters.

They had collected Anna, and Elizabeth was happy to have another matron to sit with her and watch the dancers. "Lydia told me that Captain

Smythe called on you today. How can the man have expected a lovely girl like you to be prostrate for his return after all this time? Surely he knew many other men—men of much higher rank—would want you for a wife!"

Elizabeth shrugged. "I have come to believe that all the agony that man put me through was the best thing that ever happened to me."

"How can you say that?"

"My perceived love for the lout kept me from marriage long enough to allow Philip to return from Italy."

A lovely smile lifted Anna's face. "I hadn't thought of it that way. Oh, my dear sister, I cannot tell you how happy I am that you've fallen in love with your own husband. Did I not tell you it would happen?"

"It is just as you said it would be, just as it was for you." Elizabeth's shoulders slumped. "Only Philip doesn't love me like Haverstock loves you."

Anna shook her head. "But, my dearest, it *is* just as it was with Charles and me. I was most passionately in love with him for many months before he came to realize his love of me."

"But I know that there was no other woman in his life, no mistress. We all believed from the start that your marriage was . . . passionate."

Anna's long lashes lowered. "From the start, it was. There was a very great physical compatibility between us." Her lashes lifted, and she peered into Elizabeth's eyes. "For the woman, I think that for the physical to be satisfying, her heart must also be engaged. That is not necessary for the man."

"It would destroy me to learn that Philip was

intimate with another woman."

Anna's huge chocolate eyes regarded her intently. "Keep him satisfied every night, and he will be incapable of looking elsewhere."

The heat rose in Elizabeth's cheeks and she quickly looked away. She was disappointed to see that Clair had no partner for the current set. The poor young woman stood alone at the side of the chamber, peering at her sisters.

Elizabeth felt a tap at her shoulder and whirled around. Towering above her was Captain Smythe, sinfully handsome in his regimentals. "Would your grace do me the goodness of standing up with me for the next set?"

"Her grace chooses not to dance," Elizabeth snapped.

He rounded the row of chairs where she sat and came to face her. "Very well. I shall sit with my dear old friend." His gaze then connected with that of the marchioness, and he bowed. "Good evening, Lady Haverstock."

After they exchanged greetings, he plopped down beside Elizabeth. "Where is your duke tonight?"

"He's fulfilling his responsibilities at the House of Lords."

"Which is much less threatening than fulfilling one's duties on a battlefield."

She refused to look at him. "I am sure my husband would agree most heartily with that statement." Every time she referred to Philip as her husband, her chest seemed to expand with pride.

"If you were my wife, I would not neglect you so."

She gave him a cold stare. "I. Am. Not.

Neglected. My husband and I make time to spend with one another every day." Her insides fluttered at the memory of the intimacies that very afternoon.

"What does a chap have to do to dance with the lovely Duchess of Aldridge?"

Her gaze darted to Clair. "If you go and ask my sister, Lady Clair Ponsby, to stand up with you, I will favor you with a dance later."

His gaze arrowed to the spot where Clair stood. "The freckled lady in yellow?"

"Yes."

He leapt to his feet and moved toward Clair. His striking presence drew attention away from the dancers and sent Pretty Young Things tittering to one another behind their fans.

Once he and Clair were on the dance floor, Anna turned to her. "The Captain is certainly possessed of arrogance."

"I can't think why he persists in wanting to see me."

"Perhaps he's conceited enough to think you'd throw over a duke to elope with him."

Elizabeth gave a bitter laugh. "I have my doubts that he's ever truly wished to be wed."

"Then perhaps he's one of those men who likes to seduce other men's wives, especially ones who may be neglected by their husbands—not that you are."

"Most people think I am, but they are unaware of the time Philip and I carve out of each day to be alone with each other."

"That is exactly what Charles and I have always done."

"You must be my inspiration for a happy marriage. How I pray that I am doing the right thing!"

"Love conquers all. I know that sounds trite, but love trumps every force that opposes the union of two beings."

She and Anna could not help but to watch Captain Smythe as he and Clair elegantly strode hand-in-hand down the longway, every eye in the lofty chamber drawn to the stunning officer.

He waited until the night's final dance—a waltz—to claim Elizabeth. How she had loved feeling the touch of his hand at her waist before. Before Philip. Tonight, she stiffened and did her best to preserve a large gap between them. Tonight, she lamented that she'd agreed to stand up with him. Most of all, tonight she longed to be waltzing across this dance floor with her husband.

"I feel I owe you an explanation," he began after he waltzed them into a remote corner of the room that was bereft of onlookers.

"You owe me nothing."

"But you see, when last I saw you, I was but two and twenty and in no position to offer for a wife—especially one who is the daughter of a marquess."

"You don't need to tell me any of this."

"I need you to understand. I hurried back to London the moment my circumstances changed."

She lifted a brow and regarded him. "Pray, Captain, how have your circumstances changed?"

"My father's brother died, and having no children, he left me extremely well fixed."

"Then I'm very happy for you. You have come to the right place to seek a wife. I'm sure you could take your choice."

His grip on her hand tightened. "There's only

one woman in this chamber I would choose to spend the rest of my life with."

How ill-mannered it would be for her to acknowledge that he referred to her. "I do hope you refer to one of Aldridge's sisters. He has three very sweet sisters who are still unmarried."

"Confound it! I'm lovesick over you."

How different their lives would have been had he spoken those words last year! Thank God he had not. "I am sorry for it, but I know from experience that broken hearts can mend."

He understood. His step slowed and he spoke in an anguished voice. "Oh, God, what I've lost."

Chapter 19

Upon entering the house on Trent Square, the sisters scattered like ants, Margaret to the music room for her twice-weekly lessons upon the pianoforte, Clair to the mathematics' school room, and Elizabeth was on her way to the kitchen to ensure there were adequate stores of food. Mrs. Hudson, nearly weighted down with a large basket of laundry, was descending the stairs, her little daughter a step behind.

"Stop right there, Mrs. Hudson," barked Abraham, who was just behind Elizabeth. He raced up the stairs to relieve the pretty young widow of the heavy basket. "Yer far too little to be carrying such a big load. Did you not know I was comin' today? Yer to save things like this for me."

"You're too kind," she said shyly as he took the basket.

"It's you who are the kind one. Coming here today, I read the words on several shop windows, all owing to yer kindliness in instructing me."

Elizabeth was touched over the encounter but had her own duties to attend.

In the basement kitchen, she found Mrs. Leander, who smiled up at her. "As glad as I am to see you, your grace, I'd rather it be Abraham."

"He's carrying down the laundry as we speak."

"Thank goodness. I declare, I don't mean to

seem ungrateful, but we could use that dear man around here every day, not just the two days a week your visits have been pared down to."

"Perhaps I should speak to my husband to see if Abraham can be spared more." Why was it she was still so unaccustomed to thinking of herself as the mistress of Aldridge House? Shouldn't the duchess have a say in such decisions? She had yet to feel as if she were a duchess.

"I would think a man possessed of Abraham's strength and his congeniality would not easily be given up." Mrs. Leander shrugged. "We wouldn't have to have a man as fine as him, though he's uncommonly good with the children. So many of our little lads and lassies have never known their own dear fathers."

"It does seem as if Abraham thinks he has to fill their shoes." Elizabeth heard Mrs. Hudson and the footman just beyond the door and held her index finger to her mouth.

Then Elizabeth cleared her throat. "Tell me, Mrs. Leander, now that things are so settled do you not agree that my sisters and I are only needed twice a week?"

Abraham and Mrs. Hudson passed the open door and strode to the washroom at the end of the corridor.

"Oh, I do agree. Now that your grace has so efficiently organized the house and everyone's duties." She lowered her voice, "But it would be nice to have a man around."

Elizabeth pondered the idea of having a man always at Number 7. The idea had great merit, but she could not yet commit to it. For now, she would be flippant. "The difficulty with having Abraham living here is that you ladies would all fall in love with him!"

A benevolent smile crossed the elder woman's face. "If I were a dozen years younger, yes, I'd be swoonin' over that big, strapping lad." Her voice dropped to a whisper. "I'm not sayin' Mrs. Hudson has actually fallen for the fellow, but it wouldn't surprise me if he ain't responsible for curing her melancholy. She was hurtin' very badly when I met her, and you must see the bright change that's come over her."

"I have noticed her diminishing grief and am grateful for the cause, whatever or whoever might be responsible for it."

When the group returned to Aldridge House from Trent Square, Elizabeth wondered whose large open barouche was parked in front. She had expected to see Richie's smaller curricle. Her question was answered the moment she stepped into the house and saw Captain Smythe—in his full uniform—standing next to Richie.

How could she have forgotten that it was Richie who had first introduced him to Elizabeth? The two had been at Harrow together. Even before they spoke, she recalled the Captain telling her he had come into a great deal of money. Which explained the luxurious barouche. Richie certainly did not own anything so fine.

Then she stiffened as she recalled his final words to her at Almack's. She glared at the pair of them. "It appears as if someone is being presumptuous."

Captain Smythe stepped forward. "That would be me, your grace. It's been three long years since I've been able to ride through Hyde Park. Surely you would not deny a needy soldier."

From the looks of his barouche, he was as needy as the Regent! "It matters not to me if you'd like to ride in the park. Would you care to invite one of my sisters?"

Margaret and Caro had already gone upstairs, but Clair remained at Elizabeth's side. Elizabeth and Clair exchanged amused glances.

Richie responded. He stepped toward Clair. "Pray, Lady Clair, it would bring us inordinate pleasure if you would join me, my friend, Captain Smythe, and the duchess for a spin about the park."

As much as Elizabeth wanted to shout out a refusal, she knew she was incapable of being ill mannered, even though the Captain's attentions were unwanted.

How could she once have believed herself in love with him? But she now knew the answer. It wasn't the Captain she had fancied. It was his physical resemblance to the Duke of Aldridge, the man who'd stolen her girlish heart many years earlier.

Clair cocked her head, addressing Richie. "Will we be permitted to discuss politics?"

"But of course. That is the purpose of these afternoon rides with my cousin."

"Very well," Clair said.

"I perceive that you ladies are ready." Richie's gaze scanned over their lightweight pelisses. The ladies still had not removed their bonnets.

"Yes," Elizabeth said.

When they reached the awaiting barouche, Elizabeth plopped down next to her sister-in-law, and the two gentlemen were forced to face them on the opposite seat.

Elizabeth was determined not to utter a single

word to the Captain.

"Did you see the *Morning Chronicle* today, your grace?" Richie asked once the equipage was on Piccadilly.

She regarded him from beneath an arched brow. "You refer to the article about our Lord Chancellor?"

"I do indeed."

"I read it, too," Clair said, "and I think it's beastly of him to attempt blocking the tax bill. It seems as if everyone's against my poor brother."

"I have much confidence in Friday night's dinner," Richie said. "It's things like that which can influence members of the House of Lords far better than an aged windbag like Lord Knolles. It's time the leadership in that chamber gets threatened."

"Change is often for the best," Clair said.

Much of the ensuing discussion was about the stubborn Lord Chancellor and discussing the article in the morning newspaper. Even though this topic was of grave concern to her husband, Elizabeth was too distracted to follow.

She was angry over the Captain's attentions. She did not like being seen with the man she had once been so romantically linked to. She feared others would think her affair was being rekindled.

Would the fragile bonds of her marriage be able to bear any more hints of scandal? She shouldn't care what others thought. But she did. It already stung that the Duke and Duchess of Aldridge were never together, that half the *ton* believed Philip had been forced to marry her. Her thoughts also centered on Friday night's dinner. This would be her first real opportunity to make Philip proud of her. Every dish must be perfect.

The seating arrangement needed to encourage conversation. She must strive to look as attractive as she could. While not wanting to dominate conversation, she wished to contribute intelligently. Or else remain silent. In short, she wanted everything that she did or said to bring credit to her husband. She wanted to be a source of pride.

Most of all, she hoped this dinner would establish the Duke of Aldridge as a force in political circles.

The discussion between Richie and Clair was so lively that Elizabeth's input was not solicited. Which pleased her. She was so out of charity with Captain Smythe she would not be interesting. And she was determined not to address him.

Midway through the park, Captain Smythe said, "I say, your grace, do you still fancy daffodils?"

She glared at him and nodded.

Back at Berkeley Square when they began to descend the carriage, she said, "You two go on in. I beg a private word with the Captain."

They faced each other. He smiled. She did not. "I must beg that you come here no more," she said. "What's past is past. You will find another woman far superior to me."

He gazed solemnly at her. "Never."

Incapable of a response, she turned on her heel and strode to the front door.

Instead of eating at his club tonight, Philip determined to surprise his wife. He'd been feeling guilty for his many failures to escort his own wife. He'd not taken her to the park, to Almack's, or to the theatre. Not that he was going to do any of those things tonight. By fitting in a meal with his duchess he hoped to placate her. After all, he was depending upon the success of Friday's dinner. And the success of that dinner rested on Elizabeth's shoulders more than on anyone else's.

Tonight's dinner would also give him the opportunity to coordinate the dinner plans with his wife.

As his coachman turned onto Berkeley Square, Philip peered from his window at a most curious sight. His wife, along with Clair, Rothcomb-Smedley, and a man in regimentals all climbed from a luxurious open barouche. Then, oddly, his wife stayed back to speak with the officer. The man towered over Elizabeth. He was not only large, he was put together in an altogether masculine way with powerful legs and wide shoulders.

Philip felt as if he'd been thrown from a horse. Did Haverstock not tell him the reason Elizabeth had not wed earlier was because her *captain* had not offered? Good lord, could this impressive-looking officer be the Captain Smythe who had once broken Elizabeth's heart?

Philip watched as the Captain climbed back into the barouche, then seconds later, Rothcomb-Smedley joined him.

"Go on. Don't stop!" Philip instructed his coachman.

He did not trust himself to face his wife while such thunderous emotions rocketed through him. What in the bloody hell was the man doing with Philip's wife?

That blasted Rothcomb-Smedley was an ungrateful back-stabber! Such audacity! First, openly flirting with the Duchess of Aldridge; and now he was attempting to reunite her with her former heartthrob.

I'll never allow the man in my home again.

Philip found himself wishing he'd arrived at Berkeley Square two seconds earlier. He was consumed with curiosity to know what the seating arrangements in the barouche had been. Had Elizabeth sat next to that officer?

Dear lord, was he going to have to start treating his bride as one did a naughty child? For Philip most heartily wished to put down his foot and forbid her certain associations. Starting with that bloody cousin of hers!

After more than an hour of aimlessly riding through London's busy streets, Philip was in control of his emotions sufficiently enough that he instructed the coachman to return to Berkeley Square.

The smiling face Elizabeth directed at him would have—under normal conditions—made him uncommonly happy that he had come home for dinner. As it was, he stiffened as she walked up and pressed a kiss to his cheek.

"How is it I'm to be honored with your presence tonight, my dearest?"

"I thought I could join you for a meal, and we could discuss Friday night." He saw that she was already dressed for dinner. "I will meet you in the dinner room as soon as I change clothing."

Minutes later, owing to the efficiency of Lawford, Philip took his place at the head of the table. He and his wife were joined by his trio of sisters. "Where do the Ponsby ladies go tonight?" he asked.

"To the theatre," his wife answered. "Kean's to

play Hamlet. How wonderful it would be if you could join us."

She had diplomatically refrained from berating him because he had yet to share his own box with his bride. "It would be wonderful, but I must lamentably decline."

"House of Lords meeting tonight?" Clair asked.

He nodded.

"You have an exceedingly understanding wife," Caro said, watching him through narrowed eyes.

He finally tossed a kindly smile at Elizabeth. "Indeed she is. It's always been my goal for my duchess to emulate Lady Wickshire."

Caro and Margaret exchanged queried expressions, but Clair immediately grasped the reference. She spoke to her less informed sisters. "Our brother refers to the manner in which Lady Wickshire is said to forward her husband's Parliamentary career. It is even speculated that she helps him with his speeches."

Margaret's mouth gaped open. "I did not know Aldridge had spoken in the House of Lords."

"That's because I haven't."

Caro's face brightened. "I expect you're relying on Elizabeth's help with a spectacular dinner Friday night."

"Indeed I am."

Caro faced Margaret. "By the way, we will *not* be eating here on Friday." A look of mock perturbation was directed at Clair. "We are not deemed as sufficiently informed on matters of government as Clair, who will be permitted to attend."

"My cousin Richie particularly asked that Clair join us, owing to her intelligent contributions at the previous dinner."

Philip cleared his throat and addressed his wife. "My dear, I don't wish for Rothcomb-Smedley to attend our dinner."

Her eyes widened. "But I thought he had been included in the plans."

He shook his head. "We will need as many seats as possible for lords."

"Then by all means," Clair said, "omit me and allow Mr. Rothcomb-Smedley. He's far more important than I."

"Rothcomb-Smedley himself said a pretty, unmarried female is an asset to a large dinner table," Philip said.

Clair looked incredulous. "Then I will be sure to forfeit my seat."

Elizabeth shook her head. "Your brother's right. Richie said you were pretty, and you would be a valued addition."

Clair's pale eyes widened. "Mr. Rothcomb-Smedley surely did not say that I was pretty!"

A smile hiking, Elizabeth nodded. "He most certainly did. In fact, we actually discussed why you appeared more attractive than ever, and I merely said it was your stylish hair cut."

"And what did he say to that?" Clair asked.

"Oh, he agreed."

A look of sheer wonderment gentled Clair's face. Damn, Philip thought, is she too succumbing to Rothcomb-Smedley's charms?

"The guest list is not open to discussion," Philip snapped, glaring now at his sister. "You are in. Rothcomb-Smedley is not."

"I am not happy with your authoritarianism." Elizabeth glared at him. "What of the invitations that were extended to my brother and Anna and to Morgie and Lydia?"

"I shall be happy to have them here Friday."

For the remainder of the dinner his wife sulked. She neither spoke nor eyed him and answered his sisters only in monosyllables.

As the sweetmeats were laid, Barrow brought him a note.

Expecting that it was a missive from a colleague in the House of Lords, he quickly opened it and began to read.

My Darling Aldridge,

Since the recent death of my aged Savatini, it is my joy to rush to London and be with my love. Now I am free to be entirely yours. I stay at the Chiswick Hotel and count the seconds until we can be reunited. I chose it rather than the Pulteney because it is not on a main thoroughfare, and the innkeeper is noted for his discretion.

Your Angelina

Chapter 20

She had no heart on this night to partake of a Shakespearean tragedy. Ever since the coolness directed upon her by her husband throughout dinner, Elizabeth felt an Ophelia-like melancholy. Throughout the performance, she was so steeped in her own moroseness that she paid little attention to the actors upon the stage.

How could Philip have changed so much in so short a time? The last time they'd been together, he had admitted that the absence from her had made him miserable. Tonight, he acted as if her very presence made him miserable.

Nothing in her demeanor with him had changed. In fact, she felt certain that for both of them their most recent lovemaking had been the most satisfying ever.

She racked her brain tying to recall if she had done anything which could have alienated her husband. Could he resent her drives in the park with Richie? She must bring up the subject with him. All he had to do was to ask her not to see her cousin, and she would comply with her husband's wishes. Not happily, but she would comply.

As she sat there in the darkened theatre, unaware of the words spoken by the actors, she wondered how she would feel if Philip went to the park every day with his female cousin. The very thought sank her. She would never acquiesce to such a practice.

She vowed to herself then and there to terminate the drives with Richie. Now that she was reflecting on this, it was probably a good thing she had not defended Richie.

Then her thoughts wandered to Philip's coolness. If he were opposed to her spending so much time with her cousin, did that mean that Philip was jealous of Richie—which could point to a growing love of her? Or was he merely exerting his possessiveness?

A pity she could not just ask him. A pity she could not just blurt out her love to him.

Now, how to break the news to Richie. . .

When intermission came, Richie and Captain Smythe came to her box. When the Captain went to sit beside her in the seat so recently vacated by Margaret, Elizabeth protested. "There's a matter I must discuss with Richie." She eyed her cousin. "Sit here."

Richie tossed a whimsical nod to Clair, then reluctantly took a seat next to Elizabeth. "What do you wish to say?"

She lowered her voice. "I'm not precisely sure if you were invited to Friday's dinner at Aldridge House, but my husband has informed me there won't be room for you."

He whirled to her, brows hiked, anger flaring in his eyes. "I'll speak to Aldridge."

She could not recall ever before hearing such vituperation in her cousin's voice.

He leapt to his feet, drilled Captain Smythe with a glare, and said, "We must leave."

The Captain stood, and though she could tell

he looked at her, she refused to look in his direction.

Almost as an afterthought, Richie turned to Clair. "I bid you adieu, Lady Clair, with great reluctance."

Clair's lashes lowered as she shyly nodded and murmured something unintelligible. Elizabeth could not recall a time when Clair had not spoken with great confidence. Oh dear, was she becoming smitten with Richie?

Philip would have preferred it were the Contessa staying at the Pulteney. It was solid and respectable, and his presence there would never be questioned. But going to an out-of-the-way inn—albeit, a most luxurious facility, to be sure—rankled.

Why in the bloody hell had the woman rushed to England to be with him? He thought he had been perfectly clear when he terminated their affair.

When he had first received her letter, a white-hot fury had pounded within him. His first instinct was to dispatch a cold letter to her. But he could not do that. If she had come so far a distance to see him, she could not be dismissed with an angry letter. He could not deny, either, that she had once been important to him.

Another reason he needed to see her was because he must make his position toward her perfectly clear. She had to understand that nothing she could do would rekindle what was now as cold as last year's ashes.

He had taken the precaution of switching to a hack. It wouldn't do for the Duke of Aldridge's crested coach to be seen at the very hotel where the Contessa Savatini was staying. Located on the banks of the Thames in South Kensington, the Chiswick had been the villa of a long-dead nobleman a century earlier. The stand-alone mansion lay behind brick walls constructed of the same gray stone as the massive three-storey house.

Once the coach passed into the inn yard, Philip disembarked and he instructed the hackney driver to wait. "I won't be more than a few moments."

Inside, he faced a liveried footman, who spoke first. "If you're to see the Contessa, I will show you the way."

The youthful footman began to climb the stairs. On the top floor, he strode down the wooden corridor, paused in front of a door, and inclined his head. "You will find the Contessa within." The liveried servant returned to the staircase and went back to his post.

Philip knocked. "Angelina?"

She flung open the door and went to throw her arms around him. "Oh, my darling!" She wore a crimson dress that revealed her generous bosom, and she was as elegant looking as she was stunning. Yet her dark, lithe beauty no longer enslaved him as it once had.

He stiffened and backed away. "You know I am now married?"

Eyes that had sparkled at him a moment earlier now dulled. "Come in. We must discuss this marriage of yours."

They entered the private parlor, and she went to sit on a settee near the fire. It reminded him so much of Elizabeth's chamber and the cozy chats he enjoyed with her on the settee. He regretted coming here, regretted that he wasn't sitting with his duchess right now.

"Won't you come sit by me?" she asked.

"I prefer to stand." He moved to the fire and faced her, his mouth firm, no kindliness in his disposition.

"I confess. I had heard about your marriage, but just because you married does not mean we cannot be together. Remember, I was married before, and it never dulled your ardor."

"You might recall that I resisted you five years ago because you were united to another. It was you who swore that Savatini was tolerant of your infidelities, your *many* infidelities."

"But, *amore mio*, the moment I gave myself to you, I told you it was forever. Nothing that has occurred since has diminished my deep love for you."

He eyed her with subdued hostility. "Do you remember what I told you the first time?"

She pouted and did not answer for a moment. "The same thing you told me the day you dismissed me."

"Which was?"

"From the start, you said what you wanted from me was only physical." She peered up at him with moist eyes. "But you cannot deny that what we shared was wonderful."

"It is not my nature to discuss such things, Angelina. I mean to be a faithful husband to the good woman I've married." He had rehearsed what he was going to say to the Contessa, but the words he actually uttered were not the same ones. As he spoke, he came to a stunning realization.

He spoke the truth. He had initially planned to be faithful to Elizabeth only during the early, exciting days of their unification. Now, though, he found that he had no desire for any other woman.

Especially the beautiful but decadent Angelina Savatini.

Comparing her to Elizabeth was like holding up tarnished tin to sparkling gold.

She attempted a smile, but he knew her well enough to know how insincere it was. "You are trying so hard to be a good husband. It is most admirable. But no one expects a powerful English duke to be a faithful husband. It will be permissible for you and I to be lovers."

"It may be permissible to you but not to me." He moved toward the door.

She followed him with her eyes. "Your intent is a very touching, but I know she can never satisfy you as I can. And I am a patient woman."

When Friday came, Elizabeth would not leave the house. She was overseeing the most important dinner of her life. Trent Square was the most important thing she'd ever done. This dinner was second. If she could demonstrate a capability in such affairs, perhaps she could regain her husband's affection. Since the night he'd been so icy to her over dinner, she and Philip had not been alone together.

She knew he was avoiding her and suspected the cause of his disapproval was her afternoons with Richie. If only she and Philip could talk. Then she would be able to identify the source of his displeasure and work out a solution.

For now, her best hope of winning his approval was to host a successful dinner. From Philip's secretary she had gotten the guest list. For those names that were unfamiliar, she raced to the library to consult *Debrett's*. In that well-worn volume, she studied the family histories assiduously, committing the name and background of each of their spouses to memory.

She had also been faithfully reading the parliamentary reports in the two major newspapers so that she would be able to understand the political discussions that were certain to occur.

She determined the seating arrangements and once again went over the menus with the cook. The wine merchants had brought cases and cases of the finest wines at an exorbitant cost, and she had instructed the footmen which wines to serve with each course. She had inspected the table, selected various colourful fruits to display in the magnificent Aldridge epergne, and had overseen all the flower arrangements.

"Your grace, I hate to trouble you," the housekeeper said as she swept into the dinner room, "But I wanted your opinion on a minor matter."

Elizabeth whirled to her and smiled.

"Did you and his grace not say these dinners are to become a regular occurrence?"

"Yes, that is the plan."

"There's difficulty with the wine storage. There's only a small cellar—not nearly large enough for the crates you've ordered for this dinner alone. It occurred to me that –with your grace's permission—we could store the crates in the large palace cabinet adjacent to this room. It would be ever so much easier for the footman, too."

"I certainly have no objections."

Mrs. Harrigan moved toward the door. "I'll

alert Barrow that when the wine is delivered, it is to be stored in the chamber next to the dinner room."

Once Elizabeth was certain everything was perfect, she went to her own chambers to begin her toilette. A half hour later, she heard her husband speaking to his valet, and minutes after that Philip strolled into her bedchamber, sinfully handsome in his evening dress of jet black coat against snowy white shirt with dove coloured breeches.

His gaze sifted over her with what she perceived to be simmering approval. "Your selection is perfection."

She then realized she'd been holding her breath, praying for his approval of this new gown. She had commissioned the pale blue frock of gossamer-like fabric especially for this night. She had chosen blue because Philip had once said he favored her in that colour because it brought out her beautiful eyes. "Thank you."

"I had hoped you'd wear blue tonight." He then opened the velvet case he clutched. "See, I've brought the sapphire necklace."

Her pulse accelerated when she felt the brush of his hand upon her bare neck. Once the necklace was clasped, she peered into her looking glass. She would never be a stunning beauty like Anna, but Elizabeth was supremely satisfied with her appearance—so much so that it would not surprise her to hear herself referred to as beautiful. For she was a beauty on this night.

If only Philip thought so.

Then she stood and twirled around, soliciting her husband's approval. "Shall I do?"

His simmering gaze swept over her. "I will be

the envy of every man at the table."

Even though she knew her brother's wife would outshine her, nothing her husband could have said would have pleased her more. She smiled up at him. "Allow me to say that I shall be the envy of every woman at the table."

They went downstairs together, and Haverstock and Morgie, with their wives, were just arriving in the entry corridor as she and Philip reached the bottom step. She was struck over what a handsome couple Haverstock and Anna made. What man would not be mesmerized over her stunning beauty? Elizabeth's gaze flicked to Philip to see if he would be drawn to Anna, but his attentions were fully upon Morgie.

He offered a hand to Morgie. "So very glad to learn you'll be standing for the Parliament and so pleased to see you and Lady Lydia here tonight." He eyed Elizabeth's eldest sister and bowed.

Then he turned and welcomed her brother. "Pray, Haverstock, before the others arrive, you must tell me if you've come to a decision regarding the proposed tax increase."

Haverstock frowned.

Elizabeth's stomach dropped. How could she bear it if her husband and her brother were in opposition?

"How can I not support the increase when my best friend is its most staunch advocate?" Haverstock finally said.

She could have kissed her brother!

A huge grin brightened Philip's face. "I am in your debt."

"You're more than a friend," Haverstock said. "You're now my brother." His gaze flicked to Morgie. "Just like Morgie."

The other lords began to arrive, most of them with plump wives dressed in fashionable frocks. She and Philip began to circulate among the guests, offering cordial greetings before everyone moved into the drawing room.

Once every guest had arrived, they proceeded into the dinner room according to precedence. Pride surged within her when she saw how lovely the room looked. Hundreds of candles blazed from three huge crystal chandeliers that hung above the long table which was set for forty.

"I expected to see Lord Knolles here," Lord Hathaway said to Philip once they were seated.

"Since he's made his opposition to me so clear, I did not invite him." Her husband spoke stridently, purposely projecting his voice so that he could be heard at the foot of the table as well as at the head. "Tonight it was my wish to gather those lords who vote their conviction rather than to please a man who's been sitting in the House of Lords longer than most of us have been alive."

Haverstock cleared his throat. "There is room in the leadership for other men—younger men of unquestionable loyalty to their country."

"Indeed there is," Philip said. "Every man at this table tonight is capable of one day replacing Lord Knolles."

"Not that we're advocating demotion of the Lord Chancellor," Haverstock said. "Ideally, we would like to continue to work together to win this devilish war."

Elizabeth began to pass around plates of buttered lobster and kidney pies while one of the footmen was filling bowls with clear turtle soup from the huge tureen from which steam was rising.

Before conversation commenced again, the attendees continued filling their plates with food fit for a king.

"I am so pleased to finally meet the Duchess of Aldridge," Lady Hickman said. The woman was seated four places away from Elizabeth, and she looked vaguely familiar, but Elizabeth was certain she had never before met the woman.

"It is a pleasure to finally meet you, Lady Hickman. Your father was the Earl Desford, was he not?"

The woman's eyes shimmered. "What a remarkable memory you have, your grace."

Elizabeth eyed the woman who was twice her age. "I believe I may have seen you at Almack's."

"Indeed you did. I believe every eye at Almack's was on you as you waltzed with that excessively handsome officer last week—or was it the previous week? The crowd was positively droning over the beautiful Duchess of Aldridge and the officer."

Elizabeth swelled with pride that her beauty was being praised. Her gaze flicked to her husband. She had expected to bask in his approval, but he could not have peered at her with a more loathsome look.

When she had first looked to the head of the table, she noticed Philip and Haverstock exchanging curious glances. Then her husband directed a menacing glare at her.

Chapter 21

Everything had been going so well. No finer meal could be served anywhere in the kingdom than that offered to his guests tonight. No expense had been spared, and his wife had ensured that every last detail was perfect. He could not have been prouder. When Lady Hickman had praised Elizabeth's beauty, it gladdened him.

But the confirmation that Captain Smythe had indeed come back into Philip's wife's life was as debilitating as a blow to head.

All thoughts of Parliamentary matters or even the tax increase vanished from his mind like the closing of a blind. Pain surged through him. *My wife's reunited with the only man she's ever loved.*

He was vaguely aware that Morgie was addressing Lord Strickland. "Are you acquainted with the fact I've had a son, my lord? Well, I don't precisely mean *I* had him, you understand. 'Twas me wife who did the deed."

Under normal circumstances, Philip would be chuckling over his old friend's jolly comments. But nothing could give him joy tonight. Not the Regent himself favoring them with his presence. Not pledges from every man here to support the tax increase. Not even an announcement that Captain Smythe would return to the Peninsula.

For whether the officer were in London or Spain mattered not. Not when he held a place in Elizabeth's heart.

Even if she paraded through Hyde Park with the officer or waltzed with him at Almack's, Philip knew Elizabeth's innate goodness would prevent her from having an affair with Smythe.

Not until she presented Philip with the heir he desired.

Hadn't the notion of securing the dukedom been one of the primary reasons Philip had offered for her in the first place? Hadn't her aristocratic pedigree been her chief qualification to become his duchess?

Why in the devil did Philip feel so bloody beastly? It wasn't as if they had married for love. It wasn't as if he had ever been in love with her or she with him. Their marriage had been more like a business arrangement. He could not deny that a deep affection had grown between them, and the very thought of her lying beneath him, breathless and sated, was enough to make him groan with longing.

In a perverted sense of self-torture, he thought of her lying with that damned officer. Anger as virulent as thunder tore through him. At that moment he thought he could possibly be capable of murder.

What in the devil had come over him? In his entire life, Philip had never demonstrated a jealous bent. And now he was consumed with jealousy toward a man he'd never even met! More than that, his jealousy was so potent, he fancied the notion of killing another man!

As he sat there speechless while Haverstock directed conversation toward the tax bill, a nearly paralyzing thought occurred to him.

I am in love with my wife.

Good lord, what was he going to do about this? Admitting to a one-sided love was out of the question. A man, especially a duke, had his pride.

Dazed, he continued sitting there and came to another realization: this was the first time in his two and thirty years he'd ever experienced what it was to be in love.

And he did *not* recommend it!

He'd rather wish the pox on a friend than wish anyone to experience a longing so intense it obliterated rationality, threatened a man's dignity, and ignited an unquenchable hunger.

A flitting thought sent a jolt of hope strumming through him. Was it possible he could win Elizabeth's love? To conquer her heart—if indeed it were possible—would mean that her position in his life needed to be elevated. As it was now, he only had time for Elizabeth when there were no other demands on him. That was no way to show a wife that he loved her.

True, they had both insisted that duty came first, but he needed to demonstrate that she was as important to him as any duty. He could not imagine life without her. Not after knowing the pleasure of being her husband. Would the day ever come when he could convey to her how dear she was to him?

While his guests talked, he tried to decide which of his duties he could temporarily neglect. Elizabeth deserved a devoted husband to escort her to balls and to the theatre. He wanted to be the man sitting beside her as they leisurely drove through Hyde Park. He wanted to show every man in London that the lovely Duchess of Aldridge belonged to him. He especially wanted to show that damned Captain Smythe that Elizabeth was deeply loved by the man she had married.

Would Philip ever feel *he* was deeply loved by the woman he'd wed?

As soon as he and Haverstock cracked what they dubbed the Pyrenees Code, he would start taking his wife to the park. Surely they would break the French cipher any day. That very afternoon, he had discovered a vital key to unlocking the French battle plans.

If tonight's dinner could accomplish what he hoped it would accomplish, he would no longer feel compelled to attend every single session of the House of Lords. Then he could devote more attention to Elizabeth.

He finally gathered enough composure to see to it that the wine glasses of those around him were refilled, but he was incapable of directing intelligent conversation to parliamentary matters. Not when he was reeling from the force of these unaccustomed emotions.

"I have a personal reason for wanting to win this war expediently," Haverstock said, his voice clearly heard by everyone at the table. His gaze met Lydia's, then Elizabeth's. "Our brother is serving in the Peninsula, and we want him home."

Elizabeth nodded. "His youth has been sacrificed for our country." Her voice started to crack. "We pray his life's not sacrificed." She sucked in a deep breath, attempted to steady her voice, and continued. "How many of you here at the table have a loved one fighting against the French?"

Nearly every person seated there solemnly raised a hand. "We lost a son," Lord Danvers said, sorrowfully meeting his wife's gaze.

Philip had never been prouder of his wife. Her ability to tap into these men's emotions could serve his cause far more than any pleas he or Haverstock or that damned Rothcomb-Smedley could ever make.

Now, because his wife had paved the way, Philip could carry on. "We will beat the French, but we need more weaponry, more soldiers, more money. That, my respected colleagues, is why it's imperative we adopt a tax increase."

"If it will bring our boys home, I'll do everything in my power to persuade my husband to pass that bill," Lady Hickman said. "Our three youngest sons are with Wellington."

A dozen people spoke at once, most of them nodding in agreement with Lady Hickman.

This response was better than he could ever have hoped for. When the talk died down, and attention was again directed to the head of the table, Philip said, "I vow that once we've defeated the French, we'll restore the tax to its current rate."

Haverstock nodded. "What we need is for each of you distinguished peers to help unify the House of Lords."

"If each of you can sway a single fellow member who's presently opposed to the tax increase," Philip added, his gaze traveling along the table, making eye contact with each man, "we can race to end this war."

His comments met with enthusiastic approval. He peered down the table as Elizabeth looked up and offered him a gentle smile. He was unable to remove his gaze from her. She was possessed of such a fair, delicate beauty, and he loved her so much. She was the most feminine creature he'd ever known. In spite of these crippling emotions she elicited in him, he was grateful that he'd married her. There was not another woman in the kingdom who could have made a better wife. And there was not another woman in the universe he could love so powerfully.

He grew impatient for the guests to leave. He desperately wanted to take his wife in his arms and with every stroke of her silken flesh, every compulsive kiss, every breathless whisper demonstrate his complete captivation. In his two and thirty years he had never so blindingly hungered for a woman as he hungered for Elizabeth tonight.

He was happy when the sweetmeats were served. He did not even object when the conversation steered to other, non-parliamentary matters. He was happy that the dinner was coming to an end, happy that his mission had succeeded—due largely to the efforts of his wife. Soon it would be just he and Elizabeth. Soon they could be alone. Soon, he would be able to slake his debilitating need.

After the others left, Haverstock and Morgie and their respective wives lingered to discuss the success of the evening. Lydia spoke first. "You lords should be very satisfied with yourselves. I would say you were exceedingly successful."

Morgie nodded. "I calculate a one percent escalation in my tax could pay a year's salaries for a regiment. I've been poking through records at the War Office, thanks to Lord Palmerston. I want to be well informed during my electioneering."

Philip always marveled about the dichotomy

that was his friend Morgie. When it came to money and numbers, the man was brilliant. "We shall be most happy to have your voice in the House of Commons."

Morgie shook his head. "Oh, you won't be hearing my voice there." He shuddered.

"But, dearest," Lydia said, "You will have to give speeches during your electioneering."

"But we'll all try to come and provide moral support," Anna said.

Philip's gaze went to Elizabeth. She had every right to be proud over the success of *her* dinner, but she was far too modest to boast about it. "I wish to thank my wife for all the work she put into tonight's fete." His voice softened. "Everything was perfect. You were perfect." He wanted to say, "*My love*," but the words stayed trapped in his throat.

"I was very proud of my sister," Haverstock said. "It was her simple question that did more to sway those men then a thousand of our words."

"It was brilliant," Anna said, "but successful for its sincerity."

A wistful look crossed Elizabeth's face. "I do want James home. He's been gone five long years. Every girl he ever fancied has now married another."

"'Tis the same with our two brothers who are in Spain," Clair said solemnly.

"It's very sad," Lydia agreed. Then she looked up at Morgie. "Come, dear love. I need to go feed our little angel."

Our little angel. Once again, Philip was jealous. If only he and Elizabeth could have a son.

Barrow shuffled up to the Duke and Duchess of Aldridge, holding a silver tray on which a letter reposed and eying the duke. "Her grace said you weren't to be disturbed during dinner. This came while you were eating." He handed Philip a letter.

One glance confirmed Angelina's handwriting. *Damn the woman!* He directed a soft smile at his wife. "Allow me to pop into the library and read this."

She nodded, then turned and said farewells to her siblings as they departed.

He closed the library door and tore open the letter. As he read, rage tore through him.

Amore mio,

If you desire to guard your sister's dark secret, you must come to me tonight at the Chiswick.

Eternally yours,

Angelina

He crumpled the paper in his fists and hurled it into the fire.

Sarah! How had the Contessa learned about that wretched business? He wished to God he'd never met Angelina Savatini. Even more than that, he wished to God Sarah had never met that piece of dung, Viscount Morton, who'd ended up fleeing to the Continent rather than face the wrath of the Duke of Aldridge.

Over the past five years Sarah had settled into a happy marriage with the good man who'd offered her—and her unborn child—his name. All of them had been lulled into the belief that no one would ever learn of the youthful indiscretion that had stolen her innocence.

He couldn't allow Angelina Savatini to destroy Sarah's life and that of her three children.

Though every cell in his body throbbed with

desire for his wife, he must put duty above personal gratification. He had to go to Angelina Savatini.

Elizabeth could obviously judge from his thunderous expression when he stormed from the chamber that the letter had brought unwelcome news. "What's the matter?"

"A situation has arisen that demands my immediate attention."

Her face fell. "I was so looking forward to it being just you and me tonight. I've been longing to talk with you."

His solemn gaze agonizingly raked over her. He wanted to tell her how powerfully he longed for her, but he could not allow himself the luxury. His lips were a firm line. "I'm sorry."

Chapter 22

Five minutes earlier she had thought she might explode with happiness. The dinner had been stupendously successful, but even more importantly, her husband had stood right here in this entry hall and praised her. The tenderness in his voice and the glittering in his eyes when he spoke actually had her believing he could come to love her.

Then Barrow brought the letter that changed everything.

What had it said?

After her husband curtly took his leave, she dismissed the footmen and Barrow, yet she continued to stand there in the hall, dazed.

Was there a chance Philip had left that letter in the library? She raced there to look, even though she felt guilty because she had no right to pry into her husband's private correspondence. That letter had snatched away her happiness, and she had to know why.

She went to the large walnut desk where the oil lamp still burned. There was no sign of the letter. She opened the drawers and looked, but there was nothing that looked like the folded paper she'd gotten a glimpse of.

Had he burned it? Her gaze darted to the waning fire. She strode there and peered into the embers. There was a wad of crumpled paper that had only partially caught fire.

Her heart beating erratically, she dropped to her knees in front of the hearth. For the first time all night she felt warm as she carefully lifted the partially burnt paper from the smoldering coals and tried to smooth it out. The ashed edges flaked away, and the beginning of the letter had burnt beyond deciphering. She could clearly read words written in a woman's flourishing script.

come to me tonight at the Chiswick.
Eternally yours,
Angelina

Had she been holding a viper Elizabeth could not have been as repulsed as she was at that moment. *Angelina Savatini's come to London.*

The dread that had filled her a moment earlier now slammed into her like the projectile from a giant catapult. The happiness she had known moments earlier was completely destroyed.

With shaking hands, she tossed the burnt paper back into the dying coals and left the library. Though she had no heart to go to her own bedchamber, that place where she'd experienced her greatest happiness, she mounted the stairs.

Tonight she would sleep in her cold bed while Philip would be making love to the Contessa Savatini at the Chiswick Hotel.

He did not need the liveried footman to show him to the Contessa's rooms. He threw open the Chiswick's huge timber entry door, stormed up the stairs, and pounded upon her door.

In transparent black lace, she opened the door

herself and stood there silhouetted by the firelight behind her. Other men would likely have found her ravishingly beautiful.

He found her despicable.

"I've sent away my maid, *amore mio*, so we can be alone."

"I'm here only to serve my sister's best interest." He stepped into the dark chamber and slammed the door behind him. "What the devil is it you want, Angelina?"

"You will never be able to deny that you and I belong in each other's arms."

How could he ever have thought he belonged in this woman's arms? "There is only one woman's arms I want to be in, and she awaits me at Aldridge House."

"It is very noble of you, English duke, to try to be so devoted a husband. Only one who knows you as do I knows that an icy English woman can never satisfy a passionate man like you in the same way I can. We were put on this earth to love each other."

"You're talking like a mad woman." He knew he should have held his tongue. This woman had the power to destroy his family.

Her dark eyes glittered menacingly. "And you'll be quite the mad man when I reveal your sister's ugly secrets to the English newspapers."

His smoldering anger seared. She must know about Sarah's shame. "How could you possibly know something scandalous about my sister?"

"Viscount Morton was my lover before you. I tossed him aside when he bragged to me about the ruination of your sister. He was an evil man." Her voice softened. "You know I am not evil. I don't want to hurt your sister. All I want is to love you."

"Why would you even want a man who loves another?"

"You are newly married. Affairs of the heart always burn brightest at the beginning, then they die. Then, *amore mio,* you will want me—not that girl you've wed. It is me and only me who is truly meant to be with you."

He shook his head. "You cannot force someone to love you, Angelina."

"I don't believe I'll have to. I think if you will allow yourself to be with me, here in your city, you will come to love me again. I know I cannot be your wife, but I will be content to be your lover. As we were."

"It's over, Angelina."

Anger flashed in her dark eyes. "I did not come to your frigid country to be turned away. I ask only to be allowed to spend time with you. Then, I know I can win back your heart."

He knew if he slept with her now he could placate her demands, but the very thought of lying with her repulsed him.

Her mind was so twisted he had difficulty understanding what it was she was asking of him. "Tell me what you want."

"I want you to drive with me in Hyde Park. I want you to dance with me at Lady Wentworths' ball next week. I want all of London to believe we are still lovers."

"Why? Why does it matter to you what people in London think?"

"It doesn't. But once all of London believe we're lovers, word will reach your fair duchess." Her dark eyes glittered with pure evil. "I mean to destroy your marriage."

A swift, hot wave of anger rolled over him. How he hated this woman! She wanted to destroy the thing that mattered most to him.

He forced himself to speak calmly. "What you ask of me is impossible. My duties at the War Office and in Parliament keep me from ever being with my own wife." He stopped and eyed her with unmasked hatred. "I know of no peer in all of England who drives in the park with his mistress. That is not our way in this country. We do not publicly humiliate our wives."

"A pity. Though it's apparently not the way with English maidens. Your sister Sarah most certainly defied propriety when she allowed Viscount Morton to get her with child."

Rage exploded within him. If Morton were in this room right now, Philip would happily send him to the fires of hell where he belonged.

These past five years Philip had thought that ugly affair had been put to rest. He would forever be grateful to the devoted Tremayne, who'd excused Sarah's serious indiscretion and wed her after Morton cast her aside. Thank God she'd come to love the good man who was her husband. Theirs had become an exceedingly happy marriage.

Philip would not let these monsters destroy Sarah and Tremayne's family. He must think of a way to get rid of the Contessa while preserving Sarah's good name. For now, he needed to appease the Contessa.

He drew in a deep breath. "Since what you want is for my wife to believe you and I are lovers, I have a proposal that I think might satisfy you."

She raised a brow.

"Move into the Pulteney and start mingling in

Society. I will make certain that every day the coach bearing the Duke of Aldridge's crest will be parked in front of the Pulteney."

Her eyes narrowed. "An excellent plan. I will get to be with you every day!"

"I never said I would be at the Pulteney," he snapped venomously.

"But. . ."

"Within a week, my wife will have heard that we are lovers. Is that not what you want?" God but this was painful. Less than two hours earlier he was excitedly planning an assault to win his wife's love.

Now he was burying every hope of ever securing it.

He stormed to the Contessa's chamber door and left.

When Haverstock entered his office at the War Department the following morning, he woke up Philip, who'd fallen asleep at his own desk in the wee hours of the morning. "What the devil?" Haverstock boomed. "Do not tell me you slept here!"

Philip opened a single eye. He winced and slowly raised his head to peer at his oldest friend. No one knew him better than Haverstock, but not even Haverstock could know about Sarah's shame. Philip would carry her secret to his grave.

"Should you like me to send for your valet?"

Philip's first thought was that he should send a note around to his wife. She might think he'd been set upon by cutthroats. Then he slumped back. It was better to keep her in the dark. In order for the wretched Contessa to be satisfied, Elizabeth must believe Philip and the Italian woman were lovers.

He had spent the first two hours after leaving the Contessa's trying to devise a plan to extricate himself from the evil woman's trap, but no solution had presented itself.

For some peculiar reason, he had thought to come here last night to elucidate the undecipherable French code. "Yes, do send someone around to summon my valet. He can bring fresh clothing—and be sure to ask him to bring shaving implements."

Haverstock rang for a clerk, and when the young man arrived, sent him to Aldridge House with Philip's instructions. Then he faced Philip, frowning. "How in the bloody hell did you get in here last night?"

"The night porter let me in. Then we had to round up candles to aid me in . . . " Philip pulled himself erect and scanned the top of his desk where copies of the Pyrenees Code were strewn. "Examining our mystery cipher."

Haverstock frowned at him. "You could have done that from Aldridge House. You know every word in that document as well as you know the names of each of your siblings."

Philip nodded dejectedly. "So I do."

Haverstock's expression softened. "Did you and my sister have a disagreement? You two looked so happy last night. In fact Anna commented on how much in love the two of you appeared."

It was as if a rapier were twisting in his heart. The memory was still palpable of watching his adored wife last night and of the soaring realization of how potently he loved her. He would give everything he possessed to be able to hold

Elizabeth in his arms, to have the opportunity to earn her love. But such pleasure must be denied as long as Angelina was wielding her demands like a deranged general.

If he did not satisfy Angelina Savatini, the lives of Sarah, Tremayne, and their innocent children would be destroyed.

This was perhaps the only time in his life Philip could not be honest with Haverstock. Better to let him think Philip and Elizabeth had argued. It might help to explain the estrangement all of London was sure to know about within the next week. He shrugged.

Haverstock's gaze flitted to the pile of crumbled papers with scratched-out French words. "Any luck last night with the Pyrenees Code?"

Frowning, Philip shook his head.

"At least last night's dinner was successful. Very successful, I would say."

Funny, a week earlier, even a day earlier, he would have said his duty was the most important thing in his life. The greater good. Now the bloody tax increase and the greater good meant nothing without the woman he loved. If only he had been able to let Elizabeth know how much she meant to him, how deeply he loved her.

Now those bonds were being destroyed to satisfy a mad woman.

Nothing in his life seemed important any longer. Nothing except Elizabeth.

Once she came to believe he and Angelina were lovers, would she turn to Captain Smythe?

This was the day she was to go to Trent House. Was there anything she could do that would help eradicate the worst sort of melancholy? She did not feel as if she were capable of putting one foot in front of another.

Philip had spent the entire night with his Contessa.

She sank even further when the clerk showed up at Aldridge House to fetch Lawford. Her husband had no intentions of returning to his own home. It was with a heavy heart she watched Lawford leave with clean clothes for her husband.

During her long, sleepless night she had pondered her marriage. How she wished she could start over. She would never have spent those afternoons at the park with Richie. She would have insisted that she and Philip make the effort to establish their marriage as a *real* marriage from the day of their wedding. She would have brushed aside pride and coyness and revealed to him the affection that was in her heart.

But now it was too late.

It seemed as if her life were over even though she was only one and twenty.

Then many hours later, she realized that in Trent Square she did have something to live for, and after the war in working toward the widows' pensions.

Once she understood that her husband was not going to come home, she knew she would not be able to discuss with him the situation with Abraham. She had been wanting to ask his permission to allow the capable footman to move to Trent Square and expand his duties there. That would mean he would have to be replaced at Aldridge House. She did not feel right about making such a decision without consulting her husband.

Then the situation clarified itself to her. *I am the Duchess of Aldridge.* As duchess, she would thereafter be responsible for decisions involving the household staff.

Once she dressed for the day, she went downstairs and addressed Abraham, who was in the entry corridor. "May I have a private word with you?"

His green eyes widened. "Of course, your grace."

She went to the library. He followed, then she shut the door. "I have decided—if you do not object—that you need to take up permanent residence at Number 7 Trent Square. A man of many talents is what is needed, and I think you're that man. But if you don't- - -"

He interrupted. "I would be honored to go there. Do you really think I 'ave many talents?"

She nodded. "First, I should like Barrow to train you in the various duties one must undertake when one is responsible for the running of a house."

His brows elevated. "You mean I could be like an upper servant?" He was unable to suppress a smile.

"After Barrow trains you."

"I will do everything in my power, your grace, to demonstrate that I am deserving of your confidence."

"I'll speak to Barrow, and you can start working with him after we return from Trent Square this afternoon."

Later that day as she and her sisters were returning from Trent Square, Clair commented on what a fair day it was. "We will be riding in the park later with Mr. Rothcomb-Smedley, will we not?"

"Actually, I sent around a note telling him I wouldn't be able to ride today."

Clair's brows lowered. "You have made other plans?"

"No." She did not want to tell Clair why she was no longer going to be riding in the park with her cousin. After coming to understand how unhappy it would make her for Philip to ride in the park every day with a female cousin, Elizabeth knew she could no longer so openly be with Richie. Even if it mattered not to Philip.

"I shall be disappointed," Clair said. "I'd reread Paine with the intention of discussing it with him today."

"Would you like me to ask him to drive you today?"

Colour rose in Clair cheeks. "Pray, do not do that! It would look as if I were foisting myself upon him. I am sure a handsome, powerful man like Mr. Rothcomb-Smedley has a bevy of admirers. Women much lovelier than me."

"I really wouldn't know." Elizabeth was so distracted by her own morose situation she did not at first realize that Clair must be falling in love with Richie. She eyed her sister. She had made a good effort to dress beautifully, and her hair was styled most becomingly. Could Richie be responsible for this transformation which had come over her? Elizabeth wanted to ask but decided such a question would only embarrass Clair, who had no prior experience with flirtations.

Then it occurred to Elizabeth that she did have

advice to give Clair. "I know it is not my concern to delve into your affections, my dear Clair, but I have learned a most painful lesson I would wish for you to avoid."

Clair raised a brow. "What is that?"

"When you care about someone, you should let them know. Don't worry that you'll humiliate yourself if your feelings are not reciprocated. All you risk by disclosure is the embarrassment of a single moment with a single man. If, though, he feels the same, you've gained everything your heart could ever desire. Is that not worth any risk?" Her gaze met Clair's.

The two women stared at each other for several seconds. "You think I am in love with your cousin?"

"Quite possibly."

"I have no experience in such matters, but I assure you there is no way I could ever declare such feelings to Mr. Rothcomb-Smedley."

"Just remember that he may be reluctant to show affection for you because you're a duke's daughter with an attractive dowry, and he's a younger son with no title and little money. He may very well think you're above his touch."

"Oh, dear! Surely he couldn't think that. Why, he's . . . " Clair's voice softened. "He's deserving of a princess."

Finally, something to make Elizabeth smile.

As the duchess's coach rode along Piccadilly toward Berkeley Square she saw her husband's coach.

It was in front of the Pulteney Hotel.

Chapter 23

"Haverstock!" Excitement coursed through Philip. "I think I've got something."

Haverstock bounded through the door that connected their offices, rounded his friend's desk, and leaned over Philip's shoulder. "What did you find?"

Philip pointed to a series of underlined words. "If you will notice, every time a word with the letter *i* following an *e* is used, the next word is typically a place name in reverse. Every fourth place name follows a geographical sequence. I believe the names of every fourth town or village is significant. Could it be that's where the couriers are?"

"Let me see." Haverstock studied the document for a moment. "By Jove! I think you *are* on to something. That could explain why we've had the devil of a time following the men. They must be handing off to new couriers along the prescribed route."

"There's something more. You remember the part about Lieutenant Connover's murder?"

Haverstock nodded gravely.

"I believe the bloody Frenchies brought in an Italian beauty to seduce him, steal his dispatches, then murder him whilst he slept."

Haverstock's brows lowered. "But he died in Dover! Are you saying they had a French spy operating on our shores?"

"It looks that way."

"How were you able to make this deduction?"

"Revod."

"Oh yes, I see. Dover backward. Now I understand the reference to the alluring signora in that same paragraph. She *lured* him to his death."

"We shall have to alert all our couriers to beware of Italian beauties." If only Philip had heeded such a warning four years earlier. He would not be so miserable today.

He stood and stretched. His back ached from bending over his desk all day. His head was still throbbing from the excessive drink of the night before. And he was exhausted. "I will dump this in your capable hands. I'm whipped."

His friend eyed him as he somberly nodded.

On the pavement below, Philip summoned a passing hack when he was sure no one he knew was watching. He had the hackney drop him near the Pulteney Hotel's rear door, then he made his way through the hotel's opulent lobby and out the front door, where he climbed into his waiting ducal coach which had been there all afternoon.

Others might believe he'd spent the day with the Contessa, but he refused to even look at her.

When his coach drove alongside Hyde Park, he found himself wondering if Elizabeth was riding there with her cousin. Or worse. Could she be with Captain Smythe? The very thought was like a swift kick to his gut.

Why would she not fall back on her old lover? Her own husband had never shown her that she mattered to him. Then last night, that night Philip had so hungrily wanted to show her how thoroughly he loved her, his actions could not have been more rude.

What was she to think when he abandoned her immediately after dinner? And when he never came home? She would come to believe exactly what Angelina Savatini wanted her to believe.

Elizabeth had every right to flee to the Captain's arms.

The pity was there was nothing he could do to plead his own case. Not while the Italian she-devil had the power to destroy his sister. He had once vowed to Sarah to never reveal her secret. He could not do so even to his wife.

All Philip had left was his word.

Barrow tapped at her study door, and she bid him to enter. "Mr. Rotten-Smedley to see your grace."

It was all she could do not to burst into laughter over his mispronunciation of Richie's name. "Is he alone?" If Captain Smythe had come, she was prepared to have Barrow and the footmen toss him out.

"Yes, your grace."

"I will meet him in the drawing room."

A moment later she and Richie greeted one another in the huge, light-filled chamber that was furnished in the formal French style with an abundance of gilt and silk and ornate looking glasses. "Won't you sit?" She turned and took a seat at a settee covered in pale blue silk.

He sat opposite her, the sunshine squarely striking his fair eyes.

"Did you not get my message?" she asked.

"Indeed I did. I would like an explanation. First I was excluded from the dinner. Now this. What's the problem?"

Oh, dear. "There's no problem. It's just best that I avoid possible scandalous speculations about my relationship with you. I should be riding with my own husband instead of with my cousin."

He started to say something, then clamped shut his lips and eyed her with sadness.

Did he know about the Contessa Savatini? Did all of London know? Did Richie pity Elizabeth? She knew her cousin was too much the gentleman to reveal her husband's infidelities.

For Elizabeth was now certain her husband had resumed his affair with the Contessa. Since that night he'd received the letter from the Italian noblewoman, Philip had avoided the woman to whom he was wed.

"Of course. It was insensitive of me to hoard so much of a bride's time." He stood and gazed down at her with another pitying glance. "I shall miss the opportunity to talk government with Lady Clair."

"She is perfectly capable of driving in the park without me."

His eyes widened. "Would you object if I asked her?"

"Of course not."

"I would think a lady like her would be beating away the callers. Do you think she'd consider driving with me?"

"The only way a man can impress Clair is with intelligence. I would say you can fulfill that requirement most ably."

"But she *is* a duke's daughter."

"And you, my dear cousin, will be prime

minister."

At least that gaudy barouche wasn't there. Rothcomb-Smedley's curricle was parked in front of Aldridge House when Philip arrived home.

"Where's my wife?" he asked Barrow as he strode into the entry hall.

"She's with Mr. Rotten-Smedley in the drawing room." Barrow cleared his throat. "Your grace, I beg a word with you."

"Of course, Barrow." He faced him, a congenial expression on his face. Barrow was something like a favored grandfather to him and his siblings.

"I have always considered it the highest honor to be a servant in the household of the Dukes of Aldridge, but I cannot stand by silently while that upstart Mrs. Harrigan allows swine to roam in this fine house."

Philip's brows hiked. "We've got pigs running around the house? Where?"

"They're to be delivered tomorrow."

Philip placed a hand on the old man's stooped shoulder. "I'll have a word with Mrs. Harrigan. Don't you worry. I won't allow pigs the run of my house."

He started up the stairs. Philip was too out of charity with Rothcomb-Smedley and with that damned Captain to even smile over the way Barrow had mispronounced the man's name—though he most heartily would enjoy calling Elizabeth's cousin Rotten-Smedley.

As he neared the drawing room, he heard his wife's sweet voice. "You, my dear cousin, will be prime minister."

His step froze. Her words sickened him. It seemed every man could offer more than Philip could. He strode into the chamber, nodded at her cousin, then solemnly met his wife's gaze. "Hello, my dear." His breath hitched as he beheld her. She looked utterly girlish in her soft muslin dress sprigged with lavender. The sweep of his tender gaze went from her lovely face along the ivory column of her neck, to the rise of her breasts tucked beneath the bodice of the frock. His pulse drummed. His loins ached. He had never before known what it was to long for someone as he longed for Elizabeth.

She offered him a sorrowful smile. "It is a most pleasant surprise to see you home. Will I have the pleasure of dining with you?"

Before he could respond, Rothcomb-Smedley said, "I heard that Friday night's dinner was a resounding success. You must tell me all about it."

Philip sat on the settee next to his wife. "I could not have been more pleased. Such success, though, could not have been achieved without the considerable help I received from Haverstock and. . ." He turned to Elizabeth. "My wife. You were brilliant."

Her brows hiked. "You refer to the menu and the table?"

"It goes without saying that every detail, every single offering was perfection, but what I refer to is your ability to tap into the guests' emotions."

"Emotions?" Rothcomb-Smedley looked puzzled.

"Yes. My wife asked for a show of hands on how many had a loved one fighting the French. Every man and woman at the table responded in the affirmative."

Rothcomb-Smedley smiled at his cousin. "That

was brilliant."

Philip addressed her. "Did you not think every lord left our home that night with the intention of supporting a tax increase?"

"That was certainly my impression."

Rothcomb-Smedley eyed Elizabeth with an admiring gaze. "Bravo!"

"The whole mood in the House of Lords has changed. Men are challenging Lord Knolles' absolute authority."

"You've been doing a fine job," Rothcomb-Smedley said to Philip.

At least Philip had one thing of which to be proud. “To change the topic of conversation,” Philip said to his wife, “Can you explain to me why Barrow says we’re to have swine running amuck in our house tomorrow?”

Her eyes widened. “I cannot, but I assure you this is the first I’ve heard of swine at Aldridge House.” Then she began to giggle.

Philip nodded. “One of us should speak to Mrs. Harrigan about it. Barrow’s blaming her for the pigs.” Philip sighed. “We really must get to the bottom of it for poor Barrow is beside himself with grief. Thinks we’re turning our home over to filthy swine.”

“I will, my dearest.”

He settled back, shifting his gaze from Elizabeth to Rothcomb-Smedley "So, have you two been to the park?"

"No. Your wife no longer desires my company."

Thoroughly puzzled, Philip whirled around to face her.

She shrugged but obviously did not want to discuss it in front of her cousin.

He desperately wanted to continue with those

intimate talks with his wife. But not at present. What if she asked him about the Contessa? How could he even try to articulate that situation without telling her of that dark secret he'd promised never to reveal?

How long before Angelina understood he would never return to her? He wished to God he'd never left England five years ago, wished to God he'd never succumbed to the Contessa's seductive ways.

"How's the ciphering going?" Rothcomb-Smedley asked. The man knew everything and everybody who had a function in the government.

He turned to Rothcomb-Smedley. "We made considerable progress today. I feel like we're very close. In fact, as soon as I take a nap, I plan to return to Whitehall. I may spend all night trying to decode it."

Rothcomb-Smedley's face was inscrutable as he eyed him. He looked skeptically at Philip, as if he did not believe the Foreign Office was Philip's destination that night. Rothcomb-Smedley was coming to believe what the she-devil wanted everyone to believe: that Philip would be in her arms that night.

Philip stood. "If you'll excuse me, I'm headed to my bedchamber for a few hours to refresh me for the night's tedious work." He bent down, his lips brushing against Elizabeth's silky cheek.

"Is there anything I can do for you?" she asked sweetly.

If only he could tell her what was in his heart. *Hold me in your arms. . . Send Captain Smythe back to Spain. . .Love me as I love you.* But he could not say any of those things. "No." He began to walk away, then turned back. "But thank you."

When he got to the chamber's door, he turned back, grinning this time. "Good day to you, Mr. Rotten-Smedley." Then he left.

"What the devil?" the other man asked.

Elizabeth's eyes sparkled with mirth. "Allow me to explain. . ."

“Pray, Mrs. Harrigan,” Elizabeth quizzed, “What is this about having pigs being delivered at our house tomorrow?”

The housekeeper’s brows lowered as she shook her head. “The only thing being delivered tomorrow—to my knowledge—is the wine. Several crates.”

It suddenly occurred to Elizabeth that poor old hard-of-hearing Barrow thought *swine*, not *wine*, were being delivered. “Oh, dear me. I daresay poor Barrow misheard you. He understood swine were to be delivered tomorrow.”

Mrs. Harrigan began to giggle. “So that explains why he’s been such a curmudgeon lately! He’s been walking about talking about pigs under his breath! Leave it to me, your grace. I’ll see that he understands and I will try to speak slower and more loudly in the future.”

In the hopes that when her husband awakened from his nap he would come to her, Elizabeth stayed in her bedchamber. How she wanted to be able to have one of their talks. Even more needily, she thought of how thoroughly she wanted to make love with her husband. Surely when they were entwined in each other's arms he had to feel some of the love that flowed through every cell of her body.

Her expectancy built over the next two hours until she finally heard him speaking with his valet. She waited patiently on her settee. Had she not intimated to him earlier that she had something to discuss? Would he not be here any moment? After all, it had been many days since they'd had one of their intimate talks.

She raced to her dressing table and examined her reflection in the looking glass. As she stood there peering into the mirror, she found no fault with her appearance. Her hair still looked much as it had earlier that day when her maid had so flawlessly styled it. She had changed into a more elegant dinner dress of soft pink and awaited her jewelry.

Satisfied, she returned to the settee. And waited. And waited. Then she heard the door of his bedchamber close, heard heavy footsteps in the corridor. They did not pause at her door but kept on to the stairway.

Had he left without even saying farewell to her? Her heartbeat roared as she went to her chamber door, then to the top of the stairs where she could peer down to the marble hall below.

And see her husband taking his leave.

Chapter 24

I must not think of it. For the past several days she had been unable to purge from her mind the tortuous thoughts that her husband no longer came home, that he was in love with the Italian noblewoman. She must try to forget her obsessive love for a man who married her because she fit the requirements of a duchess. She was nothing more than a aristocratic breeder, like Princess Caroline, whom all of Europe knew the Regent had *not* married for love.

Breeder. The very memory of lying with Philip, the wistful hope that she could be carrying his heir stole away her breath.

She was climbing the stairs from the basement at Number 7 Trent Square when she saw Mrs. Hudson awaiting her.

"I've just finished the reading lesson with Abraham, your grace, and I thought you might be interested in a report on his progress."

Seeing how cheerful the formerly forlorn widow had become gave Elizabeth something for which to be thankful. The young woman's eyes sparkled whenever she mentioned the handsome footman. "Indeed I am."

"He has far exceeded my expectations. His proficiency increases dramatically each day."

The two women began to climb the stairs to

the next level. "I daresay that's quite a testament to the skill of the teacher."

Mrs. Hudson vigorously shook her head. "Not at all! He told me he spends anywhere from one to three hours studying by candlelight each night before he allows himself to fall asleep."

As proud as Elizabeth was of Abraham, it saddened her to think that the only time his pressing duties allowed him to study was at the expense of his sleep. She frowned. "I told him he was at liberty to study in our dinner room by the light of day."

"A less conscientious man would have, but Abraham takes his new duties very seriously. He told me your butler is teaching him how to run a household." Mrs. Hudson's lashes lowered. "Dare we hope that means you may allow him to come to us every day?"

"He didn't tell you?"

"Tell me what?"

"I've decided that you ladies need a man here at all times, and Abraham has consented to be that man."

A huge smile broke across Mrs. Hudson's face. "That is happy news, indeed. I cannot convey to you how indebted we all are to you and your family."

It was scenes like this that lifted away Elizabeth's melancholy. "You ladies and your sweet children have brought my sisters and me great joy."

Before they reached the music room, the banging of piano keys by clumsy little hands filled the whole second story with a sound that was somewhere between music and annoyance.

"I wonder why Abraham hasn't told you about

his impending new duties."

"He's a most modest man. I daresay he was afraid he might not come up to scratch with his new duties."

Elizabeth burst out laughing. The fellow's talents were wasted as a footman. "I expect you're right."

"Everything he does, he does well."

"I know. Now, Mrs. Hudson, you must help me come up with a title for him that will befit his new duties."

They peeked in the doorway and watched as Louisa studiously eyed the sheet music and tried to transfer the notes to her little fingers. Elizabeth looked from mother to child. The look of love in Mrs. Hudson's eyes was palpable.

"What do you think, your grace," Mrs. Hudson said a moment later, "about calling him house steward?"

"That's brilliant! I suppose, too, that we will dispense with Abraham in favor of his surname. Do you know what it is?"

"Yes—only because he's been practicing writing it in both script and print." Mrs. Hudson's voice dropped. "Though I will own, his handwriting has a very long way to go before I can boast on it!"

Elizabeth chuckled. "What is his last name?"

"It's Carter."

Elizabeth chanted the name twice. "Do you not think it has a very good ring for a house steward?"

"Indeed I do. How kind it is of the duke to allow this new expenditure."

Mrs. Hudson need not know that Elizabeth and the duke had never discussed it. They never discussed anything anymore. How could they when he was only home when his wife was presumably asleep?

After leaving Trent Square, the sisters and Elizabeth rode back to Berkeley Square in the duchess's coach. Once more, the duke's coach was in front of the Pulteney Hotel on Piccadilly. It suddenly became clear to Elizabeth that the Contessa must have moved from the Chiswick to the Pulteney.

It also became clear to her that if Philip was there each day, all of London knew it. All of London knew he was in love with the Contessa Savatini. She felt as if the death of a loved one had just been announced. In a way, it *was* like a death. It was the death of all her hopes, the end of her marriage as she had known it.

She eyed Clair on the opposite seat. Clair was noted for her inherent honesty, even when the truth might be painful. She saw that Clair too had seen her brother's coach, yet she said nothing.

"I beg that you tell me the truth," Elizabeth said to her in a grave voice. "Is the Contessa Savatini staying at the Pulteney?"

Clair's countenance softened as she shot Elizabeth a pitying gaze and nodded somberly. "I'm so sorry."

For weeks now he'd thought that single-handedly cracking the Pyrenees Code would bring him more joy than anything he had ever experienced. But as he sat before his desk, the waning afternoon sun providing just enough light to read his scribbled decipher, he glared at it—the solution—strangely void of elation.

His life was so miserable, nothing could bring

him pleasure. Nothing except Elizabeth.

He had best inform Haverstock before he left for the day. They needed to act upon the newly discovered information. He crossed the chamber and went through the door connecting their offices.

Haverstock looked up. Though he was dark, and his sister was fair, there was something about his mouth that looked like Elizabeth's. Little observations like that had the power to pluck at the heartstrings Philip had not known he possessed.

"Any luck?" Haverstock asked.

Philip nodded. "In fact, I believe I've managed to solve the whole bloody riddle."

His eyes rounding, Haverstock leapt to his feet, snatched away the paper Philip held, and began to read.

Perhaps Philip was capable of experiencing emotions after all. For as he stood there while Haverstock read, pride swelled within him, and when Haverstock looked up, admiration and exultation shining in his face, Philip could not suppress his overpowering feeling of accomplishment.

"This is bloody brilliant!"

"It would have been bloody brilliant had I solved it the first day. Have you forgotten how many hours it's taken us?"

Haverstock continued to study it. "We've notified the War Office about the location of the various French couriers. Did I tell you they have already captured each of them?"

"No, and it's not as if we don't see each other every day."

"Sorry, old chap. We had men dressed in

French uniforms to draw them out. I meant to tell you yesterday."

But Haverstock had obviously gotten distracted yesterday after seeing the Aldridge coach at the Pulteney whilst its owner was ensconced in Whitehall. Being his sister's advocate, he had demanded an explanation from Philip.

It had been exceedingly difficult for Philip to withhold information from his oldest friend, but he refused to divulge any portion of the truth. "It pleases the Italian woman," was all Philip would own.

"It's a shabby way to treat your wife."

"Believe me when I say nothing could ever hurt me more than inflicting pain on Elizabeth."

Haverstock had eyed him with suspicion, then dropped the topic.

"We must get this information on troop movements immediately to the Duke of York."

"Exactly what I was hoping you'd say. I would suggest sending battalions to intercept them before they reach Spain."

"If we cannot attack this flank before it reaches our troops, we will be seriously outmanned and overpowered." Haverstock looked back up at his brother-in-law. "Your country is deeply in your debt. Well done."

"Thank you."

Haverstock started toward the corridor. "Do you want to go with me to see the duke?"

Philip frowned. "No, I have some correspondence that demands my attention."

He would not tell Haverstock that correspondence was a letter from the Contessa. Fury still pounded through him that she had tracked him to this building and had the offensiveness to have her servant deliver her letter here. His anger was so intense, he had refused to open it.

Now that his work here was temporarily finished, he felt rather like an uncaged bird. How he longed to rush to Berkeley Square and see Elizabeth, but the she-devil was succeeding in her efforts to destroy his marriage.

He must make it clear to the Contessa that no matter what she did, he would never love her. Back at his desk, he eyed the letter and finally tore it open.

Amore Mio,

Tonight is the Wentworths' ball. You will dance with me. Failing to do so would result in a disclosure to the newspapers that no one in your family would wish to see.

Forgive my ruthlessness. It is only that I love you most dreadfully.

Your Angelina

An anger like nothing he had ever known surged through him. Were the Contessa to die tomorrow, he would feel not a shred of remorse. Were she to die by his own hand—an appealing notion—he would be no better than that she-devil, certainly not a man worthy of Elizabeth.

More than anything, he wished to be worthy of the fine woman he had married.

Now he just hoped to God that Elizabeth was not going to the Wentworths' tonight.

He had to return home to dress for the ball. While he was changing his clothing, he was aware that his wife too was dressing for the night in the adjoining chamber. Dare he allow himself the pleasure of dining with her? It might be difficult to concentrate on eating when the desire to drink in her loveliness was so strong.

Once Lawford had finished with the final inspection of his master's inky black coat against snowy starched cravat, Philip was powerless to keep from striding into her chamber. He stood there for a moment, watching her sit at her dressing table before an ornate looking glass in which he could see her face. Her maid babbled on as she styled Elizabeth's golden hair. How lovely she looked in tonight's silvery blue gown. How desperately he wanted to gather her in his arms. His heartbeat accelerated, his breath shortened.

Suddenly he realized she was peering at him through the mirror's reflection, and he felt rather like an Eton youth becoming aware of his first love. This woman—his wife—truly *was* his first love. "You look lovely, my dear." His gentle voice sounded alien to his own ears.

"Thank you." She turned back to offer him a smile. "Have you brought me sapphires, your grace?"

He thwacked his forehead. He'd been so impatient to behold her he'd entirely forgotten. "Allow me to fetch them."

When he returned to the chamber a moment later, the maid had been dismissed. He fastened the sapphire necklace with trembling hands. Then his head bent as he nibbled at her silken neck.

A knock sounded upon the door, and Clair came into the bedchamber. She stopped and eyed him beneath lowered brows. "You've been quite the stranger." There was no affection in his sister's voice. No doubt she believed exactly what the Contessa wanted everyone to believe.

"Your brother has many important duties that prevent him from being home," Elizabeth defended.

Clair still glared. "So, Aldridge, will you come with us tonight to the Wentworths' ball?"

Chapter 25

He was no better than a mute throughout the light dinner he shared with his wife and sisters prior to going to the Wentworths'. His own appetite had vanished the second he had learned Elizabeth's destination. Not only did he refrain from talking at dinner, he ignored the conversations that bounced about around him.

All he could think of was that he had to get out of attending the bloody ball. Thus far he had complied with the Contessa's wishes. And were his wife not coming tonight, he could have danced once with the she-devil in order to satisfy her malicious demands.

But he could no more hurt Elizabeth than he could publicly humiliate her. Even if she did not love him. No gentleman could openly treat his wife in such a way.

Nothing could prevent a man from dancing with a woman to whom he was not married. It was done all the time. Though a man's code of honor permitted dancing with other women, that same code forbade a man to dance with a woman all the *ton* knew to be his mistress. Such shabby behavior was not to be countenanced. Ever.

He felt Elizabeth's gaze but could not look up from the plate where his fork was nudging at uneaten food. "Philip? Are you unwell? I declare, you haven't taken a single bite."

"You may be right, my dear." He offered her a smile. "My appetite seems to have eluded me. I daresay it's owing to the many things that occupy my mind."

"You never told us what your plans are tonight." Elizabeth eyed him with concern.

His gut clenched as he was forced to make a decision. "I fancy dancing with my wife and sisters tonight."

The dazzling smile his comment produced upon his wife's pretty face made him feel like a beast. He hoped to God he would be able to manage this tightrope act without jeopardizing either his wife's or Sarah's happiness.

For he had decided he would dance with the Contessa Savatini in his wife's presence. *After* he danced with Elizabeth and each of his sisters. Hopefully, by the time he got around to dancing with Angelina it might look as if she were just another acquaintance.

Except, he told himself, all of London would believe what the she-devil wanted them to believe.

No queen could have felt more regal than did Elizabeth as she glided onto the ballroom floor of Lord and Lady Wentworths' grand mansion on Piccadilly. She had no doubts that Philip was the most handsome man at the gathering—along with her brother, when he arrived. Just weeks ago, the Duke of Aldridge was unquestionably considered the best looking unmarried man in all of England. It pained her to realize that even were he not a duke, women would be making cakes of themselves to merit a glance from her husband.

As a girl, she had been one in his legion of

admirers.

Now she was his worshipper.

"I shall wait to claim my beautiful wife for the first waltz of the night," he murmured into her ear as their family lined up against a wall and watched a country set that was in progress.

Beautiful wife. Many times he'd told her she was lovely, but she did not think he had ever before referred to her as beautiful. She felt as if she had grown a foot taller under his praise.

The chamber was quite full—though not yet, she thought, at capacity. Already the heat was coating the dancers with a fine sheen of perspiration, and she found herself unfurling her fan and putting it to use. Her gaze swung up to the ceiling where two massive crystal chandeliers ringed with blazing candles gave off even more heat.

It suddenly became clear to her that she and her husband were drawing a great deal of attention. Several times she'd heard Philip's title mentioned. At first she was inordinately pleased. This was, after all, the first time her husband had appeared at a public function with her since they married.

Then she heard the name she dreaded most. *Savatini.*

Was the Contessa here? Her heartbeat roared. Even though he had quickly recovered, she remembered the look of shock on Philip's face the moment he learned she was coming here tonight. Had he come home to change for the evening in order to meet the Contessa on the Wentworths' dance floor?

Even though her husband had not married her for love, she had difficulty believing a man as fine and noble as Philip would publicly flaunt a mistress. *Mistress.* The very word sickened her. She fleetingly thought she would gladly trade the title of duchess to be the woman who slept in Philip's arms each night.

She knew not what the Contessa looked like, other than the fact she was possessed of great beauty. As a young girl, the Italian noblewoman had been married to an aging Count. Just this week Elizabeth had learned that Count had died. Elizabeth's gaze circled the room, casually at first. Then she was certain the dark-haired beauty in the stunning black lace dress must be the Contessa. Across the room from each other, their eyes met. And held. Elizabeth's pulse thundered. *She is possessed of the same kind of beauty as Anna.* Extraordinary beauty.

Then Elizabeth's gaze snapped away. Her fingers dug into her husband's palm for they still held hands.

The first complete set after they arrived, he stood up with Clair. Other young men claimed Caro and Margaret, then Richie arrived with Captain Smythe. She was sorry to see the captain and was preparing herself to refuse to stand up with him when he presented a courtly bow to a pretty young blonde, and the two of them were gliding onto the dance floor. It occurred to Elizabeth that Captain Smythe's partner's hair was the same shade as her own. She would be most grateful if he could transfer his affections to the comely lady.

Richie strolled across the chamber to keep her company. "I see you're being chaperon to all the duke's unmarried sisters," Richie said as he came to stand beside her and peruse the dance floor.

"How novel! The Duke of Aldridge attends. To what do we owe this honor?"

She was unable to voice her opinion that he had previously planned to meet the Contessa Savatini here tonight. She merely shrugged.

"Would you care to dance?" he asked.

She shook her head. "I'm only dancing with my husband tonight."

"Yet your husband is being the gallant." His gaze swung to the beautiful woman in black.

"Indeed he is, though I daresay he's prodded by a guilty conscience."

Richie grinned. "Lady Clair is a most graceful dancer, is she not?"

His comment pleased Elizabeth. She was beginning to believe that Clair was falling in love with Richie. How wonderful it would be if he too was attracted to her.

The trembling that had thundered through her subsided when she glanced to the door as Morgie and Lydia, accompanied by Anna and Haverstock, strolled into the chamber. "Our family is certainly going to be well represented tonight."

Elizabeth could not remember a time in her life when Lydia's presence was not comforting. For Lydia was not only her eldest sister, she also treated her younger siblings with the loving affection neither of their parents were capable of showing.

Elizabeth's gaze swung from Lydia to Anna. There had never been a time when Anna's beauty did not dazzle, but tonight she glowed. If anything could reduce this veil of melancholy the Contessa's presence had thrown over Elizabeth, it was the circle of her loved ones. "How happy I am to see you! As you can see, I've been deserted."

Their gazes went to the dance floor where the duke and his sisters all stood in the longway with hands clasped. Lydia faced Elizabeth, rolling her eyes. "I am well aware that if you have no dancing partner, it is by your own choice." Her voice lowered. "I daresay you are so besotted over that husband of yours you won't dance with another."

Elizabeth had never been able to hide her emotions from her eldest sister. Morgie was as besotted over that sister as Elizabeth was over Philip. He stood at Lydia's side, his hand possessively cradling her elbow and glaring across the dance floor. His brows lowered, and he spoke in a low voice to his wife. "The devil take it! The Contessa Savatini has some cheek. Can you believe she's showing her loathsome self in the same room as . . ." He eyed Elizabeth, saw that she was watching him, and clamped shut his mouth. "My, my, my dear. Have I told you how lovely you look in that fetching green?"

Lydia smiled at her husband. "Oh dearest husband of mine, this dress is not green."

Morgie's brows lowered. "Is it not?" He looked dejected.

"No, love. It's blue. Azure actually."

"I'm not blue. Not even my eyes."

Lydia giggled. "I daresay you thought I said *as you are* instead of *azure*!"

"Did you not?"

"Azure, my dearest, is the colour of a body of water. As opposed to cerulean, which is a blue the colour of the skies."

"Bloody glad I am I didn't have to study watercolours. The demmed vocabulary is worse than Latin!"

"My brother says you were a tolerable Latin

student. Not as easy for you as mathematics, of course. And," Lydia looked up at her husband, "You do dance with perfection."

"I mean to claim you for the next set."

"As I mean to claim my marchioness," Haverstock said to Anna.

Anna's shimmering, almond-shaped eyes met her husband's, and she nodded. She and Haverstock still joined hands—as Philip had done with her before the first set. How she longed for a waltz and the opportunity to feel herself in his arms once more.

She sidled up to Anna, who was radiant in a snow white gown. The contrast of the bright white with her rich dark hair was stunning. Perhaps because her mother had been French, Anna was possessed of the most unerring sense of fashion Elizabeth had ever seen. And the Ponsby sisters were touted among the most fashionable women in all the Capital. "I haven't seen you looking so well in many, many months."

Anna's spectacular smile displayed teeth that perfectly matched the white of the gown and were as even as they were white. "It is because I am so very happy."

Elizabeth's heavy heart instantly lifted. "That can mean only one thing, my dearest sister! You must be increasing!"

Haverstock had stayed next to his wife throughout the conversation. Both he and Anna—each of them beaming—nodded at once.

This promptly sent Elizabeth into tears. She was truly happy for Anna and Haverstock but was aware that her own unhappiness accounted for a portion of the tears. "This is. . ." Sniff. Sniff. "The best news I've heard in a very long time. I'm so happy, I am making a cake of myself."

Before the end of the current set, Philip came rushing up to her. "What's the matter? Are you all right?"

Elizabeth was touched that he he'd been watching her while he danced, touched that he terminated the dance to come to her. She offered him a smile. "They're tears of joy. My brother and his wife have a wondrous announcement." She eyed Haverstock.

"You, Aldridge," Haverstock said, "can be the first to offer my beautiful wife and me felicitations upon a forthcoming addition to our family."

Philip's gaze swung from one to the other. "That is, indeed, very good news, and I shall be honored to be the first to offer felicitations."

Just having her husband near comforted Elizabeth. And when his hand rested at her waist, she could have swooned.

Behind her, Richie asked Clair to stand up with him the next set.

"I pray you do not abandon me as my last partner did," Clair said in a lighthearted voice.

Richie chuckled. "Your brother was merely a concerned husband, but I vow *not* to come rushing if the duchess erupts into tears again."

The next set turned out to be Elizabeth's longed-for waltz. Her heartbeat accelerated when Philip turned and peered down at her. "I believe this is our dance."

She waited until they were dancing where no one was close enough to listen. "I've missed you."

His hand tightened at her waist. "As I have missed you."

"I have difficulty believing that."

"Because I've been a wretched husband."

"Don't say that. You've just had many other things occupying you." She paused as a she thought of something. Something different about him. "When you first entered my chamber this evening I thought at first—before Clair came—that you might have good news to report."

He was silent for a moment.

Her chest constricted. Was he going to tell her he was in love with Contessa?

"I am amazed," he finally said, "over the depth of the connection between us. How could you know me so well that you knew I have been relieved of my most pressing duty?"

"You solved the cipher!"

A smile tweaked at the corners of his mouth. "You are not supposed to know about the nature of my work at the War Office."

"You're changing the topic. Pray, tell me, did you solve the cipher all by yourself, or did my brother make contributions?"

"Hang it all, Elizabeth, you're trying to make me boast."

His humility was another attribute of this man she'd wed. Just another reason why she loved him so madly. "You did solve it without anyone's help, did you not?"

"Just this afternoon, as a matter of fact."

"And you came straight away to share the news with me! This is thrilling. Now we'll be able to be together more."

Her husband stiffened. He made no response.

It then occurred to her that he had come home merely to change clothing so he could meet the Contessa at this ball. He had not accounted for the fact his wife and all his family had agreed to attend the same fete.

She only then allowed her gaze to swing to the woman in black. Ogling men surrounded the Italian beauty, but she only had eyes for one person: she watched Elizabeth, her large dark eyes malevolent.

Elizabeth's gaze flicked away.

Her husband drew in a breath. "There are times, my dearest wife, when things are not as they seem. You must always remember that."

He spoke in riddles. "Whatever can you be talking about?"

"Allow me to say that my greatest joy of this day is not that I broke the cipher. It is that at long last I can waltz with my wife."

Those persistent tears returned to her eyes as she clutched harder at him.

During the musicians' short break following the waltz, Philip was stoking himself for the single act Angelina demanded, the single act that was sure to humiliate the only woman he had ever loved.

When he saw the musicians return to their seats, he turned to Elizabeth. "Pray, excuse me. I see an old friend I am compelled to stand up with."

His heart hammering, he turned his back on his wife and strode directly across the dance floor to the evil woman in black.

The Contessa's red-stained lips lifted into a smile as he came to stand before her. She offered her hand, and he held it as they went to join the other dancers. They stood side by side, awaiting the music.

His furtive gaze lifted to allow him to see his wife. Her face had blanched, a stricken look on it.

Then a gush of tears came, and she spun around, racing from the chamber, sobbing.

Chapter 26

Had a knife plunged into his chest, he did not think he could experience a more searing pain than he felt at that moment.

He'd never wanted to have to choose between hurting his sister or hurting his wife, but now he knew that nothing was more important to him than Elizabeth. He didn't even know if she loved him, but he knew he had to unburden his heart to her.

His eyes met the Contessa's, who had been watching Elizabeth. "Are you satisfied now?"

"Yes."

"I have complied with your every request, but I can do so no longer." With those words, he stormed away from her, crossing the ballroom in a straight line to the door. The closer he got to the door, the swifter he moved. Hc had to catch up with his most cherished wife.

He raced down the stairs, and when he reached the entry corridor he saw Lydia assisting his wife with her cape. As he drew near, Lydia saw him first and glared, anger flashing in her eyes.

Then Elizabeth's gaze lifted. God but it hurt to see her like that! Her eyes were red, her face blotched with tears. She spun away, as if to hide her face from his view.

He spoke to Lydia. "I beg that you leave me to speak privately with my wife."

Lydia nodded and went to move away, mumbling under her breath. "Damn you, Aldridge!"

He rushed to Elizabeth and clasped both her hands. She tried to pull away, and the cape slipped from her shoulders. He stooped to pick it up. Then, his eyes never leaving hers, he came to his feet, gently placed it around her, and drew her into him, his arms closing tightly around her.

Only one thing could hurt her this much. His heart soared as he allowed himself to believe that the angel he married must be in love with him.

It was as if the heavens had opened up to admit his tortured soul. It was as if a brilliant light brightened the darkest night. It was as if all the happiness in the world had been heaped upon his unworthy shoulders.

He wanted to kiss her and tell her how deeply he loved her, but not here. Uncertain if she would even come with him, he scooped her into his arms, strode to the opened door, and left Wentworth House. His long stride swiftly covered some fifty feet to the waiting Aldridge coach.

The coachman leapt down and opened the door for them. Once Philip set her inside, he knelt before her, his hands lifting to reverently cup her face. "You cannot know how deeply I have come to love you. You and only you. I have come to realize the day you made the mistake of entering my bedchamber—the mistake that made you consent to become my duchess—is the luckiest day in my life."

Her sobs commenced again. What the devil? Was she crying because his words had made her unhappy? He sat next to her. Once again he drew her into his arms.

Her arms closing around him affected him more profoundly than any previous physical contact ever had. Through this mind-numbing haze of pleasure, he remembered earlier when she told him she was crying tears of happiness for her brother and his wife. "Please tell me those are tears of happiness."

"Oh, my dearest love, they are! Do you truly love me?"

"More than I have ever loved anyone. I would jeopardize my family, my king, my countrymen for you."

She wept even more wrenchingly. "But you won my heart a very long time ago," she finally managed.

Now it was his turn to be incredulous. He drew in a breath as his hands traced sultry circles upon her back. "What about Captain Smythe?"

She drew away and regarded him with a puzzled look. "Who told you about him?"

"Your brother let something slip some time ago."

"I may once have fancied myself in love with him, but when I saw him again recently, I found him repugnant."

Philip smiled. "I am very happy to hear that."

It was her right now to ask him about the Contessa. Even though he had once vowed to Sarah never to disclose her transgression, to save his marriage he must. "There is something I will now tell you. A family's dark secret that I'd vow to never disclose. It explains the hold the Contessa Savatini had over me for I assure you, I have no love for the woman."

He proceeded to tell her about Sarah's secret and the Contessa's threats. When he finished, Elizabeth's eyes were still misty. "Oh, my darling, I had no notion what a terribly wrenching position your were placed in." She sniffed. "We cannot let that evil woman destroy Sarah and her children."

Suddenly, as if a thunderbolt had cleared his foggy brain, a solution presented itself. "We're going to the Pulteney."

"We?"

"Indeed. I won't have it be said that I've gone to see my mistress." He lowered his voice to a husky growl. "You are the only mistress I ever want."

How had her husband known that the Contessa, humiliated after he had stormed away from her on the Wentworths' ballroom floor, would rush back to her hotel chambers? He pounded upon her door, and she opened it herself. Her hostile glance flicked to Elizabeth.

Elizabeth was struck by how much this beautiful woman looked like Anna. Both women were possessed of butterscotch complexion, rich dark brown hair, large brown eyes, and flawless faces. But where Anna was nearly saint-like in her goodness, this woman reeked of evil.

"I suggest you let us in," he said.

Still wearing the black lace, the Contessa's eyes rounded, but she swept open the door. "Why have you come?"

Even though it was only a hotel parlor, there was something decidedly palatial about the chamber that was lighted by ornate gold and crystal wall sconces, furnished with opulent

French pieces, and draped in silks. Even the surround of the fireplace was of costly marble.

"Because I have a deal to make with you."

"Sit down." Anger flared in her dark eyes.

"You are aware," Philip began, "how I don't know—but you know that I have duties in the War Office?"

The dark-haired beauty nodded.

"You have been identified as the French spy who's responsible for murdering a British courier in Dover. The penalty is death."

Her eyes widened. "I am not a French spy! And I never killed anyone!"

"We have several statements describing a well-dressed, beautiful Italian woman who seduced our officer prior to killing him." Philip glared at her. "I can produce witnesses who will swear you're the murderess."

"I see what you are doing. If I remain silent about your sister's sin, you will remain silent about this so-called crime you have framed me for."

"You understand correctly."

"I have a no desire to remain in this cold a country. I came a here because I hoped to win you back." Her gaze arrowed to Elizabeth. "I did not know you had fallen in love with your wife."

Philip took Elizabeth's hand.

The Contessa stood. "I leave a tomorrow."

Elizabeth and Philip stood and moved to the door.

"Do not worry about your sister. I have never told anyone, and I never will."

As soon as they returned to his coach, he hauled his beloved wife into his arms. "God, I've missed holding you."

"I have longed for you to hold me."

"Why did you stop riding in the park with Rothcomb-Smedley?"

Her fingers slid into his dark hair. "I asked myself how I would feel if you were riding in the park each day with a female cousin."

"And how would that make you feel?"

"Like a murderess."

He brushed back her ermine-lined cape and nibbled at her neck. "I will own, I contemplated killing the Honorable Richard Rothcomb-Smedley."

She giggled. "I love it when you speak so romantically."

"From now on, I will be the one to take you to the park, to take you to the theatre, to take you . . . to bed."

Then he kissed her greedily.

The End

Author's Biography

A former journalist and English teacher, Cheryl Bolen sold her first book to Harlequin Historical in 1997. That book, *A Duke Deceived*, was a finalist for the Holt Medallion for Best First Book, and it netted her the title Notable New Author. Since then she has published more than 20 books with Kensington/Zebra, Love Inspired Historical and was Montlake launch author for Kindle Serials. As an independent author, she has broken into the top 5 on the *New York Times* and top 20 on the *USA Today* best-seller lists.

Her 2005 book *One Golden Ring* won the Holt Medallion for Best Historical, and her 2011 gothic historical *My Lord Wicked* was awarded Best Historical in the International Digital Awards, the same year one of her Christmas novellas was chosen as Best Historical Novella by Hearts Through History. Her books have been finalists for other awards, including the Daphne du Maurier, and have been translated into eight languages.

She invites readers to www.CherylBolen.com, or her blog, www.cherylsregencyramblings.wordpress.co or Facebook at https://www.facebook.com/pages/Cheryl-Bolen-Books/146842652076424.

Printed in Great Britain
by Amazon.co.uk, Ltd.,
Marston Gate.